Praise for
Name Not Taken

"*Name Not Taken* is a mind-bending tale of obsession that brings new meaning to the phrase 'mother-in-law from hell.' If you're looking for a compelling new voice in crime fiction, look no further than Madeleine Henry. I absolutely devoured this book."

—Alison Gaylin, internationally bestselling author of *The Collective*

"I could not stop reading Madeleine Henry's riveting psychological thriller, a complex and captivating story of couples, class, and the war between two powerful women for control of their family and themselves."

—Pamela Redmond, author of *Younger*, now a TV series by Darren Star

"Madeleine Henry makes a fine art out of gaslighting in *Name Not Taken*, a novel that exposes meeting the in-laws as its own form of hell. A struggling artist is pitted against her fiancé's family in this gripping, unnerving thriller that explores the blurred lines between art and life, madness and genius, and love and control. Readers won't be able to stop flipping pages—or keep a steady grip on reality—as they follow the narrator down an art-filled rabbit hole. This is a devilish and dizzying accomplishment that rivets from beginning to end."

—Ashley Winstead, author of *Midnight is the Darkest Hour*

NAME NOT
TAKEN

NAME NOT TAKEN

A Novel

MADELEINE HENRY

Little
a

Text copyright © 2025 by Madeleine Henry
All rights reserved.

Published by Little A, New York

www.apub.com

Amazon, the Amazon logo, and Little A are trademarks of Amazon.com, Inc., or its affiliates.

ISBN-13: 9781662517488 (hardcover)
ISBN-13: 9781662517471 (paperback)
ISBN-13: 9781662517464 (digital)

Cover design by Eileen Carey
Cover image: © small smiles / Shutterstock; © Catherine Delahaye / Getty; © Caryn Drexl / ArcAngel

Printed in the United States of America

First edition

for the intruder
in the family portrait

PART ONE

PART ONE

ONE

There are many dark turns on Waverley Road.

Richard and I pass another estate on our way to meet his parents, each driveway longer than the last, dimming more and more distant yellow windows. The new diamond glimmers on my ring finger, the only piece of fine jewelry I've ever owned. I hold it up and watch the twilight splinter through it.

"You like it?" he asks.

"Of course," I say, dropping my hand to reach for his. "You know me, I'm just not used to jewelry." Most of the time, I'm in secondhand khakis and an oxford flecked with paint, my hands as bare as a surgeon's.

"That's what I love most about you."

"My bare skin?"

"Your depth." He smiles at me.

We're still on a high from last week, when Richard proposed on our road trip through Maine. We were at the Colby College Museum of Art—leaning so close to a fuchsia landscape, I felt like we were inside its world—when he knelt and asked me to spend the rest of my life with him. Of course I said yes. When he stood up, I told him that in my heart, I'd felt married to him since we met.

He touches my long, inky hair.

I never expected to fall for my opposite. Richard comes from a loving family of four and has a steady friend group dating back to his days at Princeton. He thrives in sales at Morgan Stanley but thinks about his job with emotional distance, as something that isn't a vital part of his identity. Meanwhile, my art is who I am. I'm a full-time painter who's given up nights and weekends for a decade, only to end up dead broke and unknown. I've bet everything on my passion, taking odd jobs when necessary, in pursuit of my own masterpieces. Unlike Richard's, my troubled family is scattered across the Midwest—but that's in the past, I remind myself.

Richard is my family now.

I feel the car slow down and glance at him in the driver's seat. Even physically, we complement each other. We're both twenty-nine, but Richard has a sunny complexion: bright-blue eyes with white chevrons around his pupils; short, almost platinum hair. His blazer hugs his strong frame. Meanwhile, I'm bone thin and canvas white, with dark eyes that make even my belly laughs seem melancholic. Together, we're a bold pair who stimulate every part of the eye.

Richard turns left into a driveway.

"So, what do you see?" he asks, one of his common refrains. He's always been fascinated with my artistic eye, as if I can see secrets.

I look forward.

Trees flank us on both sides of the longest driveway yet. At the end, his parents' house glows in the sunset. My chin retreats, though I've already pored over photos of it online: a ten-bedroom Tudor estate. It's so grand—with several chimneys, an army of shuttered windows, and a stone turret—that I feel as if I'm looking at a surrealist work, an illusion created by carefully placed mirrors. I'm not that kind of painter, but the house is so improbably vast that these are the images that come to mind. I imagine the Belmonts climbing staircases that lead up to where they begin.

"Devon?" he asks.

"It looks surreal," I admit.

"Well, if a clock starts to melt, it's time to leave." He laughs.

I imagine the house getting smaller as we get closer—or an eye blinking in the center of a window—but nothing happens that should not. We drive up to the entrance. The enormous bushes on either side are symmetrical except for a sparrow nestled in one, almost hidden by leaves. Our headlights whiten its eyes.

I get out of the car first, expecting Vanessa and Clarke Belmont to open the front door at any second, as eager to meet as I am. Richard and I have been dating for two years, and I've only spoken to his parents on the phone. Those conversations were friendly but brief. I keep looking for them. Richard and I didn't tell anyone that we got engaged until this morning—we wanted to savor the moment to ourselves for as long as possible. Even today, we shared only the news and none of the details. I'm sure they're going to want to hear all about the proposal.

The front door stays shut.

There don't appear to be any lights on inside. The orange sunset reflects off a few windows, but the rest are a bottomless black. Richard steps up to the front door and knocks with an iron ring. He smiles at me, but his expression fades in the deepening silence. He knocks again, then starts to look as perplexed as I feel. I take a few steps back to get a better view and search every pane. Did we get the date wrong? But this house looks too desolate. It feels more permanent than getting the date wrong, almost as if they don't live here, as if no one lives here at all.

PART TWO

TWO

Richard and I are late to Vanessa's sixty-fifth birthday dinner in Greenwich. Hopefully, this will go better than our last attempt to see them. Standing in their driveway two months ago, we called them, only to realize that we *had* mixed up the date. That's what it sounded like, at least. The connection was full of static.

Richard keeps checking the dashboard clock. He passes two cars in the fast lane before racing over to our exit. We're now on the fringe of suburbia, where leafy trees are black against the sunset. He stops short at the first light.

"You okay?" I ask.

His thoughts are so loud, he doesn't hear me.

It's my fault that we're late. As we were getting dressed up for tonight, though, he looked so handsome that I had to kiss him. The kiss kept getting longer. We both whispered that we'd better stop, even as we undressed each other and threw the clothes into dim corners. Now it's almost seven, though he promised Vanessa we'd be there by six. He's driving too fast through this quiet neighborhood. I check driveways for children who might sprint into the road, but all I find are closed gates.

Around the next bend, his parents' estate appears all at once, in radiant glory. Outdoor lights beam like fallen stars. The house itself glows in amber patches, offering glimpses into tiny chandeliers and doll-size leather sofas. This sparkling place is so unmistakably inhabited, unmistakably their home. I wonder what strange crack in the universe we fell down last time, where everything was dark.

Richard doesn't slow down in their driveway. The torque pushes me back in my seat. I look at him, curious. It's odd to see him so . . . frantically obedient. He's usually so confident. That's one of the reasons I fell in love with him: he's comfortable wherever we go. He has a relentless sense of belonging, even in places he's never been before. When I'm with him, I get a taste of what that's like.

But now, he's on edge.

He throws the car into park, hops out, and shuts his door before I can take off my seat belt. He grabs the bag with Vanessa's gift from the trunk. Outside, a cool September wind blows across my face and spins my hoop earrings like mobiles. My heels clomp up the stone front steps while Richard waits for me at the door.

"Are you nervous about introducing me?" I ask.

"Not at all. She just cares about her birthday."

I rub his chest. "Trust me, Richard, no woman really loves her birthday."

He doesn't laugh.

I reach for the handle—and yank my hand back.

"What is it?" he asks.

Static electricity? I open it this time with my sleeve over my palm. Inside, no one is waiting for us. I hear voices in the distance.

"Mom?" Richard calls.

Nothing.

"Mom?" he tries, louder.

"You are seriously regressing," I mutter humorously.

Richard and I walk hand in hand toward the murmurs, through rooms lit by Louis Comfort Tiffany stained glass lamps. Every shade is a floral canopy with petal-shaped edges, drooping over a bronze base like it's a stem. I've seen these lamps in museums but never at dusk. The contrast lets their brilliance come alive.

We pass Vanessa's cat, Woolf—named for Virginia, I've been told—lounging on a chesterfield sofa. His lively eyes glisten. His gray tail curls like a question mark. We keep walking through room after room. I sense Richard itching to move faster, but the art in this house is slowing me down. A few landscapes from the Hudson River school hang in golden frames.

Eventually, Richard stops. We face a library with walls the color of red wine, an iron chandelier, and a black brick fireplace. Vanessa sits on the sofa with Oliver, Richard's twenty-seven-year-old brother. Clarke is snug in an armchair, swirling a generous glass of bordeaux in his right hand until his wrist goes suddenly still.

Their conversation vanishes.

"Happy birthday!" I say.

"Happy birthday," Richard says at the same time. "Mom, Dad, Oliver, I couldn't be happier to introduce you to Devon Ferrell."

His family's jaws drop to reveal thin black gashes of surprise. All three of them stand, Vanessa closest to me. She's petite but with strong, handsome features: high cheeks, pointed nose. She's beautiful the way that Jodie Foster is, or that Sigourney Weaver is, under a bright-yellow bob.

Behind her, Oliver is a couple of inches shorter than Richard. He still lives at home after a bad breakup two years ago. Finally, there's Clarke, the heaviest set, with full, ruddy cheeks. His white beard is thick and neat. Together, the Belmonts are a portrait of tamed extravagance: a gold watch just visible under Vanessa's sleeve, a subtle monogram on the hem of Oliver's cashmere sweater—the initials *OAB* no bigger than the head of a cuff link—and not one logo in sight. Clarke's silk tie drips behind his tailored blazer, only silently claimed by a luxury brand.

"Ray Ray, we wish you'd told us," Vanessa says, glancing at me.

"I did!" Richard says.

The new miscommunication doesn't faze me. I smile and shake everyone's hands. Clarke ruffles my shoulder and makes a self-deprecating joke about being a broken clock that's only right twice a day. I remember now that I was painting when Richard's parents called and invited us over to celebrate. They told him it would be a quiet night, just with family.

I take an armchair, while Richard sits next to his mom. She straightens his collar, pulling on the pointed ends. Only once we're settled does he seem to relax. He leans back on one elbow, elongating his torso as if he's showcasing his own body. His red sweater ends on his belt buckle, drawing my eyes.

"Now, I know you all have a ton of questions for Devon," Richard announces with friendly authority. He holds up his palms, as if he needs to physically caution everyone to slow down. "But please, go easy on her."

I reach out and squeeze his hand.

"You're right, I do have questions," Vanessa says with an elegant smile. Richard mentioned that she double majored in literature and art history at Columbia. Now she spends most of her time volunteering for nonprofits. Apparently, she's on the board of the New York City Ballet. "I suppose my first one is—how did you two meet?"

A beat of silence.

"We've told you that, Mom," Richard says.

I told Vanessa and Clarke on our first call last year that I'm from Cleveland, came to New York to paint at NYU, and never left. They asked me if I knew two families in Cleveland. Neither rang any bells. Does she really not remember? I glance at Clarke to see if he's going to remind her, but he waits with a frozen smile. I look back at Vanessa, who's still expecting my answer. They must not have known back then how serious Richard and I were, that our story would become family lore.

"You'll have to jog our memories," Vanessa says.

"Well, we met the old-fashioned way—in person," Richard says.

"We were both visiting a Jasper Johns exhibit at the Whitney," I go on, figuring that a refresher can't hurt. Besides, I like telling this story, and Richard's smile is contagious. "We were looking at one of the American flags when I noticed him next to me. I still remember his opening line."

"'Excuse me, but did you see my painting over there?'" Richard says.

I laugh, picturing how he pointed at one across the room. "I asked him what brand of paint he used, and he said, 'Sherwin-Williams.'"

In front of that American flag, I remember trying to memorize Richard's eyes. Hot blue. I wanted to use their color in a painting. Richard said his audio tour wasn't working, so I explained that Jasper Johns is an encaustic painter—meaning he works with melted wax mixed with color. It was sensual, standing there with Richard, talking about ripples in the wax. At the end of my spiel, Richard looked surprised. Maybe the other women who laughed at his pickup lines only gave him more jokes back. But I was sincere, and his whole body responded to it.

"Richard asked me out to coffee," I go on, "so we went downstairs to the Whitney's restaurant. I told him that I paint, and we talked about art the whole time. He thought my perspective was fascinating. Our next few dates were all at different museums. He kept asking me what I saw—even over lunch. He thought I was able to catch the things everyone else was missing."

"She cast quite a spell on you," Vanessa says.

"Well, that's because I admire Devon," Richard says. "Most of the people I know are living in the same place they grew up, doing the same thing their parents did. But Devon"—he looks at me earnestly—"is five hundred miles from home, doing something that's never been done. She works harder than anyone I know with no guarantees, almost no days off, and I've never heard her complain. You've said, Dev, that some people are born with an artist's mind, but it takes something extra to go after it with everything that you have. I've never seen anyone take on more personal risk for the sake of their work—it's almost insane, and I mean that in the best way. Maybe serial entrepreneurs are like that out in Silicon Valley, but they're in a culture of risk taking. And even then, they have colleagues. They fundraise. Devon works completely alone. All of that makes her special. I knew right away."

Me too.

I may have a passion, but it narrowed my life down to my art. Richard has broadened me. Now there's laughing until I lose my breath. There's taking weekend trips together, sledding in Central Park, stopping to kiss in the snow, and doing things so ridiculous and sweet that I feel like a teen again. Now there are so many more people. Richard focuses on others more than anyone I've ever met. He asks me to every party he's invited to, and when we show up, he's the life of it. The heart. I don't care if his parents' connections got Richard his job at Morgan Stanley, because his greatest work isn't his title there; it's how he treats every single person.

We hold hands.

"Were you as surprised as we were?" Vanessa asks me.

She nods toward my ring, a rose-cut white diamond.

"Sort of," I say.

She waits.

"We'd talked about getting engaged, but only in a vague way," I explain. "He asked me what kind of ring I'd want, and I said that I work so much with my hands, I wouldn't want anything too high profile or sparkly." The rose-cut stone was his idea.

"It looks plenty sparkly," Vanessa says.

I sneak a glance at hers, a cushion-cut diamond big enough to be four carats or more. *Plenty sparkly.* Is she—saying something she's not saying? She's probably just trying to convey that she thinks it's a beautiful ring.

"How'd he ask you?"

Clarke's smile encourages me.

I describe the moment when Richard knelt, lit by rosy brushstrokes. I feel everything all over again—lucky, understood. By now, he's seen all my flaws, and our relationship is only getting deeper. He's seen me obsessively sketch, paint, and repaint the same shadow again and again, trying to get it exactly right. He knows the details of my family history, that my mom's still in and out of rehab. Until my dad divorced her, he coped by turning a blind eye. He'd work late managing his Italian restaurant, go out until dawn with the line cooks, and only come home to collapse. But Richard accepts me. He still asks me what I see, as if my lens is special.

He hands Vanessa cheese on a cracker.

"How funny," she says, taking it. "Didn't you used to date someone at Colby?"

"Did I?" Richard asks.

"Yes," Vanessa says. "You met her on that trip we took with the Cabots—you know, the Boston Cabots? They're old friends." The aside is for me.

Richard did mention he'd been to Colby before.

Clarke stands and uncorks another red. He's teaching us—me, I realize—about French hospitality. In France, it's impolite for guests to serve themselves. Hosts should monitor and refill wineglasses. He goes on to educate me about tonight's bordeaux before delving into a lesson about wine-cigar pairings. I listen until I catch my reflection in a dark window. For a second, it looked like I was sitting in the driveway, like I was still locked outside, waiting to get in.

～

We don't sit down to dinner until the grandfather clock chimes nine, after exhausting the platter of cheese and crackers and getting swept up in gifts for Vanessa. The Belmonts all presented thoughtful ones, including a year-long membership to MasterClass, a pair of leopard pumps with kitten heels, and a framed photo of her with Oliver. Then Vanessa insisted on cooking and made something called chicken marbella, which nestles the breasts in stewed dark fruits.

As we sit in the dining room, Clarke thanks me for putting up with their "quirky family," though I find nothing bizarre about them.

"Does your family have any quirks?" he asks.

15

"Not really," I lie.

"Come now, everyone's got one."

I remember how my mom used to take our dog out to pee every morning, and they'd pee together in the yard. Richard interjects a compliment about the chicken, then nods at me. He knows better than to discuss my parents.

"Richard says you like to paint?" Vanessa asks.

She chews a piece of meat.

"Yes, I paint whenever I can. Modern portraits."

I explain that the famous dealer Marc Zellweger has two of my paintings in his Chelsea gallery—and omit they have yet to sell. In the silence that follows, I resume eating, feeling like I've spilled some of my soul onto the table.

"We're more familiar with the greats, artists like Rembrandt," Vanessa says, "people who've stood the test of time." I'm not surprised, and I don't take it personally. I sensed as much from the Tiffany lamps and Hudson River school landscapes. For many, the value of art begins when the artist dies. "Do you care for any of the greats, or are you more focused on blazing your own path?"

"I definitely care," I insist. "They started a conversation, and artists today are all responding to their predecessors, whether they realize it or not. I look up to a lot of the legends and hope to be considered among them one day."

Richard looks proud.

"I'd be careful what you wish for." Vanessa dabs her lips with one corner of her napkin. "What's that phrase? It was about breaking out in the art world. 'Talent is cheap, and you have to be possessed or obsessed . . .' I forget the words exactly. The point is that something has to be a little wrong with you, maybe, to find lasting success in art."

"'You have to be possessed.'"

"What do you make of that idea?" Vanessa asks.

I twirl my fork, watching the tines. It isn't hard to think of artists who have gone mad. Van Gogh, of course, cut off his left ear. The sculptor Carl Andre probably pushed his wife to her death. But there are counterexamples too—like the tireless Alex Katz, still productive and sane in his nineties, and, hopefully, like me.

"Well, it's something to think about," she says. "I'm sure someone has written a master's or a PhD dissertation on the subject of mental illness in the arts."

The words stay with me as the conversation moves on to Richard and Oliver's golf game tomorrow. At one point, Oliver asks for my phone number, and I give it out automatically. He adds me to their family text group, "Belmont Banter." Still, for the rest of dinner, I feel a little fixated on Vanessa's comment, as if it's a mosquito humming around the room. I take only a couple more bites of her fleshy chicken breasts, then leave most of the meal in perfect condition.

"Something wrong . . . ?" Clarke points at my food from the distant head of the table.

"Oh, I'm full," I say.

"Well then, next time," he says, grinning, "I'll sit next to you."

He jokingly stabs his fork on Oliver's empty plate.

~

As Richard and I get under the covers that night, in his childhood bed, I push the hair back from his forehead.

"Your parents are incredible," I say, still reeling from the evening. I've never been part of a conversation so quick and sharp; I felt like it was holding me hostage. The Belmonts have a textured grasp on everything around them, from the Tiffany lamps on every table to the history of this part of Connecticut. The last thing we discussed was the sculptor Jeff Koons, and whether he's truly an artist if his assistants do most of the work assembling his massive pieces.

"So are you," he says.

His gaze fades right.

"What is it?" I ask.

"Nothing, it's just . . . it went so well," he says.

"Are you surprised?"

"No," he says distantly. "I guess I didn't know what to expect. I've never brought anyone home before."

"Never?" I gawk.

"Never."

"Not enough room?" I ask, gesturing around us.

He laughs. "Didn't want them to sleep outside." He adds with a more serious tone, "No, my parents always wanted to wait to meet our girlfriends." I ask until when. "Until we were married." His chuckle is deflated and quick. "It wasn't a rule that they had. It was just the impression I got. They kept canceling or making excuses until one of us started talking about a ring." He looks at mine, then brings it to his lips. "I think they were just waiting for The One."

It feels oddly like our roles have reversed. He seems like the brooding one now, while I'm more optimistic—and I remember how fragile our new life really is. I don't want to break it. This experience of being normal, safe, and, finally, important to someone might vanish as quickly as he walked up to me at the Whitney. I don't want to remember my life without him. I hold his hand and remind him who he is.

"My angel," I say.

He kisses me.

"My Dev."

THREE

The next morning, Richard leaves for an early tee time with Oliver. After breakfast alone, I try to find Vanessa, but the house is so vast that she's vanished within it. I wander through a cavernous wing, hoping to come across her.

An electric candle flickers in the wooden chandelier above me. It's the only part of this house that isn't perfect—unlike my childhood home, where nothing was as it should be. The constant stream of alcohol muddied Mom's thinking, leaving her prone to strange habits. She broke things without warning, so I kept everything fragile out of reach. Even if my parents could've afforded what's around me now—a mahogany floor globe, a row of black Venetian glass goblets—Mom was too wild for everything but plastic dinner plates and anchored sofas.

To be fair, she wasn't always that way. She used to be . . . more like me. Mom majored in design at Ohio State and worked in event planning before I was born. My first memory of her is when she taught me to draw. I was sitting in her lap, working on our living room floor. She kept her hand on mine, directing the pencil. We were so in sync it was like she was transferring her creativity directly to me.

Things only got really bad when I was a teenager. That's when she started drinking every day, destroying things, and talking in nonsense. I tried to keep her habits private to protect her dignity. Our house was just steps from our neighbors', but we stopped entertaining. As an unintended consequence, I disappeared along with her. We stayed at home, alone together, until I left Ohio for NYU.

I make my way back to Richard's room. As I put on another layer, I notice a photo of him as a boy on his desk. In it, he hugs his mom's knees, tucked under her mink coat. The coat is black and almost viscous, as if the night is melting on them. Lincoln Center twinkles in the background. Richard had an idyllic childhood. Despite his privilege, he grew up to have such empathy, depth, and—fortunately for me—a relentless desire to cheer other people up. Somehow, life's been kind to him, but he has the heart of someone who's survived tough times.

My fingers find the top drawer. This was Richard's room until college. What did he leave behind? Inside, there are more photos, mostly framed ones of him with family. In the next drawer, I find folders stuffed with paper. Essays from high school? I imagine him writing jokes into his footnotes. Underneath the folders, there's something smooth. It's a photo of Richard—almost. He's on the front lawn next to a beautiful girl. She has long black hair, her features dramatized with dark eyeliner and red lipstick. He wraps his arm around her, pulling her in for a kiss.

I furrow my brow.

The attempted kiss is blinding. It hovers an inch from her temple, brushing a few ribbons of her hair. Richard looks almost a decade younger, but still—he said he'd never brought anyone home before.

Footsteps approach. I stuff the photo back in the drawer, then listen as the steps pass. I move to the threshold and spot Clarke trotting downstairs in a wide-brimmed hat with dark binoculars around his neck. Dressed for bird-watching? He walks out of sight. I head to Richard's window, where I see Clarke exit and putter to the edge of the property. He sits on a bench by the tree line and goes motionless. It looks like he's just walked into a mural and become part of the scene.

I glance back at the desk.

What do I care if Richard brought someone home in high school? Isn't that a sign of being well adjusted? Besides, I should be sketching, like I do every morning. The image of Clarke so rapt draws me over to the window again. I pull up a chair, open my book, and draw the frozen curve of his spine.

~

That afternoon, when the shadows are short, I'm still sketching by the window. It's peaceful here, silent as a cemetery. If I were at home, I'd be working on my portraits by now. In Richard's and my apartment on the Upper East Side, we converted one bedroom into a studio, where plastic film covers the floor and walls. It's stained every color, as if that's where I murder people who bleed paint. If Richard gets back soon, as we planned, I'll still have time to paint tonight in New York.

I think I hear his voice.

Now, dead quiet. Maybe it was nothing.

Richard emerges suddenly, back from eighteen holes, and I sense something is . . . off. He looks confused. Or a little scared. The collar of his long-sleeve polo is popped on one side, flat on the other. I close my sketchbook.

"What's wrong?" I ask.

I get to my feet.

"Do you . . . ?" he starts.

He searches for the words.

"My mom is worried about you," he finishes.

My cheeks feel cold.

I glance behind him. We're alone except for a wooden doorstop shaped like a Bengal tiger. It crouches between the door and the frame.

"What do you mean?" I ask.

"You didn't eat much this weekend."

I didn't?

I try to remember our meals since we got here.

Last night, I had some of the cheese—smoked gouda, as I learned from Oliver. He taught me about its Dutch origins and the kind of milk it requires. For dinner, I didn't eat much of my chicken marbella.

Is that what this is about? Frankly, I got the sense that his parents don't really care about food—which is why this topic is catching me off guard. Dinner here came together like an afterthought. The conversation seemed much more important to them. In this house, it's a work of art. People don't have the bandwidth to think about their meals if they're going to keep up with forays into "the greats" and global politics, sometimes dipping into foreign languages.

This morning, I ate alone. For lunch, Vanessa was still missing, and Clarke was bird-watching, when I made myself quick slices of toast. Sure, I didn't eat *that* much, but I didn't skip meals or act like someone with a problem.

"Ok*ay*," I concede. "But so what?"

He wavers.

"What did she say?" I press.

"She says I deserve a healthy partner."

My eyes widen.

"I am healthy!" I feel a creeping sensation, as if her whispers to Richard are tickling the fine hairs on my back. Blowing them into slow circles. I squirm and hug myself. "I'm sorry, when did she say this?"

"Just now, in the kitchen. With Oliver."

I imagine Vanessa and Oliver sitting side by side on the sofa in the kitchen, the grandfather clock in the corner keeping time.

"Why would she say that?" I ask.

"She's worried about you."

I hug myself tighter.

"Do you think you need to lose weight?" Richard asks.

"What? *No.*"

I take a deep breath.

This doesn't make sense.

"You've never worried about my eating before," I say, trying to find a shred of reality. "Are you just saying this because of them? Or do you actually think I have a problem?"

"I don't know."

He sounds honest.

"You don't know?" I probe.

"They were really freaked out. They said you might not be able to have kids if you're malnourished."

My mouth drops.

"So I'm unfit to be a mother?" I ask.

"I didn't say that."

"What *did* you say?"

Knock. Knock.

"Come in," I say.

Vanessa appears in a crisp outfit and her new kitten heels. They're silent on Richard's carpet. She smiles through the growing hush, then shakes a trash bag in one hand. She starts humming as she dumps the closest wastebasket into her bag. She mentions something high pitched about tidying up and heads into our bathroom to empty the trash there too. She says we should check for our wallets and chargers before heading out. Richard and I barely move until she leaves. The image of her poring over our trash enters my mind. I don't dismiss it easily.

I cover my eyes with my hands, and Richard pulls them down. In this slant of light, his eyelashes look long and soft. His expression is kind. For a moment, I think that he's going to apologize, that he's going to reassure me.

"They just want you to be healthy," he says.

His tone is sincere, like he's trying to convince me that they mean well. That this is a sign of how big their hearts are. Of course, I've seen this side of him before. It's his oversize, superhuman empathy. His ability to see everyone's perspective and care about it. I've seen it turn him into a pinball peacemaker, running interference between friends, being persuaded by the last person he spoke to, and changing his mind again and again. Usually, it's an endearing quality.

I take my hands back.
"I am healthy," I insist.
Aren't I?
"Okay," he says. "Of course."
But the words aren't fully on my side.

FOUR

B ack in New York, I can't stop thinking about it. For days, I replay the weekend on a loop, even the moments in their house when I was alone.

You didn't eat much this weekend.

Is this really about food? Vanessa studied literature. Is she being metaphorical? If I'm not eating enough, am I . . . lightweight? Maybe what she's really suggesting is that I'm not fit to marry Richard. It's no secret that other women look better on paper. But I do have a crumb of success in a punishing creative field, don't I? I'm living out one of their passions. Besides, I make their son happy every day.

How could I have won Vanessa over? In hindsight, maybe I should've finished at least one helping of her chicken breasts. On Sunday morning, I could've called her and made an effort to see her, instead of staying in my room. Or maybe I should've followed a social code that I don't even know to observe.

How can I win her over now?

I don't have any colleagues, meetings, or reasons to leave the apartment, so there's nothing to interrupt my thoughts. They nag me even while I'm working on my latest portrait—a woman in a lush bubble bath, sinking back into soft peaks. The bubbles started out as a dazzling variety of whites. They're supposed to evoke sun-drenched diamonds and the euphoria of an engagement.

But these days, every color I mix for the bubbles comes out too dark. I'm not even using black paint, but for some reason, every combination looks like I did. It takes a lot more paint to lighten a color than to darken it, so I end every day with heaps of wasted goo like organs on the palette: a muddy kidney, a gray eyeball. Every brushstroke dulls another spark of life in the work. It started out happy, but when I look at it now, all I see is a brunette about to drown.

As the days get shorter, at least Richard's and my relationship stays strong. We still have dinner together most nights—but now, I catch him glancing at my plate when I say I'm done. Did he always do that? We still see friends on weekends, attached at the hip. We go to a costumes-encouraged thirtieth birthday party as ceiling fans, each in a sweatshirt that reads Go CEILINGS and carrying megaphones. We still hold hands in museums, and he leaves me notes in my studio before his morning commute—*You amaze me every day*—to remind me that he's proud, even when no one's asking for my work, even as my paintings refuse to sell. We still want to have a small wedding next year—one so modest that we haven't really started planning yet. So far, we've only picked the date: sometime in June, the start of summer.

Our relationship feels healthy, but how long could this last if his mom disagrees? I know that I'm engaged to *Richard*, but after being with his family at home—and seeing the quiet authority that she has—it's clear that her opinion matters. I won't get to see the Belmonts again until their golf tournament in early October, but I'm already imagining how to make a better impression. At the very least, I'll eat more—if that's what this is really about.

~

I schedule lunch with my friend Hunter. She and I met a few years ago in the Kasmin Gallery, where she's an assistant. I liked her instantly because she was blunt—so blunt, she made spot-on jokes about a painting in the show. Everyone else in the gallery was reverent, or pretending to be. Meanwhile, she roasted the painting until I had to step outside and collect myself. At the time, I figured that she came from money and was used to getting away with reckless honesty. As it turned out, she's scratching by like everyone else. I love Hunter because she's no-nonsense, and yet, she's spellbound by truly great art.

We pick a ramen place near Kasmin.

I'm here early at a skinny table for two.

I'm tapping my fingers on the table when I see Hunter crossing the street toward me. Her camel trench coat flaps over black ankle boots. She's always had a minimalistic sense of style: simple clothes with clean lines. When she leans in for a hug, it's clear that she's not wearing a speck of makeup. She doesn't color her hair, either, which bounces in a blunt cut around her shoulders.

"What's wrong?" she asks.

Of course she can tell.

We've been in sync since the day we met. I credit it to the fact that she works with painters at Kasmin, so she gets people like me. She doesn't bat an eye when I mention that I spent all weekend in one room, immersed in my creative personal bubble. She knows that if we run into another painter, I'll immediately start to talk shop about technical things—brands of paints, which fabric stretcher bars they use. Hunter respects everything weird about me. I've never had a better friend.

As we sit, I rest my forehead in my hands and download everything, starting with the first time Richard brought me home.

"But we got the date wrong," I explain. "So we showed up to this *void*. Their house wasn't just empty; it was—have you ever seen somewhere pristine look abandoned?" I remember the dark windows. Black ivy. Locked doors. Every time Richard tried to open another one, it somehow got even quieter. "It's not a big deal, but standing in that driveway gave me a weird feeling. It was like . . ." Sinking into a bucket of dark paint. Finding the last house on earth, and no one is home. I shake my head, unable to pick a comparison. "I know it was just a mix-up, but it set the tone."

"The tone for what?" she asks.

The waiter arrives to take our orders.

We rattle off our usuals without thinking.

"Our next visit went better, until we were about to leave," I say once we're alone. "Then Richard told me his mom was worried about how much I'm eating." Hunter raises a thick, untamed eyebrow. "She told him he deserves a healthy partner."

"I'm sorry, what?"

I trust Hunter's opinion on relationships. She and her husband have been happy since their days as high school sweethearts in New Jersey. He's an introverted engineer, and they balance each other. She loves that he's a logical thinker with an even keel, a relief from her volatile artists. Meanwhile, he's fascinated by her career in the art world, a strange place without clear rules, where insiders somehow get away with selling twenty dollars' worth of materials for millions.

"Back up," she says. "You were still at their place when this happened?"

"Yes, and I've been driving myself a little mad trying to figure out what I did wrong. The way Richard was looking at me, it was like she'd told him that I have a rare, communicable disease, and he shouldn't ever touch me again. Like I'm dangerous—not just to myself but to everyone, with my ferocious refusal to eat."

"And this came out of nowhere?"

"Yes."

Hunter looks pensive.

"Do they know anything about your parents?" Her tone is delicate.

"Only the basics—that my parents are divorced, my mom's still in Ohio, and we don't exactly stay in touch." I do call my mom every few months. I remain hopeful that one day, she'll get better for good. "Vanessa isn't that close with her parents, so they just accepted the fact that I'm not either. The point is, the Belmonts don't have anything against my family. This is really just about me."

Our miso vegetarian ramens arrive. Soft-cooked egg yolks melt into the noodles. We pick up our spoons and submerge them. Meanwhile, a redheaded man beside us orders crispy eggplant and a ramen with pork belly.

"Oh," I add, "and Richard's brother was there when she said this. Oliver."

"Remind me about Oliver?"

"Twenty-seven. Lives at home."

"For how long?"

"A couple years?"

Her jaw drops—and then her lips curl into a wicked smile.

"I'm sorry, *what*?" she asks.

"He had a bad breakup a while ago." I shrug.

"Sounds like there's more to that story."

Her tone is so confident, I wonder if she's right. Now that I'm thinking about it, a breakup doesn't sound like reason enough to stay home for two *years*—especially when he has the means to be somewhere else.

Then again, I don't have a good feel for what's normal.

Mom's drinking nurtured strange behavior—stories I've only told Richard and Hunter, and even then, only late at night, when shadows would hide their reactions. Back when I was a teen, Mom started to eat every meal in her underwear so she wouldn't spill food on her clothes. I remember the first time I came home from school to find her undressed, ready for dinner with me. That's when I started to keep the blinds down. Kids are programmed to love their parents, though, and I was no different. I loved her when I understood her, and I kept loving her when I didn't.

With memories like that, I never thought twice about Oliver. I just admired the Belmonts for having a home stable enough for a long-term guest. But is there another reason he's still there? Is he hiding from someone, like the police? I doubt it. Oliver doesn't have the chops to show up late to a tee time, let alone break a law. Besides, Richard told me about the breakup. He'd never lie to me.

"What's Oliver like?" Hunter asks.

"Pretty . . . tame," I admit. Her smile is relentless, and I feel the need to defend him. I tell her that he works remotely for a successful mutual fund. Apparently, he has a textbook golf swing. "And he's a genuinely nice guy, wouldn't hurt a fly. The most damage he's ever done in his life has been to a cheese plate."

Hunter shimmies her shoulders.

"Sorry, grown men at home just give me the creeps," she says. Her lip curls as if her ramen is sour. "I'm sure he's *nice*, but I can't stop picturing Norman in the Bates Motel. You know, dead pale, soft hands, obsessed with his mom. I'm sure Oliver isn't like that, but that's just what comes to mind."

I stare at my food.

"I just wish I knew what she was really trying to say."

"Don't try to make it rational. You didn't do anything wrong." Hunter tosses her noodles without any apparent desire to eat.

"You all right?" I ask.

"I've just seen this happen before."

She keeps tossing her noodles.

"What?" I pry.

"When you marry into a family like that—people like the Belmonts—you can sort of lose control. It's like, you have to go on all their fancy family vacations to the spots *they* love. You do everything on *their* schedule. Before you know it, your mother-in-law is planning your wedding, telling you which wedding dress looks best on your figure, and these are the pearls she wore on her wedding day, so wouldn't you like to wear them too?" She looks remorseful. "Sorry," she says. "I'm sure it won't be that bad. I've just seen some friends go down that road."

I lose my appetite and feel Vanessa vindicated in the war over my stomach.

~

That night, Richard and I eat roast chicken, side by side at our table for four. My legs are on his lap, dangling between his thighs. Every time he drops a hand to my knees, I lose my train of thought, without any desire to find it. I love how he makes mundane moments sexy, quiet ones loud, just by moving his body.

He catches me staring at him.

"You've got that look," he says.

"What look?"

"Like you're going to paint me."

I laugh. "Would that be so bad?"

The first time I painted Richard was the first time he said "I love you." He was in my studio apartment in Harlem, sitting on my mattress. I was kneeling on the floor six feet away, staring at him and drawing his lines. We'd been dating for only a month, but something about looking at each other for so long, immersed in that moment—*Can you lower your chin? Put your hand on your knee?*—was hyper-romantic. He said, *I love how you see things for yourself,* which became *I love how much you care,* which became at last *I love you.* We made love on my thin mattress straight through our dinner reservation, and I'd never been more satisfied.

"Maybe not," he says.

He winks.

He's definitely remembering that night.

"So, are you going to paint me like one of your French girls?" he asks.

"That depends," I tease. "Are you comfortable with nudity?"

"I was born naked."

I laugh. He squeezes my knees.

I move my legs higher on his thighs. He reaches for one of my hands and kisses it slowly, looking at me the whole time. I melt a little. The shift he makes from playful to earnest is so quick and seamless it's like magic. Even when he's joking, or turning me on, he's always just a heartbeat away from getting serious, and that makes every fun moment feel like it's rooted in something real.

I move in to kiss him, but he leans back an inch.

"Not so fast." He nods at our unfinished plates.

I pause.

He's not saying that . . . because of his mom, right?

"I was thinking about our wedding," he goes on, still holding my hand. The sentence relaxes me. So *this* is why he wants to linger over dinner, instead of leading me to the sofa. "Remember how we chose June?" I nod. "I reserved Blue Hill at Stone Barns for us on June eighteenth." He adds that we can cancel at any point over the next twenty-four hours, but he saw the opportunity and put our names in. We can have our ceremony anywhere on their eighty acres, and then, our reception in the HayLoft. "You remember that room? It's ours now, to fill with at least forty and less than two hundred sixty of our favorite people."

My jaw drops.

Blue Hill is a sprawling farm with a Michelin-starred restaurant, where he took me to dinner for my birthday last year. We fell in love with the place. It's chic with a rustic soul. The menu changes so often that the same meal never happens twice. After dinner, we wandered to the HayLoft, where a wedding reception was in full swing. We danced for a song on our own, then kissed like the event was ours.

"Richard!" I hug him tight. "That is beyond perfect. You are the most thoughtful, most generous person in the whole world. Thank you so much. I don't know how you get better every day, but honestly, you do."

He beams.

"I feel like I can *see* our wedding now," I add.

We've decided on only a few personal touches for the day, but now, I can picture them in the HayLoft, with its cobblestone walls and barn doors. Does it really seat up to 260 people? He didn't say it explicitly, but I sense we're on the same page about inviting a number toward the bottom of that range. My parents can't help pay for anything, and Richard shouldn't have to foot an unconscionable bill.

"What do you see there?" he asks.

"You."

"Well, I'd hope so."

He laughs, and I smile.

If I'm as happy as I think, then why is something itching in the back of my mind? It must be something that Hunter said. *When you marry into a family like that—people like the Belmonts—you can sort of lose control . . . Before you know it, your mother-in-law is planning your wedding.* That's not what's happening here at all, though. *Richard* and I talked about wanting to get married in June. When he booked the HayLoft, he made a decision that he knew I would love.

I should forget it. I don't want to ruin this moment thinking about my tension with his family—or about our visit to Greenwich looming next week, when Richard will enter the golf tournament with his dad. But now, his attention is shifting to a skewered bite of chicken. He studies it at the end of his fork.

"Everything okay?" I ask.

"What was that dish Mom made?"

"Which one?"

"With the fruits?"

Chicken marbella.

"We could try to make it the way she did," he says.

I tell him sure, but I want to get back to talking about our wedding. Aren't we having a moment here? Maybe we could incorporate art somehow and name tables after our favorite paintings. I'm seeing Georgia O'Keeffe's *Red Canna* and Matisse's *The Swimming Pool*—but Richard is still staring at the chicken.

"I was just thinking about our wedding?"

"Right," he says. "Sorry."

"We can finish talking about it later," I say, feeling my mood down-shift, even as Richard pecks my cheek. "You know, I was wondering . . ." I try to sound nonchalant. "Are you sure that *you* were the one who wanted the HayLoft?"

He looks genuinely confused.

"You and me," he clarifies.

"Not . . . ?" Vanessa?

I have a sudden flashback to eating dinner with Mom. She always sat at the head of the table. I'd claim the other end, the view that hid the most. Another one of her strange beliefs, fostered by alcohol, was that refrigerators aren't as harmless as people believe. She didn't trust them—or microwaves, or any other box where you closed the door and momentarily lost sight of your meal. So she kept all our groceries on the counter. A small city of Tupperware was visible over her shoulder. She and I didn't talk much while we ate. I never complained about the combinations she served—toasted ravioli, grilled chocolate sandwiches—because I loved her.

I believed that the real Grace—my lively, imaginative, and highly educated mom—was in there somewhere, even when her behavior changed. So I sat through those dinners, waiting for her to get better. The only problem was: she got worse. So, what makes me an expert on family dynamics?

I want to swallow my words.

"Never mind," I say.

I take a large bite, still surprised at my own tone a few seconds ago. I'm probably just hurt that they don't love me more. I'm probably just on edge because every day my paintings don't sell, my dream feels further away, and I become more of a burden on our relationship. I know that my income isn't my worth, but I'd like to take Richard out for once. The mounting pressure can sometimes make it hard to think straight, hard to *see* straight. So whatever the problem is, I'm sure that it's mine.

FIVE

Richard and I pack for our visit to Greenwich tomorrow. He's shirtless in our bedroom, his khakis low on his hips. He smiles at me, two clumps of hair sticking up like golden bunny ears. It's goofy but gorgeous. On any other night, I'd smile back, drag him by a belt loop onto the bed, and make his hair even messier.

But my anxiety is creeping in, spreading like a drop of paint in water—even though everything's been going so well. Last night, we ate at Kappo Masa with two of Richard's bosses and their wives, who took us out in a delayed celebration of our engagement. The restaurant sits inside the Gagosian Gallery on Madison Avenue, conceived of as a fusion between visual and culinary art. It was brilliant sushi, while staring at Picassos. And the best part was, even with a cubist masterpiece beside him, Richard talked about my work as if *that* were the art everyone needed to see. He held my hand, beaming as if he were the lucky one.

Still, I can't stop wondering what his parents might whisper tomorrow, how they might treat me, and—I'm not a pushover. I'm not just going to pretend I'm not feeling this way. People think art is for dreamers, and maybe it is. But it takes ferocity to hold on to a dream for long. It takes nails, teeth.

"So, are your parents excited to see us?" I probe.

"Of course."

Richard disappears into our closet.

He emerges with a neat pile of polos. If I were more at ease, I'd point out that he's shirtless right now but packing four tops for a day and a half. I press a cardigan into my bag, its column of buttons like a stack of eyes.

"Have they said anything else, you know, about my eating?"

"No. I don't think so."

"You don't *think* so?"

"They haven't."

He walks back into the closet and returns with two ties. He holds up the green one covered in pickles and the phrase DILL WITH IT. His grin is triumphant. He knows I find that tie hilarious. Usually, I laugh just looking at it. We have a backgammon set in the living room, which we always play for stakes. One of our go-to bets is that the loser has to wear this tie the entire next day—a prospect always riskier for him. Richard shrugs and packs it, amused enough for both of us.

"Richard?" I ask.

"Yes?"

"Did they say anything else that time in the kitchen? You know, the last time we were there? Your mom and brother?"

"I don't really remember."

"Can you try?"

He scratches his neck.

"They were just worried about you," he says. "You do things a little differently, you know? It's not a bad thing. It's what makes your art unique." Richard's never described me like this. "My parents aren't used to it yet. So when they sat down with you to eat, they just saw you go about it an unusual way. It was *overthought* or something." He shrugs. "And it made them nervous."

"They said that about me?" I ask.

"Hey." Richard takes a step closer and holds my hand. "I love you. They love you. They just want us to be happy."

~

Saturday morning, I'm on edge as we approach the Belmonts' estate. The houses leading up to theirs are all just as grand, but none seems as thoughtful. The multiple libraries, museum-quality art—and the family's deep knowledge of it—must make their home the most cerebral one in the neighborhood. They've woven intellectual luxuries into physical ones.

Richard is holding my hand when we reach their driveway—and see his parents. They're just a few steps ahead, arms linked in Barbour jackets, apparently returning from a walk around the neighborhood. Vanessa does a two-mile jaunt first thing every day, so this must be her second round. As they turn toward us, baseball caps cast small shadows over their eyes.

Richard rolls down my window.

"Hi!" I make an effort to smile at Vanessa.

She returns mine with a more subtle version. She's polished as usual, her bob sleek and characterized by precision. The style must be murder to maintain. I can almost see the flurry of shears around her, keeping the bangs just above her brows, the edge hugging her jawline.

"We were just taking a little stroll," she says, "and talking about that new article in *Vanity Fair*? About the incident at that MFA program?" I have no idea what she's talking about. I've been struggling so much with my portraits that I haven't found time to read. "Apparently, a teacher confessed to kissing a student. I know we've all read variations on this theme. But what's interesting *here* is that the student says the incident never happened and is some kind of fantasy."

"What happened to the teacher?" I ask.

Vanessa looks curiously at me.

Her fur lapel shakes in the wind.

I regret my question, suddenly feeling flustered. Of course, I should've asked about the *student*. How did I miss that? Now I look oddly sympathetic to the predator.

"Sorry, what I meant was—" I start.

Vanessa interrupts me to shriek, pointing at my lap. Clarke's eyes widen. I scream without knowing what's scaring them. I look down, but there's nothing, nowhere, and *not* knowing is even more terrifying. Richard turns me toward him, his hands on my shoulders. He scans my body gravely. Outside, Vanessa is still in shock. I feel Richard lift my arm. He points to a gruesome streak of red oil paint across my wrist.

"Is she all right?" Clarke asks.

"It's paint," Richard announces.

He licks his thumb and smears it. My heartbeat slows, but I'm so unnerved I start to cry. I thought I cleaned myself up last night before we packed. I remember washing my hands—scrubbing them so hard that they turned pink under the faucet; oils are relentless—but I must've missed this spot.

This one enormous spot.

"Paint," Vanessa repeats.

Richard rubs my back.

"I'm sorry," I say, my eyes still dripping.

"Nothing to be sorry about," Clarke's friendly voice booms. "We knew you were an artist, but now, we learn you're a work of art yourself." Vanessa recovers enough to laugh, but the sound isn't joyful. Clarke wraps an arm around his wife. "Well, kids, we'll let the both of you get settled." Before I can get ahold of myself, they've already turned their backs.

~

As we drop our bags in our room, Richard gets a work call, even though it's Saturday. He mouths an apology to me, but I silence it with a kiss.

I head downstairs and glimpse Vanessa in the library. She's reading on the sofa, her legs folded in V shapes beside her. Does she know I'm here? I'm one room away, by a leaded glass window. It blurs the view outside, melting everything down to its colors. But Vanessa's in focus, her dewy cheeks catching the light. If she's wearing anything on her skin, it's sheer, from a neutral palette. The look lets her eyes shine through, those transfixing Belmont blues.

I remember how much my mom loved makeup: vivid blushes, bold lipsticks. She was more careful with the products when I was a kid. When I was a teen, she still put them on every morning, but if I wasn't there, I don't think she would've taken them off. Sometimes, I'd come home from school to find the eye shadow smeared into knife points over her cheeks. She's as pale as I am, so the contrast was severe. I had to insist on helping her. I'd walk her into the bathroom and wipe her eyes clean with damp toilet paper squares. The worse she got, the more I drew.

The floor creaks under my foot.

"Devon!" Vanessa shuts the book. "Please, join me." She scoots sideways and taps the sofa. "Sorry again about earlier. I thought . . ." She doesn't finish her sentence, so my mind does for her. *I thought you'd cut yourself. I thought your wrists were slashed.*

I take a seat, glancing at her book as she rests it on the coffee table. It's a biography on Picasso.

"One of the greats?" I ask.

"One of the great*est*."

She drags a hand over the cubist piece on the cover. It looks like a shattered face. I ask if she's learned anything surprising. She leans back, thinking, her legs still tucked in their Vs. She might carry herself with a sense of order and control, but there's something quietly flexible about her. It's evident in the angular swirl of her body, her ankle in one hand.

"The *toll* of his creativity was a dark little shock," she says slowly. "One of his mistresses hanged herself. His second wife shot herself. His son died of alcoholism . . . It makes you wonder about the *price* of great art, doesn't it? If it requires someone to hurt, whether it's the artist or the ones they love? Maybe there's some blood in everything truly special." She smiles, saving the conversation from a grimmer turn. "You'd know better than I do, which reminds me . . ." A beat. "I'm not sure I got to mention this at your last visit, but I have a lot of respect for what you do."

"Really?"

She nods. "Richard's told us about your devotion. He says you're a force of nature. That when you're painting, nothing can tear you out of the studio. Nothing can stop you from giving a canvas what it needs." Her legs are still spiraled on the cushion between us. "I suppose I'm a different cat. Instead of spending ten years crafting my style, chipping away at a masterpiece, I'd rather go to the Met and enjoy someone else's." Her smile becomes guilty. "Is that lazy?"

"No, it's quite sane."

She laughs.

"I do think people who *make* great art and people who *enjoy* it have something important in common. Don't you? Otherwise, how could the art resonate with them? Art*ists* and art *lovers*, they must share a bond." I can't help but feel a little flattered that she'd try to point out similarities between us. I'm not sure if this is a small olive branch or if I just misread her in the first place.

The front door opens to reveal Oliver in white light. He waves to Vanessa, his fingers cutting through the glow like scissors. He parks his golf clubs and heads for us, his gaze fixed on his mom. He's thin boned, his nose narrow and jaw delicate, making him seem more aristocratic than his brother. He's just steps from us now—but still won't acknowledge me.

Richard would never do that. Even in a crowded room, he makes everyone feel like the most important person there. And yet, here's his brother, just feet away, and I'm watching him through a one-way window. Oliver is a bloodless kind of pale despite his round on the golf course—one of several this week, I imagine. A dark leather golf glove covers his left hand.

After he hugs Vanessa, he sits on the arm of the sofa. She grabs his knee, and I notice her polish is as neutral as the rest of her outfit. The only exceptions are her flats, flashes of snakeskin when she moves her legs. While they take a moment, I study my black pants and turtleneck, feeling a little out of place. Maybe I should invest in some beige pieces just to wear in Greenwich. Richard, for one, has his own wardrobe for this house, as if there's a silent dress code.

"Devon?" Oliver asks.

I lift my chin.

"Could you excuse us?" he asks.

"Of course."

"Oh, let Devon stay," Vanessa intervenes.

"Please?" Oliver asks his mom.

"I'm happy to check on Richard," I lie.

I stand and leave politely—as if I have somewhere to go.

Clearly, Richard got the hospitality genes. But I try to put myself in Oliver's shoes. Maybe they do have something private and urgent to discuss. Not to mention that living at home could've sapped some of his social graces. He could've regressed, fallen back into the mindset of a kid unwilling to share his mom.

Was he nicer to me when we met?

I think back to when Richard and I visited for Vanessa's birthday. But I was so focused on her and Clarke that now, I can't remember a single thing Oliver said. As if he did nothing but lurk in the shadows, watching everyone else. When I try to picture him on that night, it's like trying to see the subject in Magritte's *The Son of Man*: one figure in a bowler hat, face hidden by a hovering apple.

~

Before dinner that night, I find my place card on the dining room table—right next to Vanessa's. Both are wedged into the trunks of tiny silver elephants. Last time, she sat *across* from me. Did I make it back onto her good side? Or was I wrong about her in the first place? The elephants seem exuberant, trumpeting our names like a show's about to begin.

In the kitchen, Vanessa stirs a meaty beef bourguignon. I replay highlights from the last few hours as I wait my turn by the stove. Everything seems to be going well. Vanessa was a doting host during cocktails, without giving me unwanted attention. Oliver perked up and told a couple of golf stories from today. At one point, I thought he was going to reveal something—and give me an insight into his personal life—when he asked, *You know what I need more than anything?* But the answer turned out to be an umbrella stand.

After Clarke in the serving line, I load my plate as full as his. We file into the dining room and find our seats. Richard winks at me from across the table—too bad we can't lock ankles from here. I raise my water in time with their wine. Then I swallow lump after lump of— pearl onions? Unrendered fat? The sauce makes everything hard to identify.

"Devon, how is painting?" Vanessa asks.

All eyes stick to me.

"It's great," I lie.

I tell them about Marc's show next month, when he'll unveil my latest work. The bubble baths are still too dark, but I'll fix them—I have to.

"What's the marketing plan?" Oliver asks.

I furrow my brow. "The usual."

"She's an artist," Richard says. "She's not in PR."

But maybe I should learn about it.

I remember my last opening night. A few months ago, I stood dressed up next to my pieces *Not Red* and *Melted Stones*. At first, it felt like a dream come true. My work was in Zellweger. Then, I spent the night watching people swarm other artists. A young hotshot across the room was getting a solo show at the MoMA, and everyone was buzzing about it.

"That reminds me," Vanessa says, pointing her fork at me. "I put in a good word for you at the 'Quin. I said they should consider you as a speaker." Before I can ask, she explains, "It's a little private club. No stadium seating, of course, but an event there might stir some whispers about your work." Her tines swirl as she gestures, four polished teeth. "Don't thank me yet, but I'm trying. A peek behind the curtain at your process would be fascinating."

The conversation shifts to a story in the *Times*. I focus on finishing my food, feeling lost as they discuss it. I need to get back on track with work to make time again for the news. Otherwise, I might lose touch with what's happening in the real world. My attention drifts to Oliver. He's staring at me, something dark in his eyes. As soon as I catch him, he averts his gaze.

Did I imagine that?

I put my silverware down.

"I would like to take a moment," Clarke cuts in toward the end of the meal, "and request that we look at everyone's plates." I freeze. Everyone's eyes dart around, registering five clean dishes. "Vanessa, that was excellent."

But—Clarke didn't want to focus on *everyone's* plates, right? I get the feeling that he just wanted to point out mine. He was trying to show someone else at the table that I'd finished my food. I look at Richard, but he's tipsy. He gives me a fuzzy-eyed thumbs-up that seems like a complete non sequitur. Who was Clarke trying to reach? I look from Vanessa to Oliver to Richard back to Clarke. There's something unnervingly similar about them. Their eyes are all the same shade of blue. They're all in turtlenecks with leather elbow patches sewn on their sleeves. They're all swirling dark glasses of wine. If one of them is concerned about my health, are they all?

I force myself to finish dessert, thin sugar cookies that taste like icing. They're hard as bone. I reluctantly accept a decaf espresso.

"Who wants to play Ping-Pong?" Clarke asks.

I take my dish into the kitchen, trying to dodge the filling roster.

Sure, all Clarke did was point out my plate, but that means people really are talking about what I'm eating and whether it's the right amount. I don't like these lurking suspicions—about my *food*.

It's invasive. Because when they debate my meals, they're hashing out what happens inside my body. It's not far from debating my blood or a cross-section of my thigh. I help ferry in forks, knives. I might be the guest in this dark estate. But they can't choose what I eat.

The grandfather clock in the kitchen reads ten thirty. Vanessa appears at the sink wearing an apron patterned with Princeton Tigers. I hear her talking—she's telling me that she's going to start soaking her fingers in nail polish remover so that she stops biting her pinkie nails. She asks me if I have any bad habits. I excuse myself and head upstairs to Richard's room, where I shut the door and sit on his bed. Oliver and Richard creak up to the third floor, where the game room awaits. A third pair of footsteps—heavier ones—stops nearby.

"Dev, do you want to play?" Clarke asks.

He must be right outside the door.

"Dev?" It's gentle.

I know he means well—I think he does—but there are undercurrents about *me* here that I don't understand. Eventually, his footsteps head up the final flight of stairs. Ping-Pong balls crack and zip. Oliver must be dangerous with all the racquet sports that he plays. Was he really staring at me during dinner? He wasn't looking at my plate. He was looking at *me*, as if I were a shifting puzzle.

SIX

The next morning, I'm sketching in bed while Richard golfs with his dad. I've been here since we kissed goodbye a couple of hours ago. I wished him luck, but he said he didn't need it—after all, he never misses his fourth putt.

I should get up and change, or at least turn on a light.

The shadows are starting to sink under my skin.

I thrust the curtains open, and day rushes inside. I could go downstairs with his family. But I'd rather not face their creeping doubt, their slippery eyes. Instead, I pull a chair up to the window and draw the view. There are fewer leaves than last time. Branches claw for pieces of the sky. My mind drifts back to my paintings at home. I need to pump life into them. I want the woman in the bath to think for herself, *look* back at me. More sketching might help, because the practice is about capturing the heart of something. It's about that hot, quick impression.

Going on instinct, at least, is a strength in my family. Mom trusted her intuition above all else, leading to a host of unusual beliefs. For one, she was resolute that the body could heal itself. So I never got familiar with modern medicine. She'd diagnose my colds or pains, then give me homeopathic pills. As I got older, her sense of what was wrong with me declined. In high school, she started connecting my symptoms to past lives. When I got the flu, she said that in the Middle Ages, I had been poisoned. I didn't fully believe her, but I also wasn't sure she was wrong.

The front door shuts.

Who was that?

I check my phone to see a missed text from Vanessa. Oliver left for the driving range, and I'm headed out on another short walk. Do you want to come? I spot her vanishing down the driveway. Her steps are long, elegant. Did I miss my chance?

She makes it all the way to Waverley and strides into the stillness. I don't think I could join her now, but I can't ignore her offer. I text Sorry I missed this—was sketching! and watch until she disappears. But she doesn't check her phone.

~

When the clock chimes one, I close my sketchbook and stand. I probably should eat something. Isn't that what they're saying, anyway? On my way downstairs, Woolf sprints away from me. His furry claws dart out of sight.

I wander through the dining room, where five brass dial clock faces are built into the wall. They stare back at eye level. I must've spent too much time in the dark this morning, because now, they look vaguely human. The round slab inches from my nose feels like a kind of mirror image. A real clock *face*.

I cross into the kitchen, which feels thick with tension even now, when it's empty. It's been almost two hours since the start of her "short walk." The more I think about it, the more convinced I am that Vanessa's text was a fake invitation. If she really wanted company, she would've made more of an effort to include me. But why would she extend a fake invitation in a private text? Especially after being so nice yesterday—talking about our similarities, proposing me for the 'Quin? Now, she's gone, and the men won't be home from golf for another few hours.

I fix myself a bowl of cereal and text Richard that his family has abandoned me—it's a dramatic choice of words, but we have a running joke where we blame others for the situations we create. When Richard has too much to drink at someone else's party, we blame the host for overserving him. When we forget an umbrella and end up drenched on our way to dinner, we blame the rain, the vindictive rain.

Eventually, I head back upstairs.

It's one thirty, more than two hours since Vanessa left. I go back to my sketchbook and try to work, but I'm distracted. Where is she?

~

The front door opens close to two.

I hear Vanessa hum her way into the kitchen. I'm uneasy up here, but I shouldn't be. I'm probably just remembering what it felt like to be at home, listening to my mom in the next room. The older I got, the more she spoke to our furniture in her own language. She would address the chairs as "Mr. and Mrs. Ikea" and have whole conversations with them using verbs I still don't understand. I don't know if things would've been better had Dad spent more time at home. Either way, he divorced Mom when I left for college. The last thing he said to me was that I reminded him too much of her. He didn't want anything to do with me either.

Richard texts me. He emphasizes my message about the abandonment and tells me that he, Clarke, and Oliver will be back soon. I pack our things, and in minutes, it's as if we were never here—except for the chair I moved to the window. Now, it looks like a ghost is enjoying the view, watching shadows sway.

The front door opens, and Richard leaps upstairs. Soon, he's crossing the threshold, almost filling the doorway as he passes through it. His long-sleeve polo fits him well, hugging the muscles that slant down both sides of his neck. Folded aviators dangle by the buttons. He kisses me hello, and unfortunately for him, he smells more like sweat than sunscreen. His cheeks are already a dangerous pink. Even on cold days like this, I know better than most that you can still burn.

He looks more concerned about me.

"What happened?" he asks.

"Nothing, really."

"Nothing?" He looks surprised. "I thought . . ."

He pulls out his phone.

"Honestly, nothing," I say more confidently. "I've just been sketching." I try to run one hand through my hair, but it gets caught in my low ponytail. I let a clump of dark strands fall loose and hide an ear.

"The whole time?" he asks.

"Yes."

"I thought you would've spent some time with Mom." He looks hopeful, his eyes rosy with veins. "You know, girl talk?"

I remember her hustle down the driveway.

He checks his watch, saying that he's going to grab a coffee before we go. He asks if I want to join everyone downstairs. I tell him I'd rather not, after the abandonment and all. I'm clinging to the joke, but he doesn't smile. He kisses me on the mouth, the ear, then leaves.

Alone again, I feel uncomfortable. All day, I've been in alternating roles of avoid*ed* and avoid*ing*. I should probably just focus on my drawings, as usual. I walk up to the chair.

"Do you mind?" I ask the ghost.

I'm only kidding, but the light on the wooden seat shifts.

I'm sketching a spiderweb outside—it's skirting the line between visible and invisible, glinting every few seconds—when Richard comes back upstairs. He looks redder than he was just a few minutes ago. His burn is setting in. Tiny vessels swell on his cheeks, looking like shrunken handprints. I close my book as Richard grabs two of the suitcases by the door.

"How was it?" I ask.

"I told them it wasn't very nice how they abandoned you."

"You *told* them that?"

"Isn't that what you said?"

"To *you*. Not to them. To *you*."

"Well, it's true!"

"Richard, I was exaggerating."

I can't see his expression now with his back to me.

Richard and I head downstairs, our steps loud with the weight of our luggage. I hate that most of my relationship with his family happens when I'm not there. When the foyer comes into view, he turns around and stops short. I'm two steps above him. My frustration must be all over my face. He puts the suitcases down and faces me with prayer hands.

"Can you pretend for a second that you don't hate my family?" he asks in a stage whisper. In the foyer ahead of us, Clarke is hanging a wide-brimmed hat on the coatrack. He freezes momentarily, his arm lifted. He definitely just heard.

I don't know where a comment like that comes from. *Can you pretend for a second that you don't hate my family?* I've never acted like I hate the Belmonts. Ever since I met them, I only ever wanted to be one of them. I only ever wanted to belong here. Hate them? This is just like when Richard said that I do things a little differently, his eyes flat, tone automatic—I just knew those words didn't belong to him. *Can you pretend for a second that you don't hate my family?* That idea isn't his either. I can feel it. And if we weren't within earshot of his dad, I'd say exactly that.

I motion with my chin for Richard to keep going.

We make it to the first floor. Clarke turns around.

"Oh, you're leaving?" he asks.

"Yes, didn't Richard tell you?" I ask.

Clarke looks lost.

Vanessa strolls in with Oliver, both sharing a dumbfounded expression. They protest we're leaving too soon—but this has been the plan all along. Richard and I have a grocery delivery arriving at four. We were planning to cook an early dinner and talk more about our wedding. Richard didn't tell them? Did they expect us here tonight? Vanessa asks why we're leaving, and Richard only says that he wishes we could stay. His voice is congenial, dodging specifics. I don't know why he's not clarifying things for everyone, because now this looks reactive. It looks like I'm forcing Richard to clear out because I'm resentful.

He heads outside, hoisting our bags to the car. Vanessa and Clarke are a step behind. I'm just with Oliver for a second before he follows and shuts the door. What's going on? The window in front of me blurs them. The only clear thing in sight is the landscape painting over the front door. It looks like an Albert Bierstadt, and it might be authentic, judging by its quality and devoted picture light. In the piece, a red sun bleeds behind a volcanic peak.

I open the front door.

When it shuts behind me, the four of them startle. They lean back so fast from their huddle, Vanessa takes a step for balance. I'm not sure what to make of it, so I say a quick thanks for the weekend, buckle myself into the passenger seat, and wait while Richard says less clipped goodbyes. From inside the car, their voices sound garbled. Eventually, Richard's door opens, and he slides into the driver's seat without taking my hand like he usually does.

We start to move, passing trees on both sides.

"You know, you can't hold my family emotionally hostage like that," he says.

"*What?*"

Silence.

"What do you mean, Richard?"

"Someone told me—"

"*Who* told you?"

He looks conflicted.

"Are you keeping something from me?" I ask. "For them?"

Waverley twists through quiet lawns.

"This is not how this works." I'm adamant. "*We* are together now, Richard. You don't keep secrets from me, not even if your family asks you to. *Especially* if they ask you to." Isn't that what marriage means: We make our own family now? How are we on such different pages?

I look over at him, but he still looks like my Richard, the man who walked up to me at the Whitney and hasn't left my side since. With his skin turning red, his hair looks whiter by contrast. It flares around his crown, full of messy waves and flyways so faint they blend into the space around him.

"Someone said—"

"Richard, please," I beg.

"Will you let me finish?" he asks.

He's flustered, but there's no edge in his voice.

We've never had a confrontation on the road before. We're not going fast, but something about the situation is unnerving. There's too much emotion in too tight a space.

"Someone said your moods were difficult."

"My *moods*?"

I don't know what he's talking about.

Richard and I have lived together for a year. My *moods*? If I had them, wouldn't he have noticed before? Besides, I do the same thing almost every day. The wildest, most violent part of my life is my work.

"Who said this?" I ask.

"I don't want to say. You'll have to deal with them for the rest of your life, so I'd prefer if you get along with them, please."

"Who." It's not a question.

Meanwhile, we pass a private tennis court with a black lattice fence. The slats intersect to create an illusion of diamond eyes. As we move, they blink and blink.

"My dad," Richard admits. "When I was loading up the car."

"What exactly did he say?"

"He said, 'Between you and me, her mood swings are not normal.'"

I fall silent.

I almost don't believe it. Clarke is the one person I was sure liked me in that family. *Mood swings*. My dad would use the same phrase to attack my mom. Whenever he came home to find something broken or defaced, he'd confront her. *Mood swings.* I did my best to defend her. Sometimes, I even told Dad it was *my* fault—that *I* was the one who kicked the leg out from under the kitchen table, that *I* threw our coasters into the walls—but he never took my word for it.

Now, who's here to defend me?

SEVEN

When Richard and I make it back to the Upper East Side, the words *mood swings* are still hot in my mind. Our heels click across the marble lobby. Richard gabs cheerfully with our doorman, Paul, as if there's no sour air between us.

"How's Carla?" Richard asks.

"We're going to spend Thanksgiving with my parents, so I'm hearing about that at home already." Paul gives us a wry look. "I promised her we'll leave as soon as they start to cause trouble. So she says it doesn't make sense to fly to Florida just for breakfast." Richard laughs. "How was the golf?"

"I got sunburned and shot a hundred ten," Richard says.

"The higher the better, right?"

"Exactly."

They laugh.

In the elevator, Richard's still beaming from the exchange. I never imagined that this part of him I love—this desire to entertain—would put distance between us. I want to finish the conversation we started in the car. Richard got a work call as we were leaving, so we haven't had time to reconcile. Before I can open my mouth, though, he checks his phone.

Two missed calls from Clarke stack on top of each other. The alerts are strange. Clarke never calls Richard. Clarke also texted him, asking to get lunch this Friday. I remember Clarke did mention that he and

Vanessa will be in the city then for a birthday party. I notice that I'm not invited. I haven't been explicitly excluded, but I have been in the way this family always excludes me, as if by a magical sleight of hand.

"What do you think the lunch is about?" I ask.

"He's probably worried about me."

I'm incredulous.

"What do you mean?" I ask.

"I don't know."

We cross into our dark apartment.

"Think, Richard."

"He probably wants to make sure I know what I'm getting myself into."

Richard and I have only had a couple of fights, both after we moved in together. We were already starting to talk about marriage, and he wanted to meet my parents. I told him that wasn't a good idea. My dad still won't have anything to do with me. I only call my mom a few times a year, and it's always hit or miss whether she's sober. Richard kept insisting. He wanted to at least talk to her on the phone. I told him that I didn't want to unbury my childhood traumas.

Each time our conversation came to a head, I locked myself in my studio. Then, when I couldn't paint anymore, I went on a long walk to cool off. I'd never known myself to get so heated. Part of me feared that if Richard spoke to Mom, he might view me differently. It's one thing to *know* that she's unstable. It's another thing to *hear* her. On those walks, I'd trek all the way down to the bottom of Manhattan, listening to music so loud the city was silent.

I feel a familiar wave of emotion come over me now. This time, though, I don't want to run away. Richard and I are engaged—and commitment means that you stay. I sit on our dark-blue sofa. Richard turns on the lights.

"I am a good person," I say.

I don't know why I feel the need to say this. Richard collapses on our bed in the next room. I make my way to the threshold. He's put a pillow over his eyes.

"Richard?" I ask.

I sit next to him.

He removes the pillow.

His eyes are watery.

"I love you," he says.

"I love you too."

"I'm sorry, I'm just . . . trying to make everyone happy."

"Okay, but what about you?" I ask.

He looks grateful.

"Forget about all the voices in your head," I go on. "You have your mom in there, your dad, your brother, me. Everyone has an opinion, but what do *you* think about us, Richard? What do *you* think about *me*?"

He takes my left hand in his.

I palm one side of his face. He hasn't shaved yet today. The yellow shadow around his mouth is a gentle scratch. He pulls me closer and closer into a kiss. I want to keep talking, but now, I feel his fingers at the bottom of my shirt. He's playing with the hem.

"Richard," I say quietly, "are you sure now's a good time?"

He kisses me again. It's soft, sorry.

I feel like we're still talking, like he's answering my questions in the way he strokes the back of my head, then rubs a thumb across my cheek. He knows that there's nothing wrong with us, that there's nothing wrong with me.

"I'm sorry, Devon."

"It's okay."

I kiss him back like I want to forgive him.

We stay like this for so long, I think I do.

"I love you," he whispers.

"I love you too."

"You are the best part of my life."

It's a messy moment. I can feel that he's sorry, and I'm still hurt. But this close, our bodies have minds of their own. He moves my hips on top of him. I straddle him while he slips his hands under my shirt, up to my bra. A moan oozes out of me. I grind into his fly. He rolls us over and pulls his shirt off with one hand. When he kneels to toss it aside, I rise with him, running my hands up his chest. He stays kneeling while I fiddle with his buckle.

He looked this handsome the day we met.

~

On Friday, I'm early for lunch with Hunter. I've been antsy all week leading up to now, when Richard will meet Clarke alone. I did consider asking Richard to include me or even to cancel. In the end, I figured that if Clarke wants to tell his son something in private, he'll find a way to do it—no matter what.

I'm on the other side of town at Hunter's and my favorite Vietnamese restaurant. A yellow scissor gate blocks part of my view outside. It's twelve fifteen. Richard might already be at Smith & Wollensky for their twelve thirty reservation. That steak house is usually full of corporate groups expensing premium meals to their firms. I imagine Richard walking through the bar toward his dad, dark suits parting around him. I'm jostling my knee, shaking the table, when Hunter crosses the threshold. Her smile fades. She hurries over and gives me a tight hug.

"Thanks for coming," I say.

"What's it now?" She winces.

I cover my face. "I don't want to make this all about me."

"Well, I do."

As we sit, I rehash last weekend, including Clarke's comment about my moods. Now, he and Richard are having a private lunch.

"I just know it's about me," I say.

"That's horrible."

She gives me a compassionate look.

"You have any idea what they're saying?" she asks.

"My 'mood swings.' Something about how crazy I am."

"*That's* insane."

I feel validated that Hunter is on my side. After all, she knows *real* mood swings better than most. The art world has long attracted the unsteady. The eccentric and ultrasensitive. At Kasmin, she works with an artist who paints the most cheerful abstractions to combat his depression. All his pieces are sunny and smooth. When people see his work, they're uplifted, not knowing the man with the brush was fighting suicidal thoughts.

"Originally, I thought it was Vanessa who hated me. But maybe she likes me, and it's Clarke who thinks I'm nuts. Or maybe it's Oliver. Or all of them." I unfold the plastic menu, facing a hundred options. "I have no idea anymore."

"You know, most of the time, people aren't upset about what they *think* they're upset about." Hunter's brown-eyed gaze is steady. "So, when they're making these accusations about you—whoever's behind it—maybe it's not really about your health or your mood. Maybe they're just upset that you're taking their son away from them. Maybe they're not ready to let him go." She shrugs but with confidence. "Have they treated his other girlfriends well?"

"I'm the first woman Richard's ever brought home," I say, then remember the photo I found in his desk. "First or second," I clarify.

Hunter looks shocked.

"I've been bringing guys home since fifth grade," she says. It feels good to laugh with her. "My parents had to make a rule that they wouldn't meet any more boyfriends until we'd lasted for at least six months. That got rid of everyone I dated in middle school."

When the waiter arrives, we order two pho soups. Usually, nothing lifts me up like a steaming bowl of pho. The broth here is a work of art:

savory but transparent, heaped with sprouts. Hunter asks for bubble tea as the waiter leaves.

"What about Oliver?" she asks. "He with someone?"

"Nope."

"Has he *ever* been with someone?"

I shrug. "He used to date a girl at Columbia, but that ended badly. He went home after the breakup and never left." The image of Oliver eating beef bourguignon returns, his hands limp on the cutlery, curating soggy bites. "Anyway, his most significant relationships are with his parents now. I'm on their family text chat, and Oliver uses it all day long. He texts his parents dozens of times a day. There can't be much room for anyone else."

"Sounds insular."

I'd agree, but I don't exactly have a pedestal.

"How's the extended family?" she asks.

I nod my head from side to side.

I've met some of Clarke's family, but none of Vanessa's. Apparently, she's been growing apart from her parents for decades. They stay in touch with the Belmonts, but otherwise, they're not particularly involved.

I only talked to her parents once, the week after Richard and I got engaged. It was a strange call—because they were so happy for us. So warm and eager to connect. Richard's ninety-year-old Grammy did most of the talking. She asked about the ring, Richard's exact words, who cried first, and then she wanted to know all about the *wedding*. In her mouth, that word sounded magical. At the end of the call, she said "I love you already" in a way that made my heart ache. Afterward, Richard explained that Vanessa can't relate to her parents because they don't value arts and culture. Vanessa grew up to be so different that they can't get a conversation off the ground. And without his mom spearheading family get-togethers, the branches just grew in different directions.

"I just worry that Richard's family could damage my relationship with him," I say. "If they don't want him to marry me, then maybe

Richard will have to choose between *them* and *me*, and I just don't know—"

Hunter's bubble tea arrives.

Dark beads swirl around the bottom.

"You don't know what?" she asks.

"If he could let them down." I wince. "Richard loves me, but he has this need to make everyone happy. This sixth sense for who needs his help. He still volunteers at that no-kill shelter when he really shouldn't, because it tears him up inside. Last month, I had to talk him out of adopting this senior boxer there, Freckles. Richard kept saying he wanted to take Freckles home, throw her a fifteenth birthday party, and take her to the vet every week." Hunter's expression lifts. "Exactly. And if he can't disappoint a dog he just met, how could he disappoint his own family?"

"It's simple."

"Is it?"

"He just tells them to mind their own business."

I can't imagine Richard saying that.

I massage my temple and roll my neck, making eye contact with a redheaded man sitting two tables over. Is he watching me?

"Devon?" she asks.

"Yes?"

"Where is this insecurity coming from?"

"I'm not insecure."

"You're acting like it. Remember who you are, for crying out loud. You wouldn't have made it this far if you didn't believe in yourself."

"It's not about what *I* think."

"Then what?"

"It's about what the *Belmonts* think," I say. "If *they* are looking for reasons to reject me, I don't exactly make it difficult to find them. I spend whole weekends in my studio when Richard's away, painting something I felt for a second. I know the Belmonts love art, but really, I have nothing to do with *art*. Do you know what I mean? I'm the mess of making it. As soon as it's *art*, I disappear." Hunter of all people knows I mean that literally. I have a superstitious habit of never looking at my paintings again once they're done. "And then there are all the class differences. I still don't know how the score works in golf. I just don't want to lose him." I cover my eyes and feel—tears. All of a sudden, I'm crying. My body isn't shaking, and my voice isn't out of control, but tears run down my cheeks. "Now look at me."

"I am looking at you."

"I'm falling apart."

"Stop it." Her tone is severe. "You are the bravest person I know, so start acting like it." I drop my hands back in my lap, the tears warm on my fingertips. "And if they're as smart as you say, they're going to recognize everything special about you and value it. You're actually betting on yourself, Devon, and you're doing something you believe in. Most people are too gutless for that."

Hunter's being generous, but maybe my path was less of a choice than she's making it seem. Only a less reactive version of me would've been able to hold down a normal job. Maybe the idea of mood swings cuts deep because it's true.

Our food arrives, piping hot.

As we eat, Hunter lifts me out of my downward spiral. She says that I can work with Richard to set boundaries with his family. We should let them know they're not allowed to intervene in our relationship. I nod along, my gaze drifting over to the redheaded stranger. He doesn't look at me again, but I can't ignore the suspicion that he's listening.

EIGHT

After lunch with Hunter, I check my phone.

It's 1:11 p.m. I imagine Richard's done with his steak. The fatty edges of his porterhouse are probably discarded, bleeding pink juice across his plate. Maybe he's swirling the last of his french fries in ketchup. I text Richard and ask how he's doing. How long will this lunch go? He promised that he'd stop by our apartment after and work the rest of the day remotely.

Was that a bad sign?

Close to home, I stop in a coffee shop and order a hot matcha latte. When the barista says that will be $5.50, I do a double take.

I still have yet to sell a painting in any legitimate deal. I've sold a couple to Richard's friends, but those transactions felt like charity. His friends made their offers in front of him. Richard responded by telling them how "nice" they were. This year, I won't break the poverty line, despite working every single day. Richard may be wealthy, but that hasn't taken away the feeling that I'm treading water, my chin always skirting the surface.

It's after one thirty by the time I'm home.

I text ?! to Richard.

Distracted, I still try to work.

In my studio, I mix colors for a new piece, having given up on the baths. This one was inspired by a moment in Central Park. A mom and daughter were sitting next to each other, sharing two halves of the same sandwich. They looked poignantly in sync, like an echo across generations. I'm trying to blend them together, but I'm running into the same problem I had with the bathers: the piece is too dark. Every day, they look more and more like a twisting devil.

The front door opens.

"Richard!" I try to sound happy as I jump into the hallway.

He's staring at his phone, apparently displeased. His strong chin is clean, shaved specifically for this lunch. His starched blue oxford is immaculate, as if he didn't have anything to eat at all, as if he went to Smith & Wollensky and got so swept up in their discussion that his steak cooled and cooled until it was taken away. He tucks his phone into a pocket before giving me his full attention.

"How was it?" I ask.

"Good!"

Before I can really read him, he runs into the bathroom and relieves himself. I wait as our conversation is interrupted by an aggressive stream of urine. He stays in the bathroom for a full minute even after the noise stops, before he finally returns.

He sits on our sofa.

"Just . . . good?" I probe.

He wipes his face. I sit next to him and look down. Usually, Richard wears Allbirds to work—and on some Fridays, Crocs—but today, he's in shiny loafers. They point ahead, parallel to me. The distance between us is tense and uncomfortable. I reach out and hold one of his big hands.

"He said that he and Mom love you," Richard says.

"Okay . . ."

"And that you are always welcome at their house."

It takes a moment for me to realize how underwhelmed I am by that. *Welcome.* I'm *welcome*? As in, I'm permitted to visit? Of course I am. I'm engaged to their son. My skin is starting to crawl, but I plaster on a fake smile. There's no way I'm sharing how offended I already am by this conversation. I don't want to blow it up before it's even begun.

"That's nice," I lie.

Richard nods. "He said we might need to work on our communication." His voice sounds like it's retreating. "So, we might want to see a therapist."

Old memories creep back.

Dad asked the same of Mom. Our walls were so thin I heard everything from my room. *Grace,* he'd beg, *it's just talking. I'm just asking you to fucking talk to someone who isn't Devon.* But of course, Mom didn't believe in doctors.

Sophomore year at Mayfield High, I did seek out the school counselor to get her opinion on what was happening at home. I'd always sensed that things weren't right, but I didn't have the formal terms. Didn't have solutions. So I saw Mrs. Campbell and framed my problems as a friend's. After just one session, it was clear that seeing a therapist would only destabilize my situation more. I was overwhelmed by how much needed to change and had no idea what life would be like on the other side. I've been too spooked to go back since.

"Clarke wants us to see a therapist," I repeat.

"He said that if we want to have a successful marriage, then we have to learn how to be . . . steadier." I squint, confused. "You know, we can't get into fights so bad that we have to take off in the middle of the day."

"That didn't happen to us," I say.

He's silent.

"Did you tell him that didn't happen to us?" I ask.

He looks at the rug.

Of course he didn't.

"Forget what your dad said," I say. "Do *you* want to see a therapist?"

He touches his chin.

"Do you?" I press.

"He says it might be a good idea."

"But what do *you* think?"

"Why not?" he asks.

"Because I don't like therapy."

In college, I read some Sigmund Freud after I learned the Surrealists idolized him. I stopped once I saw how much he tied to our parents. At the time, I was trying to start a new life in New York. I didn't want to hear about the lingering imprint of home.

"Therapy tries to tie everything back to your childhood," I say, "and I don't want to dig into my past. You know that. Besides, Richard, we don't have any real problems between us. The only thing we fight about is your family."

"Then let's talk to her about them."

"I really mean it when I say I hate therapy." I enunciate each word with cold clarity. "This is going to push me over the edge, Richard."

"Therapy?"

"I mean it."

"Why are you so upset?"

"I mean it, Richard."

"What's the harm in—"

I pick up the ceramic coasters in front of us and throw them. Some shatter against the kitchen island in high-pitched tings. Richard raises his forearms over his face, bracing himself. The rest of the coasters roll to a stop.

I stare at the mess.

"I'm sorry," I manage.

When we look at each other again, he seems . . . not quite scared, but close. His pupils are wide, pushing his irises into thin blue rings.

He blinks multiple times.

What did I just do?

I stand up and collect the pieces. The beautiful coasters used to be luxuriously smooth, each inky with a lion in the center. They looked like antiques—I hope they weren't family heirlooms. They're sharp now, full of corners. I have to be careful as I pile them in my shaking palm and then stack them on the table. After I pick up the final shards, I return to the floor just in case I missed one. When I sense Richard standing over me, I feel sinking shame.

"I'm so sorry," I say.

Nothing.

"I just really don't like therapy, but . . ." I look up at him. "If you ask me to go, then as your partner, I'll go for you."

He offers me a hand. I take it, trembling.

He helps me stand and then rubs the back of my hand, as if he's trying to soothe me, as if he loves me just as much as he did on the day he proposed. He opens his arms, and I step into them. When I try to kiss him, though, he tucks his chin into his neck, as if he's not quite ready for that. I try again. I find his lips, kiss him, and throw my arms around his neck because I *am* sorry. Because I love him. Because we've grown so close, he's my favorite part of myself.

"My angel," I say.

"My Dev."

He lowers his hands to my waist. When he holds me like this, I never want him to let go. I know we should be talking about what just happened, but maybe we still are. I reach for his shirt and, button by button, peel it away. He does the same for me. We're picking up speed now, because I'm desperate to apologize, and maybe he's just as thrilled to move on.

He kisses me down my neck before picking me up. The upward whoosh makes me feel giddy. I'm not happy, but I smile as he carries me to the kitchen counter. When he sets me down, I keep my legs around his thighs, as if just one more inch between us would ache. He unbuttons my khakis and tugs them off. He looks calmer now, focused. It's the most connected to him that I've felt all day. Neither of us is perfect, but maybe, we're perfect together.

I feel the hair on his abdomen as I undo the last button on his shirt. It falls to the ground, vanishing with our conversation. From where I sit, with my chin angled up to him, his jaw looks wider. His shoulders look broader. I pull him down on top of me. He slips one palm protectively under the back of my head. Soon, we're moaning together.

I fade into bliss.

Eventually, Richard steps back, kissing my fingers on his way to the bathroom. I turn and glimpse the broken coasters on the table, arranged like a graveyard of crooked headstones. I toss them quietly into the trash, then ball a couple of paper towels and throw them onto the mess. Whether I'm hiding it from Richard or myself, I can't say that I know.

NINE

The next morning, while Richard's in the shower, I eye his phone. It's within reach on his nightstand. He's singing in a low voice, his words blurry.

My heart thumps as I reach for it. I've known his code for years. He's never hesitated to unlock his iPhone right in front of me, never finger-pecked the five digits in any rush—6-5-4-6-5, after his parents' address on 654 Waverley Road. I did go through Richard's phone once before, when I was about to move in with him. Back then, I figured that we were on the verge of a big step. No matter how perfect someone seems, you never know what they might be holding back. I didn't find anything. I haven't felt the need to check again, because I trust him.

I'm just not sure I trust his family.

6-5-4-6-5. Apps populate the screen.

I open his most recent texts with Clarke and skim the logistical ones before lunch. Then, close to two, Richard texted his dad, **Love you!!** It's a new window into their relationship. Of course I've heard Richard tell his dad "I love you," but never in a way that suggested two exclamation points. This looks more youthful, insistent. There's an implied *I mean it*.

Clarke did not reply.

Back in Messages, I see Richard on a new thread with a number that's not in his contacts. This three-person thread was initiated by Clarke.

Gretchen, I'm putting you in touch with my son, Richard. He may schedule a session for him and his fiancée, Devon. This should only be interpreted as an expression of how much we love them and want them to succeed. I will not pry or check in again. I will step back now, thank you. Clarke Belmont

The water stops.

I replace Richard's phone quickly. He didn't mention that his dad actually *gave* us a therapist. So, we wouldn't just be seeing *a* therapist because Clarke suggested it. We would be seeing *the* therapist Clarke chose. That feels like an important distinction.

I'm making the bed when Richard emerges with a towel around his waist. He smiles cautiously as water trickles down his torso into the hard knot of cotton. We never did finish our conversation about therapy yesterday. If our chemistry weren't so magnetic, maybe we could have. Last night, we ended up in each other's arms, watching *Seinfeld*. Our wounds were healing.

And now, Gretchen.

I smile briefly at Richard on my way out of our room. Usually, we make breakfast together: my banana, his eggs and sausages, and plenty of Dark Magic Keurig coffee. Today, I walk straight into my studio, to the place where I've always gone to exchange one reality for another. I sit on the stool in front of my twisting demon, the back of the canvas to the door. I stare at the girl's black eyes. Why won't you *look* at me? Her gaze is static, lifeless. I pick up a tube of red paint and squeeze it on top of her. I take a wide brush and smear the paint until she's buried.

Knock. Knock.

"You in there?" Richard asks through the door.

He knows that I like my privacy here.

I walk toward his voice and crack the door.

"Hey," he says, "you mind if we talk for a second?"

His voice is unusually soft.

He holds out his hand. Of course, I take it and follow him to the sofa. When he sits down, I lose his grip. We end up sitting a foot apart, which feels like a formal amount of distance. He looks uncomfortable, like he's being pulled in two directions. This isn't the Richard I know. The Richard *I* know is obsessed with making sure everyone has a good time, and he leads by example. If he's not in charge of the atmosphere right now, in our own home, then who is?

"I'd like to talk to you about your eating," he says.

I use self-control to wait.

"I'm seeing some things that worry me, and I'd like you to see a doctor."

"What worries you?" I ask calmly.

"You know, you don't eat . . . in a relaxed way," he says. "When you have your banana every morning, you cut it into pieces first."

"Yes." I pause. "And?"

"It's just unusual, chopping it into these paper-thin coins. I've never seen anyone do that before. I'm surprised they don't melt in your hand." His shoulders rise. "And . . . sometimes, when you put a meal together, you make these combinations—it's just very intentional. I can tell a lot of thought went into them." His voice is becoming more delicate. "And . . . your hairbrush in the bathroom. I don't think anyone should be losing that much hair." I picture the round brush he means. It *does* cling to a black inch of hair, but that's accumulated over years. I haven't cleaned it because I'm busy. I haven't replaced it because I'm cheap. "I love you to pieces, Devon. I just want you to be healthy. I really want you to see a doctor."

"Does this have anything to do with your lunch with Clarke?"

"No."

"Is my weight acceptable?"

The question makes me picture raw steak on a hanging scale, the shaky red arrow going still. Richard stares at my knees, uncomfortable. Yes, the topic objectifies me down to my meat, down to the mass of my bones. Yes, it's deeply weird to ask him to depersonalize me like this, but I didn't lead us here.

"Yes."

"Then aren't I healthy?" I speak so clearly, I'm practically spelling the words as they leave my mouth. Richard seems to struggle with this question. His hair and temples are still damp from the shower—now, I wonder if he might be sweating. "Fine," I say, cracking the silence. "If you need me to see a physician, I'll do it, even though you're being absurd."

He relaxes. "You will?"

"I'll get every test they have," I say, my tone sharp, "but I need you to be honest with me: Are you sure this has nothing to do with your dad?"

He nods vigorously.

I'm not sure if I believe him.

He reaches for my hand and squeezes it. When he leans forward to stand, I hold on, keeping him here. He looks at me, expectant, earnest. And something about him is so gentle, so well meaning, and so unintentionally handsome that I want to kiss him. But if we keep having sex when we should be talking, we're never going to solve our problems.

"Also," I go on, "I wanted to talk to you about the therapy."

"All right."

"You reached out to anyone yet?"

"No, but I have someone."

"Where'd you get the reference?" I ask.

He pauses.

"A friend."

"Which friend?" I persist.

He looks down.

"A friend," he insists.

"Tell me, Richard."

I feel him thinking.

Why can't he tell me the truth?

Why is he choosing them over me? We're going to spend the rest of our lives together. We're going to have children. We already picked the name for our first: Whitney. Richard melts with kids. Still, whenever we've talked about having them, he's always made it clear that what I want to do with my body comes first. Where is that sentiment now? Why is he letting his family pick at my flesh, my mind?

"Who gave you the reference?" I demand.

"My dad."

I drop his hand.

"Why didn't you tell me that?"

I'm as sad as I am angry.

He looks apologetic.

"Why did you keep that from me?" I press.

"I'm sorry."

"So, we're not only *going* to therapy because your dad suggested it, but we're seeing *the therapist* he picked out?"

"I don't see the downside."

"I *told you* I hate therapy." I eye the four coasters left. I didn't want to feel this again so soon. I ball one hand in the other. "Do you even know what her specialty is?" He doesn't say anything, and all I hear is, *No.* "This is already turning into a nightmare." My voice strains, on the edge of splitting. "Do *you* have any problems with me, or is it just *your parents?*"

His rising eyebrows ask me to calm down.

I should feel some sympathy for him—for my fiancé who just wants to make everyone happy. But I'm too mad that he's not fighting for me.

"Why won't you stand up for me?" I cry.

He sits motionless as my tears fall.

I wipe my eyes.

"Why aren't you reacting to me?" I cry, louder.

Nothing.

"Can you *hear* me?" I shriek.

"Look," he cuts in assertively. "Therapy was my dad's idea, but this reaction to it is scaring me. I know you're afraid of talking about your mom. But something doesn't feel right about this conversation." He points a strong index finger between us. "I don't understand why you're shouting at me and throwing things. I know you don't want to look back and . . . manhandle raw nerves. But maybe you haven't dealt with something. You can't avoid talking about your past forever. I'm sorry, but the more you fight it, the more I think therapy is exactly what we need to do."

Richard stands up.

"Where do you think you're going?" I demand.

"Can I get some water?"

I drop my head in my hands and remember Mrs. Campbell. *It sounds like your friend is in a situation where social services has grounds to remove her: emotional abuse, medical neglect . . . If you brought some evidence, I could help your* friend *get to a better place.* Then, her wobbly, fearful smile. But of course, I never turned in my parents. Who knows where I would've ended up? If my new guardians would've been even more warped, even more broken by life?

The cushion next to me sinks. Richard's back.

"No matter who suggested therapy, I'm the one following through," he says evenly. I wish he didn't have their eyes. I feel like I'm back in their dining room, under their constant observation. Richard puts a hand on my back, but I shake him off. When he tries again, I slap his wrist—harder than I intended. The sharp *smack* is loud. The feeling of his wrist bones stays with me even after I pull away. He holds his arm crooked against his chest, looking more than a little betrayed.

~

Repentant, I make the doctor's appointment.

I'm in the orange waiting room at One Medical a few days later, unsure what to expect. My experience with doctors is scarce, given my mom's aversion and my lack of insurance. My best reference point might actually be *The Gross Clinic*, Thomas Eakins's 1875 painting of a brutal operation. In that piece, the patient is so contorted that it's hard to tell which of his limbs has been cut open, which part of him bleeds on the surgeons' bare hands.

Richard offered to walk me here, but I refused. I don't need any more help that feels infantilizing. He was also the one to suggest this office. Did the Belmonts choose this doctor too? While I wait, I put my headphones in and listen to what Richard and I picked as our first dance song: "Home," by Edward Sharpe and the Magnetic Zeros. It reminds me of better times, that it's not such a bad thing to see a general physician every ten years.

"Devon Ferrell."

I follow the voice.

In Dr. Raja's examining room, she offers me a chair without arm-rests. I grip the edges as she collects information about my family's medical history: my dad has high blood pressure, but he's a restaurant manager, so that might explain it; he also has high cholesterol. She asks what's brought me in with a pleasant tone, as if it must be a cheerful thing.

"My fiancé is concerned about me. His family is too." I'm suddenly more nervous than I expected. I'm having trouble putting words together. "They're worried about the way that I eat." That's it. "I'd like to get some tests to show that I'm healthy."

"I'm sorry to hear that."

It's hard to read her tone exactly: it's a strange blind spot of sound. This room is starting to smell like antiseptic, metal. She says that she can run panels for diabetes, cholesterol, and other biomarkers, even though they aren't routine until I'm thirty-five.

"What about minerals? I think he'll want to know if I'm eating what I need to . . ." Survive? Give birth? For the first time, I see my visit in the context of patriarchal control. I'm reminded of the ritual that some women endured, having their hymens inspected before marriage.

"We can run metabolic panels," Dr. Raja says.

She asks me to recite what I eat in a day.

I list everything down to the contentious banana. I don't describe the daily autopsy, but she doesn't ask. She gives her professional opinion that I'm eating well, before imparting some advice about portions. I'm supposed to fill half my plate with vegetables, a fist-size amount of meat, and a fist of carbohydrates. As she shares these rules, I can't help but notice the Oreo wrappers and soda cans in her trash bin. Does she follow her own advice?

If not, does she even believe it? What world is this where healthy people visit doctors who dole out rules they don't follow? I look up at the ceiling, in case there's a flipped version of this situation over me, or an audience of seated fish watching with amusement.

She takes my vitals—normal—then tells me I'm free to see the technician next door for my blood test. I thank Dr. Raja and linger on the threshold. After all, I never see doctors. Maybe there's something else I could ask to make the most of my visit. Now's my chance for any health questions flickering in the back of my mind. She stares at me from behind her computer.

"Anything else I can do?" Dr. Raja asks.

I put on a smile. "No, thanks again."

Next door, the technician's expression is hidden behind a surgical mask. I sit and confess I have a fear of needles. He asks if I want a warning as he rips the sterile package. I shake my head, fumbling to put in my headphones. I'm crying before he even touches my arm. When the needle pierces my skin, it really does feel like just a pinch. I'm sobbing more than it hurts.

My blood recedes in two containers.

When it's over, I wipe my face, embarrassed. I apologize quietly and leave with a cotton ball taped to the red dot. On my way outside, I almost recognize the man on the other side of the street. He's standing still under a dark umbrella in the rain. When I turn left, he starts walking in the same direction. It's so simultaneous, it's almost like he's mirroring me. How do I know him? He's as tall as Richard, with red hair and a dense spray of freckles. Did I see him—at the Vietnamese restaurant? Two tables over? He turns again before I can get a better look.

Now, Richard's calling.

"How was everything?" he asks.

"Fine, I guess."

"I'm sorry, Dev." He must be in his office on the landline because the sound is crystal clear. I imagine his tie knot pulled down a few inches from his collar. "I feel terrible that you're out doing that in this weather—"

"It's not your fault it's raining."

"I know, but you're out in the rain because of me. I just kept looking outside and thinking about you." He sounds sincere. I stop under an awning next to our building. I don't want to lose him in the elevator up to our place. "And I'm sorry that things have been off between us because all I want to do is make you happy. That's all I care about. I love you and I always will, until you are 'old and grey and full of sleep.'" His reference to our favorite Yeats poem is a nice touch.

"I love you too."

Silence.

"So, are you free this Thursday," he asks, "for therapy?"

TEN

Richard and I sit in Gretchen's office that Thursday night. He keeps trying to hold my hand as we settle into the sofa. I prefer my arms crossed.

How exactly does Gretchen know Richard's parents?

She looks polished but approachable, with her silver-streaked hair in a loosely assembled low bun. Her oxford shirt is cuffed up to her elbows—the way I wear mine at home. I push that thought aside. I don't want to feel comfortable with her and accidentally reveal too much, sending us all down a rabbit hole into my childhood traumas.

Gretchen: Thanks for coming across town to my little office.

Me:

Richard: Thank *you*, Gretchen, for making the time and having us on short notice. It's really nice of you to work us into the schedule.

Gretchen: Happy to help. Why don't we start with a little about you two. Where are you from?

Me:

Richard: I grew up in Greenwich, Connecticut. What about yourself?

Gretchen: I'm from Florida, but let's keep this focused on you, if you don't mind. So, how did you two meet?

Me:

Richard: Devon and I met a couple years ago at a Jasper Johns exhibit. I was on the other side of the room when I saw her staring at an American flag. She was beautiful in a way that was very . . . strong. I kept checking on her, and she didn't move. She was just standing there, staring at the painting. You know how most people in museums take a photo and move on? Or they're in a group, sort of gliding by everything? Devon was alone and completely absorbed. I just knew she was going to be . . . interesting.

Gretchen: And what do you remember about that day, Devon?

Me:

Richard: Dev?

Me: When I saw you, I just felt happy.

Gretchen: Is there anything else you remember?

Me:

Richard: Devon?

Me: You were beaming. You were practically on the balls of your feet, leaning toward me. I could tell you were a positive person before you even used your opening line. You seemed like everything good.

Gretchen: And how has that impression changed over time?

Me:

Gretchen: So, what brings you in today?

Me:

Richard: Devon and I love each other. We have a great relationship. We're just here to make it even better.

Gretchen asks a series of innocuous questions. Richard could use any of them as a launching pad to talk about why we're actually here. But he doesn't. It's as if he's trying to entertain Gretchen, as if he's using *our* session to help *her*.

Me: Do you want to just tell her why we're here? That your dad sent us to therapy because he's worried about us?

Richard:

Gretchen: Is that true?

Richard: Yes. I got lunch with my dad last week. But before I get into that, I'd just like to say I love Devon. My dad loves Devon. My whole family loves Devon. But my dad is worried about her eating disorder.

Me: What?

Richard:

Me: He said that?

Richard: I'm sorry.

Me: What were his words exactly?

Richard: He told me not to tell you. But the more time he spent with you, the more he got . . . nervous. [rubs neck] For one, you don't eat your meals like other people. You play with them, rearrange them. Like it's . . . doll food. And your clothes are all baggy, as if you're trying to hide how thin you are. Your pants are so wide, they've never seen your knees *bend*. And the last time we left their house, you had this mood swing. He said you had a look of "unbridled rage" in your eyes. Undereating can make people . . . "unsteady."

Me: So you lied to me?

Richard: I'm sorry.

Me: I'm healthy.

Gretchen:

Me: Are we seeing the same things here? Look at me, I'm completely fine. Besides, I just went to the doctor and got all my blood work back today. Richard and I went over the results on our way here. All my calcium, potassium—everything was normal.

Gretchen: This sounds like a painful experience for you.

Me: Why did you lie to me?

Richard: I'm sorry. I was prioritizing my relationship with my dad.

Me: I just don't understand why you'd lie.

~

Richard and I file into a taxi outside Gretchen's office and sit on opposite sides. We look out different windows. I feel like we're in an Edward

Hopper painting: dramatic lighting, somber atmosphere, and not a word being spoken.

See you next week, Richard told Gretchen as we left. How long are we going to be her clients? Does he think that session did any good? We just talked for an hour, and our relationship only feels weaker, more vulnerable to creeping rot. Gretchen didn't ask about my parents, but who's to say that she won't next time?

"I hate therapy," I say.

"I know. Thanks for coming."

"That's not the point."

We stop short at a red light. I lurch forward a few inches, without my seat belt on to catch me. Meanwhile, Richard's holds him securely in place. My heart hammers as a man in a bowler hat crosses ahead of us, biting into an apple. He glides past a group of pigeons pecking the curb without disturbing them. Our car speeds up again.

"The *point* is that I don't want to go back unless we absolutely need to. And we don't need to." My tone cracks toward the end of the sentence. "The only thing *wrong* with our relationship is that we've let other people into it. We've let their opinions matter."

"Are you going to put your seat belt on?"

"Richard, focus."

"Can you please just—?"

I click it angrily.

"I feel like we're getting somewhere with Gretchen," he says.

I'm too riled to respond.

For the rest of the trip, I see Richard only through his reflection in my window. Headlights flicker over us, making shadows move like smoke. When we arrive at our building, Richard pays while I open my door to the street—to see a black Honda hurtling toward me. The redheaded driver honks and swerves dramatically, rejoining his lane at the end of the block. I slam my door shut and hurry toward the lobby. Richard gabs with Paul while I call the elevator.

"I've been meaning to ask you . . . ," Paul says.

"What's that?" Richard asks.

"Are you behind the Wi-Fi name 'It Burns When IP'?"

Richard laughs. "I wish. We're 'I Believe Wi Can Fi.'"

Paul wags a finger as the elevator doors close.

Richard hits our floor number, still beaming from the interaction. Why does he always have to pretend like he's doing well—like *we* are—even when it's not true? Paul would understand if we had a bad day once every few years.

"Do you want me to gain weight?" I ask.

His expression falls.

"I love you, Devon."

"Then answer me."

He sighs. "I don't know what to say."

"Do your *parents* want me to gain weight?" I wait for an answer that doesn't come. "If it's that ambiguous, then we should ask them. We should call them up right now and ask how much I should weigh." I dislike even pretending that the Belmonts have authority over my body, that they have any say in the width of my arms, the mass of my legs.

I check my phone as Richard turns the key to our place. Twenty-six new texts wait on Belmont Banter. They began with Oliver's question, Is there still interest in movie night? His parents agreed to meet him in the home theater. Now, all three of them comment on a movie live. Messages stream in, even though they're clearly together, maybe just feet apart.

"Is Oliver okay?" I ask.

"Of course."

Richard opens the door.

We take a long step into the dark.

"Why is he still at home?" I ask.

Richard walks straight to the kitchen sink. He takes a mason jar off the drying rack, fills it with tap water, and empties it in three gulps. I stride up to him and stand just inches away. He stares at me through the glass bottom of his jar, his eyes blurred. When he lowers the cup, I raise my phone open to Belmont Banter. More texts arrive from Waverley.

"Richard?"

He shrugs.

"Maybe *he* needs therapy. Anyone dared to say that? Everyone's so worried about the healthy young woman, but no one even blinks at that sick fucking man." The venom surprises even me. Richard winces, as if I offend him when I attack his brother. I should get out of here before I say something worse or do something we won't forget.

I head into my studio. When I shut the door, it slams so hard that I might've chipped paint. *Unbridled rage.* Is that what I have? Or is that what his family wants to provoke? I feel like I'm at war with these people, and every fight is indirect.

My hands tremble as I remove the mother-daughter painting and lean it against one wall. A new canvas takes its place on my easel. I pick up a brush, sit on my stool, and start to move. The strokes come out dark. I'm not thinking about anything—not about consequences, nothing. All I want to do is gush onto this canvas until it absorbs how I feel. My inner life takes on shocking color. Depth. Time slides through my fingers, greasier than the oil. Every so often I come to my senses, and tiny chills sweep through me when I face what I've done.

ELEVEN

In the days after Richard and I see Gretchen, my work comes to life. Our session lit a fuse inside me. Now I dream of painting—of painting the future and watching it come true around my canvas; of painting children who walk out of my art and brush my hair; of painting staircases and then climbing them.

I start waking up earlier than usual, still on the hazy edges of my dreams, with an urgent need to work. While Richard's asleep, I creep out of bed and change into the outfit I wore the day before, left on the rug. I pull the khakis on without unbuttoning them and tuck the oxford deep inside. I keep my hair in a braid now for simplicity. If it unravels overnight, I redo it quickly on my way to make coffee. Does the Keurig wake Richard up now, before his alarm? I don't stay long in the kitchen. A cup of Dark Magic is all I need on my way to the studio.

Usually, I do my best work in the mornings. Now, I paint all day, deep into the blackest part of night. The hours dissolve in my studio. I barely think as images arrive. My hands move on their own, and paintings emerge. Van Gogh must have felt like this when he wrote, "Paintings have a life of their own that derives from the painter's soul." I keep going even after Richard comes home. Aside from checking on me before he goes to bed—with the door closed—he doesn't intrude. It's nice that he respects my privacy in here, even when we're fighting.

I do leave my studio—for water from the kitchen sink, a late lunch at five p.m., and rushed trips to the bathroom. It's then that I remember feeling this way as a kid. Whenever Mom got worse, and life got more bizarre, I'd draw nonstop. Sometimes, my art was pure fantasy. I'd fill pages with bright homes and clearheaded parents. Other times, I took my reality down in detail: opening a medicine cabinet to a skyline of liquor bottles. Either way, my creativity fed on intense emotions. Without them, I would've made nothing.

My next show with Zellweger is a month away, in late November. I only promised him two new paintings, but the work is pouring out of me. I complete three in just a few days, a new personal record. As soon as the pieces are done, I turn them around to face the wall. They look like stiff white ghosts haunting the room.

The prospect of unveiling them is a thrill.

TWELVE

I leave our building for an afternoon walk, a rare break in my recent spree. It looked warmer from my studio, but it's still nice to be outside, to see something other than half a face. The other side without skin, without shape. Just the white beginnings of an eye. On my way up Fifth Avenue, I feel my phone in my jacket pocket. I run my fingers over the smooth glass, the rounded corners.

Am I really going to do this?

I don't call my mom often, but I check in with her around major holidays. Calling her *on* a holiday is too risky, so I try to get her before celebrations begin—before she has an excuse to raise a glass to something.

I take out my phone.

Am I nervous? I'm pinching my shoulders now, pulling the flesh up from the bone. The last time Mom and I spoke was in April for our Easter call. She was fresh out of rehab and making all the promises she usually does. Ever since her first time in rehab after Dad left, it's been the same routine every time: lofty goals followed by disappointment. In April, she swore that she was going to get that temp job back in Cleveland and be in the office three days a week. She said that she was going to reconnect with her AA sponsor, Teresa, and go to meetings again. She would start cooking, drinking water, and getting outside every day.

I pull up her contact.

Our calls are different every time. Sometimes, she answers on the first ring but says nothing. She just breathes heavily, leaving me to wonder if she's drunk or worse—if she's lost, hurt. Other times, she answers with a string of nonsense. In those cases, I still do her the dignity of saying goodbye. Then I tell myself that I can't help someone who doesn't want to be helped. I go so far as to say it out loud, as many times as I need to hear it. The hardest calls of all, though—the ones that cause the most pain—are the few when she's crystal clear. Because those give me hope.

I dial her number.

As it rings, the crowded sidewalks are calming. If something strange happens, I'm not alone. I'm surrounded by sane, productive people surviving in a challenging city. I pass a man in a suit sucking a tobacco pipe, his prominent nose above the smoking bowl. His red tie is a lone stripe of color.

"Well, if it isn't my Devon," Mom says.

Her voice is throaty and—sober. Has she been clean since the spring? Richard and I only texted her in July to let her know that we'd gotten engaged. She replied, Congratulations!, spelled correctly. I didn't push my luck.

"Hi, Mom. Do you have a minute?"

"Several."

Her TV sounds in the background.

I imagine her in the living room at home, where our TV faces a sagging sofa. When I was fifteen years old, I stood on that couch in an artistic fit and painted two figures directly on the wallpaper. Both were distilled down to their essentials. The shorter girl was just one arcing contour. The taller woman was similar but overrun by zigzagging black scratches that followed the shape of her silhouette. I painted the zigzags with such force that afterward, the bristles on the paintbrush held a permanent curve. Dad wasn't home enough to insist that we cover it. Mom didn't seem to care. I wonder if the painting is still there, hovering over her.

"I just wanted to check in on you," I say.

"No, I don't think you did."

Her bluntness reminds me of myself.

"What's on your mind?" she asks.

I rub my neck.

"It's actually about Richard's family."

The words slip out before I mean to say them.

Now, I'm doubting if that was wise. I don't really want to talk to *her* about this. I want to talk to the *idea* of her. I want a strong maternal figure to help me cope with the Belmonts. Unless—is she better now? Whenever she stops drinking for long enough, she starts acting like a rational person again. It's always so tempting to believe that this time, it will be for good.

"Oh, really?" she probes.

"I've only seen them a few times, but they're convinced that we have problems. Richard's dad told him that we should see a therapist—"

"What? Why?"

"He told Richard that I have an eating disorder, which might be triggering mood swings. He said that I'm 'unsteady.'"

"*What?*"

Her shock is validating.

"Don't tell me there's more," she dares.

"It's just . . ." I've spent two weeks with these accusations, wondering who's right. "I'm not close to that many people, you know? Richard's parents have been married for decades. They raised a family that's stuck together. Their kids have jobs working with real people. Meanwhile, I've spent my life making things no one's asked for, things no one wants. If the Belmonts think there's something wrong—is there?" Ants maul a fruit salad at my feet, darkening split grapes and chunks of melon.

"No. They shouldn't be meddling."

"Ok*ay*." I'm not convinced. "I just don't know if they're onto something. Maybe there *is* something the matter with me, and I've just carved out a life where I can fake it. But really, I have an instability or something—"

"You don't."

She sighs.

"You know," she goes on, "I have half a mind to say something—"

"Don't. You can't."

Fear almost stops me short as I imagine Mom on the phone with Vanessa. On Mom's side of the line, I see her at home—lights off, blending into the dark. When I lived with her, she wore her hair in a long braid down her back. At any given moment, half the braid had come loose. On Vanessa's side of the line, I imagine her perched in neutrals, thoughtful words on glossed lips. Her nails now so clean there's no polish on them at all, nothing but a trace of acetone.

"All right," Mom relents. "Just forget about what they think."

"I'm trying, but . . ."

"Yes?"

"I don't like who I am right now," I admit, remembering the coasters and then hitting Richard on the wrist. "Richard and I don't even have real problems between us. All this chaos just came from letting other voices into our relationship. This isn't us. Or me. Or is it?"

"Don't overthink it," she says.

"I'm trying, but—"

"Devon, please," she says. "You just said it yourself. 'This chaos came from letting them in.'" Her TV goes mute. "No matter what you do—or don't do—there's always going to be someone to judge you for it. You know this. It's like driving: keep your eyes on the road. If you keep looking at trees, sooner or later, you'll hit one." As an aside, she adds, "Rich people think everything's their business."

I smile, stopping at a curb.

Mom taught me to drive. She kept one hand on the wheel from the passenger's seat, her fingers over mine. She started letting go long before I had my permit—once again, trusting her gut over the rules.

We had some good conversations in that car. I remember asking her once why she and Dad didn't have more kids. Was parenting that bad? Was I? She told me that it wasn't meant to be, that the universe gave her one perfect baby instead of three or four average ones. I laughed, but I sensed part of her was being earnest. She always believed in me.

Mom and I haven't had a conversation like that in a while—one where we're actually connecting. It scares me to think how quickly her clarity could be taken away. When the feelings become overwhelming, I change the subject.

"Enough about me," I say.

"If you say so."

I laugh. "How's the neighborhood?"

"Same as always. But a new neighbor did come over last week to complain about my lawn." I brace myself for the worst: sky-high piles of trash, furniture she broke and threw outside. When I lived with her, I was always there to clean up the mess, to keep the neighbors' suspicions at bay. "Too many dandelions, he said. The lawn's covered in them. Apparently, they're weeds, bringing down the value of his home."

That's it?

"Did you . . . ?" I picture how she might've evened the score. Mom never hurt anyone, but it's not a stretch to imagine her tossing a chair through their windows.

"Do anything? Of course not."

"Nothing?"

"Flowers never hurt anyone."

It's encouraging to hear.

"Do you have plans for Thanksgiving?" I ask.

"Yes, good ones."

I laugh because I know what that means: she will spend the holiday alone at home. Whenever she sobers up, she avoids the places and people that used to trigger her. She claims to love the peace and quiet, the chance to start over. Sometimes, she even starts to draw. I hear Mom laugh too—and it's so touching to be in sync I have the sudden urge to say goodbye. I don't want to hear something that would undo the magic, that would erase this feeling of being connected.

"Love you, Mom. Take care."

"You too, girl of mine."

THIRTEEN

After almost a week of progress—a nonstop indulgence in new ideas—I'm in my studio, blowing dark hair out of my eyes. Every now and then, it slides back down like a crow's wing. My back is starting to ache, but I keep working. Inspiration is precious.

The front door shuts.

"Hey." It's Richard on the other side of the door.

I lean back from my canvas and roll my neck in a circle. Outside, the city is midnight blue and twinkling all the way to the East River. I like the lemony yellows, little citrus dots up the skyscrapers, and look back at my piece. Can I use that color anywhere?

"Do you have a second?" he asks.

I rest my brush on a palette and walk to the door. It's hard to find space, the floor packed with canvases, sketches ripped out of my journals, and containers stuffed with brushes. It's a good thing Richard never comes in here, because some of these containers are valuable things I grabbed in haste: a Baccarat vase, a crystal pencil holder, and a porcelain bowl.

"What's up?" I ask.

"Don't forget our session with Gretchen tomorrow."

I look at my bare feet.

"Same time tomorrow night," he adds.

I feel a buzz of fear like static electricity. I don't feel comfortable with Gretchen. Richard knows this. I told him after our first session that

I didn't want to go back. Why isn't he listening to me? Why can't we talk without a chaperone? When I open the door, Richard is so surprised he steps back. A plastic bag of to-go food swings in his right hand. As soon as he recovers, he lifts it.

"I got enough for you too," he says. "Your favorite dumplings."

I hate that he means well.

And I hate that he looks so good. Richard's in a pearl-gray cashmere zip-up, his bright hair ruffled after a long day at work. I've barely seen him since last week, when he admitted that he lied for his dad. The only face-to-face conversation we've had since then was over the weekend, when I ran into him in the kitchen. He asked if I wanted to talk about anything, and I said no—the only way to stop fighting is to go to the source. We need to confront his parents and set boundaries. Richard said that was a bad idea, that we should wait to have this discussion with Gretchen. I felt so busy I didn't even stay to argue. I just returned to my studio with fuel.

"Richard, I can't make it tomorrow."

"Why not?"

"I have a lot to do."

"Can you make time?" His voice is soft, kind.

"No." I massage my brow. "I went once. Please, I've told you I don't want to go down this road. I don't want to retraumatize myself."

"I'll be right there with you."

"Richard, please. What do you want to talk about? Let's do it right now. We can work through it together, and you'll see that we don't need someone else to translate. We've always worked things out. What is it?"

I look deep into his eyes.

"I would like to talk about your mom," he says, "and I would like Gretchen to be there." He sounds so lucid I wonder if he's rehearsed. "Everyone's in therapy these days. It helps to have someone calm in the room, someone who knows how different parts of your life are related. If we work with her, and we talk through some of this stuff, I think we can get to a place where you aren't as reactive, frankly. Where we can talk to each other without screaming."

"Are you trying to punish me?"

"*Punish* you?"

"Torture me?" I raise my voice.

"Can you talk to me like you respect me?"

"You think I don't respect you?" He flinches at my volume. "I'm sorry, but we are engaged. I'm committed to spending my life with you. You are my whole world. And you think I don't respect you? Are you serious?"

He's silent, as if he's protesting my tone.

"I'm sorry, how about *you* respect *me*"—I'm shouting now—"and what it was like to grow up with people who terrified you? How about that? You want to just pry open the cuts and poke around? Like it's a growth exercise? Because you read it on WebMD?"

He stays silent.

"Richard—"

He holds up his hand.

I swat it down.

He points at me with a stiff finger. His body is so big it can be scary even when it's immobile. Just the suggestion of it is powerful.

"Don't hit me," he says, his voice low.

I swat his hand again.

"Or else what?" I've never seen Richard get mad. He's never raised his voice at me or anyone else since we met. Is now going to be the first time? I keep swatting his hand, faster and faster. He doesn't move. "You want *me* to respect *your* boundaries? Then how about *you* respect *mine*? I'm asking that we don't see Gretchen. I don't want to unleash my own demons. Is that clear enough?"

"I'm not *asking*," he says quietly. "We're *going*."

I give up and turn around.

"For your rage," he adds.

I stop next to Richard's desk, between my studio and the front hallway. It's a beautiful antique with two computer monitors, two framed photos of us, and a laminated block with his first business card. A hanging mirror beside it enlarges the space.

"Don't," he says warily.

I stare at him, feeling just as frustrated and, now, hurt to think that he expects me to wreak havoc. Hot tears prick my eyes. He doesn't get any closer. I hate this. Before I know what's happening, I'm reaching for his business card block and throwing it at the mirror. Richard cowers as it shatters beside us, spraying shards of glass across the room. I raise my hands to cover my face and feel something nip my forearm. I'm crying too hard to see what I've done. It's only when I sink onto my knees that I make out the hundreds of radiant pieces on the ground.

"My bubbles," I mutter between sobs because here they are. All the colors I needed in my bath paintings are right here on the floor, in these starry and shimmering shapes. When I lift my chin, Richard looks afraid.

~

The next night, Richard and I sit down with Gretchen. He's in a tailored suit on the other side of the sofa. Damien Hirst–like dots speckle his Hermès tie. He must've just come from a meeting with some powerful clients. If we called each other during the day anymore, I'd know who he saw. Meanwhile, I'm in my painting clothes. Black streaks dry on my shirt cuffs. My khakis are worn to threads at the knees. I thought about changing into something nicer, but then I realized that was the conceit of therapy: to change *me* into some*one* nicer.

Gretchen has her notebook ready.

I still don't want to do this, but I'm here for Richard. After I broke his mirror last night, I felt so ashamed that I needed to make it up to him. He asked again for therapy. There was only one answer I could give.

Gretchen: How are you doing?

Richard: Starting with the tough questions already. What about you, Gretchen?

Gretchen: Just grand. How have things been at home?

Richard: On the bright side, I've been happy to see Devon so inspired. She's been painting all week. She doesn't share her work until it's finished, but I know these will be . . . important. She's been pouring herself into them. To be honest, we haven't really seen each other since our last session here.

Gretchen: Haven't seen each other at *all?*

Richard:

Gretchen: Last time, Richard, you shared that your dad has some concerns about Devon. Your dad told you these privately.

Me: Yes, and at this point, the only way forward is for us to confront his parents over what they said. I can't solve this with Richard. He's just trying to make everyone happy. We need to get to the root of the problem.

Gretchen: You want to confront his family.

Me: Yes. Otherwise, they're just going to keep whispering in Richard's ear. I want to set boundaries and make it clear that they aren't allowed in our relationship. Ideally, before we stay with them for Thanksgiving.

Gretchen: You want to set boundaries.

Me: I'd do it today, but Richard won't have any of it.

Gretchen: Is that so?

Me: I brought it up over the weekend. He said it was a bad idea. Then he refused to talk more about it until *you* were here. It was so demeaning—and hurtful, to hear my partner push me away like that.

Gretchen: Richard, is this true?

Richard: Yes. I believe that a "confrontation," as she puts it, will ruin our relationship with them. I've seen her when she "confronts" me.

Me: [laughs]

Richard: You think this is funny?

Me: That's not how I "confront" someone. That's how I act when the one person who used to understand me now doesn't get a thing I say. When you need someone else in the room in order to talk to me.

Richard: Did you ever think that I wanted to wait for Gretchen because you're starting to scare me?

Me: No. Do you actually believe that? After two perfect years and a couple bad weeks, you suddenly can't be alone with me? That's not reality, Richard. It's your family putting that idea in your head. Your underhanded, undermining family.

Richard: So, when she says things like that—my "underhanded, undermining family"—I don't trust her to have a mature conversation. I think she's going to yell at them the way she yells at me.

Me: You're doing it right now! Do you see what I mean? You're not talking to *me*. You're talking to *her* about me. You've lost all respect for my mind ever since they started to *warp* your opinion of it.

Richard: Do you hate my family?

Me: Tell me why I shouldn't.

Richard: See?

Me:

Richard: Well, since we're getting nowhere with this topic, I'd like to talk about something else.

Me: Don't, Richard.

Richard: Enough about my family; I'd like to talk about her family, actually.

Me: Don't, Richard.

Richard: I want to be as sensitive as—

Me: MAKE IT STOP.

Richard: possible, but—

Me: OR I WILL LOSE MY MIND.

~

The next night, feeling guilty for losing it, I cook one of Richard's favorite dinners: a roasted half chicken with buttery baked potatoes and even more buttery broccoli. We sit across from each other at the table. The air is dead silent.

I pick at the chicken.

It's a miracle that Richard keeps forgiving me. Ironically, the quality that's causing some of our problems is also what keeps bringing us back together: his drive to delight. While *he* might not hold grudges against me, this room hasn't forgotten what I've done. The wall next to Richard's office is now asylum white, with nothing but a metal stud left where we hung the mirror.

"You know," he starts cautiously, "I called my parents today. They said they're looking forward to seeing us for Thanksgiving." I nod, feeling wooden, and pet the meat with my fork. Vanessa and Clarke might've said that, but I doubt they meant it. How am I supposed to respond? I can't tell Richard that his parents are lying. I just want us to have one conversation that doesn't detonate, one that doesn't leave me feeling better understood by my art than by my fiancé.

He clears his throat.

"Also," he says, "they had some good news."

"Good news?"

"Yes, they offered to help pay for our wedding."

I put my fork down silently.

"They know weddings can get expensive. My parents just went to one where the flowers alone were seven figures. Mom sent me the name of the florist. Anyway, we don't want everyone to leave our reception talking about how much it cost. That's not very romantic. The point is just that my parents said not to worry. Nothing is off limits. They'll make our dream come true."

I should be grateful. If I were another woman, I would be. But *my* dream wedding is cozy, and it doesn't involve coordinating with them. I try to control myself. One more outburst might convince him that I am a woman of "unbridled rage." But has Richard thought about how this might develop? If they're paying for the wedding, who's to say they can't invite an army of their closest friends?

"Mom said she's happy to chip in with planning too. She's at your service when it comes to invitations, table settings—you name it. If you need someone in the bridal trenches with you, she'll be there to help."

I don't need more of their "help."

This is exactly what Hunter predicted.

"That's nice, but . . . ," I start.

"But?"

"I want this wedding to be *ours*."

"Of course."

I don't feel like we're connecting.

"You and I have a specific, manageable vision." My tone is exceedingly polite. "If your parents pay for our wedding, they have control of it. Do you see what I mean? And I don't want to consult with your mom about everything—anything, really. She and I have enough friction as it is without going through the gauntlet of wedding planning. So I'm very grateful for their offer, but we should do this on our own."

Richard nods thoughtfully, then resumes eating. Are we agreeing? Was it that easy, or is he just—waiting for Gretchen to finish this?

He looks at my plate.

"What?" I ask.

"Are you done?"

I look down, where my chicken leg remains intact. The beige skin is wrinkled. The knobby end of one bone sticks out above a thigh.

"Yes, I am done. Do you have a problem with that?"

He pulls out his phone and takes a picture of my dinner.

"What did you just do?"

"I want to show Gretchen."

I push my plate away from me.

"This is going to set me off."

"What?"

"*I* get to choose what *I* eat. I'm not your family's dog."

"You don't need to be that loud."

"Then *listen* to me." I start to cry. "I don't want your family here now. Why are they in this moment with us? We're at home. Can we have privacy at *home*?" I cry harder. Would the Belmonts label this a "mood swing"?

"I'm sorry," he says. "I love you."

"Don't you have anything else to say?"

"I love you."

"No, Richard. About your family. About how they're getting in the way of us. They're in all our conversations now, all our meals. They're right here. Can you *feel* them?" I lasso an arm through the space around us. "Do you have anything to say about *that*?"

"I I—"

"That's not what we're talking about!"

My throat hurts. Is it sore just from shouting at him?

I head to the refrigerator. I'm so sick of everyone talking about my food. As if my body is Belmont property, some*thing* they maintain. I rip the door open and hear condiments slide. I drop armfuls of groceries on the counter, stack Tupperware into towers. When the fridge is empty, I turn to Richard.

"You want to stare at my food?" I ask.

Disbelief parts his lips.

"Let your eyes get a taste."

I leave the fridge door ajar—sometimes, keeping a door open is more powerful than slamming it—and head to my studio. Something bites my foot as I step inside. A thin shard of Richard's mirror is lodged in my heel. I pluck it free. I don't want to throw it out in the kitchen, where I'd have to see Richard. Instead, I place it on my windowsill. Half the splinter is red—but a beautiful red. It's bright with some cayenne in the shade. I take a seat on my stool and watch it for a bit.

Watch it bleed into the sky.

FOURTEEN

Two days later, I'm about to see Hunter for lunch.

I'm waiting for her at the Eastern, her favorite place for a Caesar salad. The decor is neat and minimalist: black wooden chairs without cushions, a lustrous black banquette with buttons in two parallel lines. Nothing hangs on the beige walls. Everything looks so clean and perfect it's as if they don't serve food here—just plastic meals that never drip, never stain. Meanwhile, my studio is messier than ever. There's even paint on the windows now, but I've felt too busy to wipe it off. The streaks glow in the afternoon, like the Belmonts' stained glass lamps.

What *am* I going to do about Richard's family? Assuming that he and I stop fighting, and I have the *chance* to do something. He's started to leave our place every morning without staying for his eggs and sausages. For as long as I've known him, he's never skipped that indulgent part of his routine—no matter how busy he gets, no matter how demonic his hangover. Now, he's gone days without it. As if, after the past few weeks, he's trying to avoid me.

"Devon!" Hunter waves.

I stand, knocking the table.

I hug her twice in succession.

"All right." She sits down. "What's it now?"

I want to laugh and cry at the same time: someone who can read me, who can tell when I'm not well. She looks magically serene. Is she usually this calm, or am I more chaotic? Her white sheath dress is as seamless as a brushstroke. Meanwhile, I can't remember the last time I showered. The hairs on my legs chafe against my pants. I tell her everything, stopping only to order a Caesar and coffee.

"I know I'm not myself," I say. "But if you push someone hard enough, they're going to fall in that direction. Do you know what I mean? The Belmonts are driving me over the edge. They're doing such a good job—it's almost like they're *trying* to provoke me. Testing how much I can take before I go insane."

"That is ten kinds of bizarre." Lowering her voice, she adds, "Why does this happen?" I ask what she means. "I'm not saying that *this*"— she gestures to my situation—"happens to everyone. It sounds like the Belmonts are taking it to an extreme. But in general, families accept the men their children bring home and not the women. Men are integrated into the family, and if the new women aren't rejected outright, they're the source of endless tension."

"You think?"

"Even with my husband. When I met Eli's parents, in high school, it caused a year of fighting on his side. His parents thought he was settling down too soon. I wasn't allowed to visit their house until we'd both graduated from college." I cringe. "Meanwhile, my parents loved Eli from the moment they met him. The point is, I've only ever heard of this happening to women. It's like internalized misogyny."

I think about it as the waitress arrives with our salads.

We dig into the roughage.

"You think so?" I ask.

"Maybe the Belmonts unconsciously think that all women are moody, crazy, or fill in the blank." The theory doesn't prove anything, but I feel like we're onto something. "Have you ever seen or read *The Handmaid's Tale*?" I shake my head. "It's about women who help men abuse other women. It's more than that, but the story gets into this idea that people can have contempt for their own gender."

I admit that might explain some of the Belmonts' behavior, then change the subject. I don't want to dominate another lunch with my issues. I ask Hunter about Thanksgiving. She tells me that she and Eli are planning to spend the holiday with his parents. There's no angst in her voice, no fear, giving me a glimmer of hope. If she can reconcile with her in-laws, maybe I can too. Then again, Eli's parents never worried that she was unstable, never sent her to multiple doctors.

"What about you two?" she asks. "Waverley for Thanksgiving?"

"That's the plan." I try to smile.

"Good luck."

~

Back at home, I paint my frustrations.

My studio is bright enough now with only natural light. The windows illuminate everything on my easel, down to the canvas weave. When the sun crosses onto the West Side, I turn on a tripod lamp near my piece. When the sun starts to drop, I turn on another. Keeping the light perfect takes constant adjustment. When I'm doing it right, every hour feels like ten in the morning. Maybe that's why I lose track of time in here. The light barely wavers all day long.

As I sit with my latest portrait, the rest of the world fades away. I mix a maraschino red so lush I can almost taste it. I mix a cantaloupe shade of orange so ripe it practically drips juice onto the floor. My work keeps getting better. Everything that can go right, does. Usually, painting the second eye in a face—and making all those tiny details match—is a challenge. Today, it's easy. Every part of the painting sings so loudly that I can almost hear the canvas buzz.

It's all overwhelmingly real.

FIFTEEN

One week before Thanksgiving, I file onto the crosstown bus. As I sit, Richard texts, Leaving work—see you at Gretchen's. Thank you for coming. I read it twice. Usually, he's a more emotional texter, expressing himself in heart-eyed emojis and hand-drawn Digital Touch messages. I've never seen him text anyone a cold hard dash in his life. It's eerie to get a message from my fiancé that looks like it was written by someone else.

From my seat in the back, I search the oily sky for stars and find only airplanes. They blink like shifting white eyes. Gretchen's building is narrow and filled with doctors' offices. When I reach her floor, Richard is already there on a call. I walk toward him through a tight hallway lined with closed doors. Each has its own brass nameplate with sharp corners. Richard starts to laugh so hard he leans forward. After his strange text, I didn't expect to find him so happy.

He greets me by lifting his chin.

"What did Mark Twain say about him?" Richard asks. "'Once you've put one of his books down, you simply can't pick it up again'?"

Incoherent noise on his call.

"Hopefully you aren't the only one who shows," he says, "and has to fill air about Henry James for an hour."

His smile is electric.

"Love you too, Mom. See you soon."

He hangs up and knocks on Gretchen's door. GRETCHEN PARKER, PSYCHIATRIST. Her nameplate looks so intelligent that it might be reading us as we read it. Neither Richard nor I say anything while we wait. He grins at me, but it's different from the one he just had. It's more muted and—guarded, even, as if we're strangers in an elevator. I can't see his teeth. He undoes the buttons on his vest. The snaps are loud. Am I overreacting to a couple of seconds, or does this feel more uncomfortable than it should?

The door swings open.

Gretchen gestures to the sofa with a royal demeanor. It's pleasant but joyless. Once Richard and I take our seats, she looks at me with her pen uncapped. I can't help but focus, though, on her blouse. It has an intricate green pattern, like a close-up of a leaf. Dark veined, branching. I wonder if I could use that design in anything I'm painting, even in just a patch.

Richard: Devon?

Me: Yes?

Richard: Sorry, I don't think she heard.

Gretchen: Not a problem. I was just saying that last time we spoke, Devon, you wanted to confront Richard's parents. You said that was the only way to "clear the air." Are you planning to talk to them before the visit next week? Or will you do it over the holiday?

Me: Do it over the holiday?

Gretchen: Yes.

Me: No, I don't plan to do it over the holiday. Are you serious?

Richard: Can we be nice, please?

Me: That's exactly what the Belmonts would want me to do. They'd want me to make Thanksgiving some big, dramatic event.

Gretchen: What makes you think that's what they want?

Me: Because they've been trying to get under my skin. Just look at everything they've told Richard—about my rage, my moods, my mental illness. Of course all that was going to get back to me and just *dig* at me. Just *itch*. I don't know why, but they want me to lose it.

They're dying for me to see red.

Gretchen: If I may, Devon, clarify something. Last time, Richard said that his dad thinks you have an eating disorder. Is that what you mean by "mental illness"?

Me: Yes.

Gretchen: That's an interesting way to interpret his words. An eating disorder *is* a mental illness, but not everyone uses those words interchangeably. Also, not everyone views mental illness the same way. This sounds like a charged topic for you. Are you sensitive to mental illness for any reason?

Me:

Gretchen: Did you ever have one in the past?

Me:

Richard: Did you?

Me: How is that relevant?

Richard: Because we are asking you now.

Gretchen: Would you be comfortable sharing what happened?

Me: It was so long ago.

Gretchen: We only want to hear what you're happy to share.

Me: In college, I was a little . . . low. So I downloaded this app to videoconference a doctor. She put me on a drug for depression, but it took away my edge. My art got so . . . lukewarm, fuzzy. So I stopped the pills. That period taught me it's okay—more than okay, it's *important*—to feel things deeply. It's a strength, not something that needs to be medicated.

Richard: Why didn't you tell me?

Me: It's not who I am anymore.

Richard:

Gretchen: Did you ever have an eating disorder?

Me:

Richard: Did you?

Me: I might've been a little underweight too. That's when my parents were getting divorced. And losing my dad—the one adult who was a little bit normal, who could've been there for me even though he never was . . . But I don't want to relive that. That's irrelevant because I'm healthy now.

Honestly, Richard, your family has gone too far. They can't *spoon* out my history like this. They can't get in this deep. I need some privacy, boundaries. I'm not going to live in a glass house with them. Do you know what I mean? Do you know what it's like to be constantly *watched?* I can't even take a sip of coffee without it feeling somehow, somewhere *measured.*

Gretchen: Thank you for sharing that with us. Richard, it looks like you're trying to put some thoughts together.

Richard: You never . . . Sorry, Devon, but you don't think *any* of that is relevant?

Me: No. I had problems ten years ago. Ten *years* ago.

Richard: But we've been talking about—

Me: *You* haven't said a word.

Richard: What does that mean?

Me: I only hear your family.

Richard: Gretchen, I really need some help. How should I respond when she gets this angry? I don't know what to do.

Me: Ask *me.* I'm right here.

Richard: I'm worried about your temper. Everyone is.

Me: No, they *want* me to break. They're—

Richard: That's not true.

Me: —desperate to disturb me.

I feel a dark urge and leave before it takes over. Her office door slams behind me. Her next patient appears to be here already. As he checks the time on his watch, it slides off his wrist, hits the floor. I stride to the exit, dodging a woman who raises thin eyebrows as if I'm a ghost. It would be too easy to startle her now. Why doesn't Richard see that we're all fulfilling expectations? If this woman thinks I'm a phantom, I could scare her just by smiling.

On the bus home, I replay the session, staring out the window as we cut across the city grid. How am I going to fix my relationship? We can't keep going back to therapy. It's tearing us apart more than it's putting us back together. I lose my fiancé more and more every week. My eyes feel hot. My wrist stings. I look down to see something black dripping across my palm. I lift my sleeve to find wet stripes across my forearm. The blood looks like oil in this light.

Did I do this?

Claw myself?

I glance around the bus. No one's looking this way. They're all on their phones, blue rays on their tired faces. I peel my sleeve back. Did I do this during the session? I check my nails, but it's too dark to tell which ones cut through my skin. My other palm pools with ink. I wipe it on my shirt without thinking, smearing a handprint across the front.

As soon as I'm home, I take off my shirt, throw it in the wash, and start a cycle. I breathe easier when it's out of sight, churning in detergent. In the bathroom, I clean my forearm and watch pink water spiral down the drain. The cuts don't look that bad up close. I only have three scratches, like I picked up a cat who didn't want to be held. My medicine cabinet is empty, so I open Richard's for Neosporin. I'm shaking as I rub the gel and hide the wound with Band-Aids. When I'm done, I gaze at my reflection: rail thin, bone white, and bandaged.

Who am I without Richard?

I text him that I'm sorry.

That I'll be on my best behavior for Thanksgiving.

That I'll keep going back to therapy for as long as he wants.

The messages form a neat stack on my phone. I wait to see if he'll answer, touching the screen when it grays. He doesn't reply. I check the time and realize that our session isn't over. He might still be there, talking to Gretchen—about me.

~

The next day, I'm tempted to call my mom. We never talk this often, but she was so clear last time. She sounded like she believed me, like she believed *in* me.

Right now, I need more of that.

I leave my studio around noon and put my jacket on in the elevator. I realize too late that I'm barefoot. My nails peek out from under the hem of my pants, like ten flipped white smiles. Elevator doors open. Paul tips his cap. I nod but stay put and ride back up to my floor, stuffing the smiles in boots before coming down.

Outside, the wind blows a few strands loose from my braid. They flick around my eyes as I dial Mom and walk. While the phone rings, I pass groups eating al fresco at Nello, famous for its giant red teddy bears sitting like patrons under the awning. I've always found it a little disorienting, as if I've just drunk one of the potions in Wonderland.

No answer.

Mom's voicemail is full.

Maybe it's better this way. Getting too close to her in good times just worsens the inevitable heartbreak. I head home, but after a few blocks, feel a prickle up my neck. I glance back to see a redheaded man. It's him—the same man from outside One Medical, from the Vietnamese restaurant. He's twenty steps behind me, holding a steady pace. His clothes are neat and neutral, white collar crisp over a beige sweater. His legs are unusually long, shrinking his torso. He lifts a phone to his ear, then catches my eye. I turn around.

So what if it's the same man?

Do I really think he's following me?

Paul tips his cap again when I return to the lobby. He hands me our mail with a tight smile. Now that I think about it, he never does chat me up the way he does Richard. It must be one of his strengths, discerning who likes to talk and who's better off alone. Today, though, I need some normal conversation. I'd really like for someone to treat me like I'm in the middle of the bell curve.

"TGIF?" I ask.

"TGIFF."

He smiles like he means it.

"How's painting?" he asks.

"Getting back to it." I point to the elevator as it opens.

"You're always at it."

I throw my arm out to stop the doors from closing.

"What's that?" I ask.

"I can tell." He points at his head. "You're always working on something."

The doors shut.

Whatever he meant, I'm sure it was nice. I go through the mail and notice an envelope from Gretchen Parker. It's thin, addressed to Richard. I open it before it occurs to me that maybe I shouldn't. There's just one sheet of paper inside, folded in thirds. I lift the flaps, my heart loud. But it's nothing more than a bill.

I drift into our apartment.

After I left therapy last night, Richard stayed for the full hour. When he came home, we sat on the sofa with enough space for a third party between us. He told me gently that I may have developed a deep distrust of others, stemming from unreliable parents. That attitude might explain why I work alone. On a related note, my temper might be quick to set off because I assume other people are working against me. Richard sounded hopeful when he said that I don't have to worry because not everyone is like my parents. He and his family want to help.

All I know is that I want to be with Richard. I leave the bill on his desk, by the glaring white wall. It watches like an unfinished eye.

PART THREE

SIXTEEN

Richard and I drive slowly through Greenwich on the day before Thanksgiving. A radio ad fills the space between us, pushing insurance. *Are you expecting the unexpected?* Richard turns the radio off as we pull into the Belmonts' driveway. The trees on either side look more skeletal than last time. Ragged hands point at us, reach for our windows.

Once we park by the front door, the three Belmonts step outside. Vanessa stands between Clarke and Oliver, slightly hidden by her son. Oliver's in an ivory long-sleeve polo, pressed khakis, and velvety leather derby shoes. He looks casually elegant and perfectly put together—except for his expression. Is he nervous? I plaster on a smile and tell myself that it's for Richard, not for them. No matter what happens during this visit, I can channel my feelings into my art. Even if I can't express myself in their house, I will always have a voice in my work.

"Happy Thanksgiving!" I greet them.

Clarke pulls me in first for a hug. As he leans back, he grabs one of my shoulders and gives it a squeeze. He's stronger than he thinks. Vanessa and Oliver are next in line with more delicate embraces. I notice a thick book in her hand, as if she's just stood up from reading. Richard seems genuinely happy to see everyone, which lifts my spirits. Clarke whisks two of our bags upstairs.

I'm the last inside.

Vanessa closes the door behind me. I forgot how immersive and self-contained this house is. The blurred windows hide the outdoors.

There's nothing in the decor to remind us that we're in Greenwich or that we're even in this century. When the front door shuts, we're in our own world. On our own time.

"We're so glad you could join us," she says.

"Me too."

"We've been preparing all week."

She sets her book down on the entryway table. It's a copy of *When the Stars Go Dark*, by Paula McLain. Pointed treetops circle the cover. *When the stars go dark* . . . I turn the phrase over as I carry our last two bags upstairs. Taken literally, it's a terrifying image.

The clocks are relentless in the background, like mechanical cicadas. Clarke passes me on his way out of our bedroom. He jiggles his eyebrows as if the stage is set, a curtain about to rise. Vanessa laughs somewhere under my feet. It sounds like her boys are with her. I try to collect myself. Have the clocks always been this loud? The ticking feels aggressive.

I take deep breaths and head down.

All four Belmonts are in the library. I sit in my usual chair, praying that no one will pay attention to me. Hopefully, they'll just pester Richard with questions and glaze right over this spot. At least my vocation is somewhat opaque. They won't know where to start, and maybe that will keep them from starting at all. Oliver is limp on the sofa next to Vanessa. It's strange to think that he and I are almost the same age. Richard sits on her other side. Vanessa keeps one hand on him, preening his shoulder, flattening his collar. She smooths his hair—I gasp.

She's wearing a new ring on her left hand. It's my engagement ring—rather, it's a ring that looks exactly like my engagement ring. It's a rose-cut diamond on a gold band. I feel my stomach twist and reach for my own. *Plenty sparkly.*

But there it is on her.

"Are you okay?" Richard asks.

He scoots forward on the sofa.

"Sorry, is that new?" I ask Vanessa.

I point to the ring.

"Oh, I've had this forever."

Vanessa puts her right hand over her left, just enough to hide the ring. She brings up Africa, moving the conversation in a new direction. She says that she's booked rooms for the family at the Lamai lodge next September in the Serengeti, so everyone can watch the Great Migration. This lodge sits on the river where hordes of wildebeest will attempt to cross without being eaten by crocodiles. Meanwhile, my injured wrist starts to ache.

When Vanessa's hands drift apart, my eyes narrow in on the ring. I can't believe she's wearing a carbon copy of my engagement ring—on her *ring* finger. Confronting her about it now would make me look crazy. I unfold my arms and interlace my fingers. My nails are over-grown, ten different lengths. The conversation drifts to Richard's new project at work. Everyone's eyes are on him except for Oliver's. When I catch him staring at me, his gaze flits away.

If part of me ever doubted that the Belmonts are trying to provoke me, I don't anymore. They are definitely trying to get into my head. Is this what happened to the brunette from that photo in Richard's room? Did he bring her home, only for his family to destroy her from the inside out?

"Devon." Richard's voice is loud.

Everyone looks at me as if I've just walked into the Diego Velázquez masterpiece *Las Meninas*. This time, the Spanish royal family has stopped abruptly to glare at *me*. Did one of the Belmonts ask me something?

"Yes?" I probe.

"Do you want to join us?" Richard asks. I look around the room for a clue as to what he means. "For the golf ball hunt," he adds after a pause. "We're going to walk the road next to the club and look for stray balls."

"Right, the tradition." I smooth my skirt and notice the fraying hem. "I'll stay here and do some sketching. But don't let that stop you."

The news ripples through them, bobbing their chins. Vanessa keeps her ring hand on Richard, the other on Oliver. She must feel me watching her, but she won't give me more than her profile, the side of one sapphire eye.

I stare at her sharp nose, pale lips. The point of her jawline pokes toward me like a challenge. This family doesn't look like a multiheaded creature anymore. Vanessa is too central, her arms like tangible influence over her sons. Clarke is blissful in a distant armchair. He might've taken Richard aside, stirred doubt about me. But my gut tells me that wasn't his idea. In this room, Vanessa is the focal point. She's where the chairs and clocks all face. And right now, she's the only one showing me deliberate neglect. She is the one with my ring.

They make their way into the foyer, where they grab Barbours and baseball caps. Oliver uses the phrase "herding cats," which doesn't get the laugh he seems to think it deserves. They file outside. Richard's about to turn around when Vanessa shuts the door between us.

The clocks tick. I'm alone.

I walk up to her book on the table. *When the Stars Go Dark.* The inside flap reveals that it's about a detective who investigates missing children. It appears to be a slow-building suspense, with a heroine motivated by her own childhood traumas. Why are you reading this, Vanessa? Are you leaving me a clue or fishing for morbid inspiration?

Do you have a slow-building plot for me?

If you do, I'm going to prove it.

I run my hand up the banister and stop next to a red tapestry on the wall. I inspect it so closely I breathe on the stitches. I'm not sure what I want to find, but if I look hard enough, I'll see something. I keep walking. Next to the final stair hangs a life-size portrait of a fifteenth-century woman. It's so realistic it might've been painted by a Spanish old master. She looks right at me in heavy jewels, a puffed collar. I follow my curiosity and check behind her. There's a ribbon of space between the frame and the wall. I slide my hand behind the woman's back but feel only dust. When I look at my palm again, it's as dark as its own shadow.

I clap to get rid of the dust.

It floats upward.

I wander into an office. It has a masculine feel, like somewhere Clarke might work, centered around a black antique desk. I tug the drawers, starting from the bottom—locked. When I pull the final one, it gives way. Felt tips roll toward me. Paper clips slide into dark buttons and a five of spades playing card. There's one flash of color in the mix: a red paintbrush.

I stare at it, confused.

No one in this family paints. The Belmonts are curators, critics. They're collectors who relish in the pleasures of art. They don't suffer in the trenches of making it. The paintbrush looks so out of place I'm afraid to touch it—but I do. It's small, something that could fit in a toddler's hand. The bristles are frayed, but the handle is bright. Shined, almost.

Why is this here?

I spin around, looking for the answer—for an easel in the corner, a canvas turned against the wall, *something*. There's nothing but more photos on a dark bookcase. Most include Vanessa or feature her alone. I inch closer, holding the brush. In the closest one, she perches with casual flexibility on a window seat. She's in a slinky, off-white cashmere dress, looking like her body's dripping with cream. The next photo shows her with Clarke in the tropics. She's chin-deep in water the color of a gemstone. I use the paintbrush to spin the frame around, but there's nothing behind the photo. As far as I can tell, there's nothing else strange about this room.

I can't see any reason for the brush.

Did Vanessa plant it here, toying with me?

No matter why it's here, I need something concrete on her. I need proof that she's trying to get into my head. I put the brush back and creep around the second floor, passing rooms with fireplace screens as tall as I am. I gaze out a window with diamond-shaped glass, like a snake half-buried in the wall. At the end of the hallway, one door is ajar.

It's the only door in sight that's almost closed. I pad toward it, slowly making out what's inside. A beige cardigan hangs on the back of a desk chair. The fabric looks like a translucent cashmere. One pearl button gleams near the neckline. I move faster toward the distant room. What am I going to find in there? A receipt for the ring? Or worse?

I push the door open.

The study is messier than I expected. Vanessa might have a meticulous look, but her personal den is chaotic. Papers overwhelm the desk. Hardcovers twist in stacks on the floor, several encyclopedias and *The Oxford English Dictionary* among them. Wraparound bookcases are stuffed with more titles, including two copies of *Rebecca* by Daphne du Maurier—her favorite novel, Richard mentioned. The slim crevice of wall space is crammed with black-and-white photos of ballerinas. It's a vertical column of dancers in striking poses, sharp shoes.

Being in this room feels like being in *her* head.

I hurry to the desk, reading the papers upside down as I turn. They're all printed emails. The one on top went to an events coordinator at Blue Hill, with the subject: Belmont wedding. In it, Vanessa asks where they might set up a tent for two hundred fifty people—two *hundred* fifty. The emails behind it are to vendors, collecting price estimates. Vanessa had a back-and-forth with Delphine Cakes, where they quote $8,500 for a five-tiered design. She also emailed a stationery store in Greenwich, asking for dates when she can see invitations in person.

The next stack is just as thick, titled BELMONT GUEST LIST. It's a table of two columns: ENVELOPE NAMES and ADDRESSES. Here, Vanessa lists a staggering number of people. I don't know a single one. Why didn't she tell me about this? She knew I wanted a small wedding. Richard must've told her that. I hate her *seeping* into ours like this, slipping through the cracks, somehow in every decision. This is just like when she got inside my *food*.

She's in everything that's supposed to be mine.

SEVENTEEN

I try to act calm with Richard's family.

We're in the library, where we sat before their walk. They only came home when it was time for cocktails, laughing at new inside jokes. Now, everyone gathers around hors d'oeuvres, dressed with holiday flourishes. Clarke wears tartan pants. Richard sports a maroon bow tie. With my art show coming up on Friday, though, I've been so busy I didn't pack well. I'm in the same outfit as this morning. My hands hide the fraying hem of my skirt.

I'm trying not to bring up the wedding. It takes effort to stay quiet, to keep my hands over the unraveling seams. Meanwhile, Oliver retells a story from a recent golf tournament. Apparently, he chipped out of sand forty yards from the hole for a birdie on eighteen, tying for second place. The first time he shared this with us, five minutes ago, no one responded with much energy. Now he's retelling the story in detail, clearly seeking a better reaction.

While he talks in a circle, Vanessa ferries between us and the kitchen, moving as if her bones are filled with air. Hosting makes her seem magnanimous, but I see it as a form of control. After all, we're forced to stay here until she calls us to dinner. No one knows when that will be. All we can do is listen to the same golf story again and again, with no end in sight.

Belmont Guest List. I remember the names alphabetized from Aaron to Zander. The printout is hidden in my suitcase. I still don't know what to tell Richard. If I show him the list, he'll know I was snooping, and I haven't discovered anything truly condemning yet. I can hear his reply already: *Are you this upset because she wants to throw you a spectacular wedding? She hasn't made any decisions yet. She's just getting information—for you.* There must be something else I can find on her, something that would prove she's trying to drive me mad.

"Dinner's ready," Vanessa announces.

We follow her into the kitchen. I find myself in the middle of the Belmonts, drifting in their cashmere fog. We line up to serve ourselves from the stove, holding the fragile rims of china plates. Clarke taps my shoulder, his eyes watery from the wine.

"How's wedding planning coming along?" he asks.

"It's coming," I say, caught off guard. Everyone else appears to have one ear in our conversation. At the front of the line, Vanessa squeezes green beans in silver tongs, her chin angled toward us. "We're still early in the planning. But we're thinking we want something small and intimate. Does that sound good to you?"

"Well, sure," Clarke says cheerily.

"What about you, Vanessa?" I speak up.

"Hmm?" she asks.

"A small wedding sound good to you?"

"No wedding is small. Every one is important."

She looks right at me, apparently unafraid. I hold her gaze as she hands the tongs to Richard. Her outstretched arm looks elegant, like the dancers' precise extensions on her office wall. I've never been physically powerful or well coordinated, but I do have grit. I can hold my ground.

"Have you thought about who you might want to invite?" I ask.

"A little." She steps out of the kitchen.

"A little?"

"Don't worry about it now."

At this point, I'd have to hold her feet to the fire to get her to admit something. It's not worth it. Badgering her now, the night before Thanksgiving, would only reinforce what they've whispered to Richard.

I don't think he would ever leave me, but with too many explosive fights, there could be lasting wounds.

When it's my turn, I serve myself some of everything. I glance sideways to catch Clarke and Oliver watching my plate. As we head into the dining room, I can almost see the Belmonts' fingerprints on my food—the marks glinting in oil, feeling the heft of my portions, the length of my green beans. Vanessa sits at the head and urges everyone to raise a glass.

I follow, feeling my hand forced.

Does every woman feel trapped in situations like these? I fell in love with Richard, not his family. Now here I am, getting married to all of them. Maybe the Belmonts feel the same way. They signed up for Richard, but they didn't sign up for me.

~

That night, I can't sleep. I feel like I've done something wrong by taking the guest list and stuffing it in my suitcase. I keep imagining it under my socks, proof that I was rifling through the house—stealing, actually. Besides, I can't shake the suspicion that Vanessa is somehow one step ahead. She probably wanted me to find it. I shouldn't have been so rash, snatching it out of her files.

Why can't I control myself?

As if every thought needs me to say its name?

Every feeling needs to crawl out of me and *breathe*?

I roll out of bed and creep over to my suitcase. Keeping a piece of Vanessa's property, however small, doesn't feel right. List in hand, I step into the hallway. I feel my way through the labyrinth, sinking every once in a while on a creaky board. Each time, I freeze in place and wait before proceeding. It's gotten easier to navigate this place, but the routes aren't intuitive yet. I still have to picture the floor plan and take tortuous stabs in the dark.

Vanessa's den is farther than I remember. Eventually, I replace the list and look around to see if anything's been moved since I was last here. The night is too thick. I only see disembodied parts of furniture and blots of pure darkness hiding everything else.

The journey back is slow.

All lamps over their art are black, turning great works into eye sockets. My arms tighten around my waist. Not even the carpet is warm. When I reach the door to Vanessa and Clarke's room—I think—I stop. Why are you trying to drive me away? I stand still, as if I'm waiting for an answer. Then again, Oliver hasn't had a girlfriend since he moved in. Maybe Vanessa thinks that no one is good enough for her sons. Maybe she wants to keep them here on Waverley.

Richard grumbles sleepily as I slide back in bed.

"You okay?" he asks.

"All better."

~

I wake up to the sound of her name. *Vanessa!* It rings in my head like a bell. I'm not sure if I'm dreaming when I open my eyes to Richard's stained glass windows. They illustrate a long river across the far wall. The light through the blues is psychedelic. *Vanessa!* Did we really not close his curtains? Yesterday was so chaotic. The river seems to move as the light shifts from the belly up to a frothing crest. The sound of her name gets louder until it's right outside our door.

Clarke strides suddenly into the center of our room. He's in a Barbour jacket and tennis shoes clinging to broken blades of grass. I scramble to sit up, my nipples like tent poles in my T-shirt. I pull the duvet up to hide them. Richard's in his boxers next to me, also fumbling for covers. Over his bare shoulder, I watch Clarke. He looks—different. His steely eyebrows are cinched together. His stare is so sharp I follow his line of sight like a wire through the air.

He looks at Richard, then me.

"Have you seen Vanessa?" Clarke asks.

"No," Richard says.

"No," I echo.

"Heard anything from her?" Clarke asks.

"No, Dad, we just woke up."

"Did she say she was going somewhere?"

"No, Dad. What's going on?"

"She's not in the house."

The clock behind Clarke reads nine. Usually, everyone in this group is up by seven. Richard must be in a vacation state of mind, as he's taken the week off work. I must've slept in after agonizing over that list.

She's been missing for two hours?

"Did you call her?" Richard asks.

"Her phone is here." Clarke pulls a black iPhone out of his pocket and holds it up for us to see. He slips it back inside. "Just like her car in the garage. Just like her wallet on the nightstand. *They're* here, but *she's* not."

"Did you call the police?" Richard asks.

"About to." Clarke turns on his heel.

"Did she go for a walk?" I ask.

Clarke stops short.

Richard's head swivels slowly.

"What did you say?" Clarke demands.

"I-I . . . ," I stammer.

It's the most harmless explanation. She goes for a walk every morning like clockwork. What if today's went long? Maybe Vanessa bundled up for a stroll and then had more energy than she thought. Instead of walking the usual route around the neighborhood, she decided to go an extra mile or two.

"You're right that her sneakers aren't by the front door," Clarke says, looking at me funny. "But she's not on a walk, Devon. If she were, she would've taken her phone, and she would've been home two hours ago."

Oliver enters our room, red faced.

"Well?" Clarke asks.

"Nowhere," Oliver says. "I went all around." He draws a lopsided rectangle in front of him, car keys swinging in his hand.

A chill sweeps up my spine.

What happened to Vanessa?

Richard jumps out of bed and strides to the bathroom with purpose. I hear a short, hard stream of urine. Clarke and Oliver leave the room without saying where they're going or what they're doing next. I'm still in bed when Richard returns. He's apparently bewildered to find me stationary in my pajamas.

"What are you doing?" he asks, confused.

I scramble to my feet.

We hurry to get dressed.

I tear a streak into my black pantyhose as I pull on my outfit. I don't have time to change into something else. Richard's already in an oxford and sweatpants, waiting for me by the door. I step into my fraying skirt. The loose threads sway like fringe. I'm trembling as we leap downstairs, toward his dad's baritone voice. But I can't keep up with Richard. In these tights, I'd slip across the wooden floors. I'm a few steps behind him by the time we reach his family in the dining room.

Clarke hangs up, his mouth in a firm line.

"What happened?" Richard asks.

"The police said they can't help us until this afternoon at the earliest." Clarke shakes his head distastefully. "They said she isn't technically missing yet, that we should give it time, but I know she's missing *now*." His voice rises in frustration. He starts pacing. I'm too nervous to swallow, to make any noise at all. "Fine, they can wait, but we don't have to. I'll get a private investigator on my own. Oliver"—he snaps fingers at his son—"start texting everyone in the family. Ask if they've heard from her. Richard"—Clarke turns to face us—"call everyone in the neighborhood, all our friends. Keep track of who you ask and what they say."

"I'll get my laptop," Richard volunteers.

While he jogs upstairs, Oliver takes a seat and gets to work. Clarke finger-pecks his phone with hard taps. I feel uncomfortably inert. The longer I stand here, the worse it gets, like I'm sinking in something dark. When Richard returns, I follow him to the table.

"Is there anything I can do?" I whisper.

We sit side by side.

He looks afraid.

"I could—"

"Not now!" Clarke cuts me off.

At this point, I'm unsure which is more frightening: Vanessa's disappearance or Clarke's transformation. I've only really seen him kicked back in an armchair, letting the conversation melt over him. Now he has an uncharacteristic rigidity. His girth is pushed forward, making him look even bigger and much more powerful. I never imagined that he could *snap* at me, that he could make his voice much louder than the polite chime of silverware.

Not now! Of course, though, he's right. I shouldn't be wasting people's time to relieve my conscience, to soothe the guilt I feel for just *standing* here. I let his tone go. Besides, he must be in a personal hell. Until we find Vanessa, they're all allowed to be short, irritable—anything they want. I look across the table at Oliver. Blue iMessages dominate his phone. The bubbles keep rising like water starting to boil. He catches my eyes. Does he look skeptical? Why is he staring at me like that? Meanwhile, Clarke lifts his phone to his ear and marches out of the room.

"Hi, this is Clarke Belmont calling from Greenwich," he begins. His words vanish more with every step. "Please call back as soon as you get this. My wife's been missing since this morning, and we're looking to hire . . ."

This all happened so fast. Outside, birds are still ringing in the new day. They whistle and squeak right outside, sounding precious and bright. How is Clarke so sure that something bad has happened? Then again, when you've been married to someone for forty years, as they have, you must know your spouse well enough to sense when something is wrong.

Is there nothing I can do?

"Do you want any coffee?" I ask the room.

Richard stiffens next to me.

Neither of them responds.

Was that the wrong thing to ask?

I head into the kitchen alone, intending to make myself a cup. It's only when I see the foil-wrapped chocolate turkeys next to the coffee bean grinder that I remember it's Thanksgiving. The birds stand on a box of orange nonpareils.

"What happened?" Richard asks in the dining room.

He doesn't address anyone in particular.

"Did she slip?" he presses on. "Did she go on a walk and *slip*?"

"I checked all the roads," Oliver says.

I try to imagine how I'd react if I woke up on Thanksgiving to find that my mom wasn't in the house. I guess I wouldn't be entirely surprised. I've worried about her so much I've experienced her death multiple times.

But Richard and Oliver have never seen any real weakness or vulnerability in their parents. At least, not according to Richard. I don't know if going through this is harder as a kid or as an adult. Either way, when one of your parents needs more help than you do, something inside changes.

~

"Does anyone want anything to eat?" I ask.

The clocks just chimed two.

Richard, Clarke, Oliver, and I are in the dining room, craning over our devices. Richard sits next to me in the Columbia hoodie that he's worn all morning. On his laptop, he faces the spreadsheet that the Belmonts set up on Google Drive. It lists everyone they've contacted and what they've learned. So far, it amounts to nothing. Across the table, Clarke and Oliver have had their heads together, poring over Oliver's phone. Now, Clarke looks at the floor with stern eyes. He's reacting as if I just suggested abandoning the effort to find Vanessa.

I retreat to the kitchen.

Was my question out of line?

We've been here all day, and I haven't seen any of them eat—not one bite. Don't people still need food in an emergency? They're acting like their basic needs vanished along with Vanessa. They haven't even had coffee. I served them each a cup a few hours ago, though none of them asked for it. Only I finished mine, drinking down to the clean bottom of the mug and savoring the boost.

The kitchen is eerily beautiful. Copper pots hang over a gleaming central island. Bay windows frame the sunny backyard, letting in a torrent of natural light. If all I had was this shining view, I'd think it was a gorgeous day.

I make a turkey sandwich on a brioche bun. On one side, I add mayo. On the other, mustard. I'm careful to stay away from bells and whistles, though: no toasting bread, no slicing avocadoes. This is a sturdy meal, but not one that would disrespect the reality weighing on us. No one joins me. They seem too nervous to leave that pulsing knot of energy, the tangle of anxiety tying them together. They must think that if they take a break to eat, they'll miss something important.

I sit at the island. My chewing is loud.

What else can I do?

I've tried to help all day, but—I've been getting the strange feeling that I'm unwelcome. Whispers seem to die down whenever I return from the bathroom. Everyone avoids my eyes. Every time Clarke thinks of another task, he delegates it to one of his sons. I've tried to be pro-active. *I* was the one who thought to call every hospital in a fifty-mile radius. However, as soon as I finished and reported that Vanessa isn't in any of them, Clarke told Oliver to call every hospital again.

I work my way through the second half of my sandwich. Are they excluding me on purpose? Maybe they think that I can't possibly grasp their pain. Maybe they don't trust me to be as thorough as her own flesh and blood. Or maybe their reactions have nothing to do with me, and this is just how people suffer.

Oliver appears on the threshold.

"Are you done?" he asks with an edge. He crosses his arms in a polo the color of his own skin. It blends into his khakis, almost making him look naked. Richard walks up behind him and jingles car keys over Oliver's head.

"We're going to do another loop," Richard says.

"I can drive," I offer.

"Thanks." His voice is grim.

I slip my plate into the dishwasher and head to the foyer, where Richard and Oliver bicker in whisper tones. I open the coat closet. There are dozens in here, organized by color. The black at the left transitions to brown in the middle, then blue, and then just a final inch of color. I grab a Barbour. Was Vanessa kidnapped?

No one's said it out loud, but it must've crossed everyone's minds. Why would someone target *her*? She's wealthy, sure, but so is everyone else in this zip code. It must've been an accident. She must've forgotten her phone, gone for a walk, and—got hit by a car? I squirm. The thought of her run over and abandoned is disturbing, but it isn't unrealistic. The more I think about it, the more certain I am that there couldn't have been any foul play. She just didn't mingle with those kinds of people. All her friends were in bimonthly book clubs or on the high-profile charity circuit. She never crossed paths with anyone seedy in her thoroughly upper-crust life.

"—Devon—" Oliver whispers.

Did he just say my name?

On the entryway table, Vanessa's copy of *When the Stars Go Dark* is gone. Did she move it yesterday? I walk closer. It used to be right here, where the mahogany gleams. Richard's still murmuring with his brother behind me. When I glance back, Oliver's staring at me.

"You didn't even like her," he says.

I look to Richard to defend me.

Nothing.

"Richard," I plead.

"Stop it, Oliver," Richard snaps with authority.

"This is all your fault." Oliver punches a finger in my direction.

"Enough!" Clarke bellows from the dining room. He emerges in a hurry and comes to a skidding stop. "You two, go." He points at Richard and me. "Oliver, stay here. We can't waste our time arguing."

"What's he going to do here?" Richard asks.

"Search the property again," Clarke orders.

Oliver glares at me like a rabid watchdog.

Richard opens the front door and ushers me outside. I'm sick to my stomach as I get in the car. Richard is quick to follow on the passenger side. It takes me a few seconds to adjust the mirrors. I feel his impatience brewing as the micro-adjustments continue. I move my seat forward a couple of inches, trying to ignore the mechanical whir as it slides. I fiddle with the thermostat, raising the heat. My trembling hand makes this take longer than it should.

Now, we're on our way.

I drive the speed limit around their neighborhood. No one's on the road except for us. None of the houses are close enough to glimpse inside, to see whether people are carving turkeys or clinking Bloody Marys. I'm about to open my mouth when Richard takes out his phone and dials someone on speaker. Clarke answers on the first ring.

"Have we missed anyone?" Richard asks.

"Let me check."

Heavy footsteps on Clarke's side of the line.

"Oh, thank God," Clarke says.

"What?" Richard leans forward.

"Thank God."

"Dad, what happened?"

Dead silence.

"Dad!" Richard presses.

"Detective McInnis . . . ," Clarke begins. "He's going to work with us. Sorry, he sent me a text. I'm still reading it. He's going to be over in a couple of hours."

"Who is he?" Richard asks.

"He worked with . . . ," Clarke says slowly, clearly preoccupied. He's now murmuring something incoherent, as if he's reading the rest of the detective's text to himself, leaking only some of it out loud. "Sorry, he needs recent photos of Vanessa, and he wants to talk live. I have to go. I love you."

"I love you too."

They hang up.

Richard taps his phone on his knee. I check between trees on my side of the road. What are we looking for, exactly? I know this search is well intentioned, but have they thought this through? We don't know how long she's been gone. Did she go missing in the middle of the night or first thing in the morning? Seven hours is the difference between New York and North Carolina. I'm not sure if scanning trees at twenty-five miles per hour is useful.

This is all your fault. But I try to forget what Oliver said. Of course he was going to snap. Losing your mom is hard enough, and his life hasn't exactly prepared him for adversity. His only social circles are at home, work, and country clubs—hyper-polite places filled with people decades older. He doesn't have any peers who challenge him emotionally. He doesn't have much experience with the darker side of human nature, with what truly desperate people can do. Blaming me might help him cope for now, but I'll be exonerated once we find a lead.

Where could she be?

Every now and then, Richard gives me a driving direction. I don't reach for his hand even though I desperately want to. I know that sometimes, when Mom isn't there, you don't want sympathy and love.

You want other people to help solve hard problems. Today isn't about our relationship. It's about his relationship with her.

~

The doorbell chimes at four o'clock.

"That's him," Clarke says, rising from the dining room table. He races into the foyer, while Richard and Oliver are slower to stand. A whole day without news is heavy. She's been missing for at least nine hours.

I'm the last one on my feet. It's just me in the dining room now, with four framed photos of her. They cluster in the center of the table, where they've been since Richard and I returned from our drive. Apparently, Clarke came across these while searching for the detective's pictures. Once he had them in his hands, he just couldn't let them go. With the candle-style chandelier overhead, and the sun just starting to set, the scene looks like a vigil.

I glance left to see the front door open. Clarke and the man who must be Detective McInnis are shaking hands, but the door blocks almost all of the stranger. I see only his pale hand rising and falling in the air.

I drift toward them in the foyer.

Detective McInnis has red hair and freckles. He's distantly familiar, like one of Richard's colleagues, someone I've seen at crowded cocktail parties but never actually met. Or one of Marc's regular clients, someone who visits the gallery alone to walk through the showroom and listen to the paint. My lips part in shock. It's him—*him*. Last week, he was trailing me on my way home. Before that, he stood outside my doctor's appointment in pouring rain. He ate pork belly behind Hunter, ears piqued. Up close, he looks to be in his forties, with light wrinkles under copper scruff. He has a thin face and taut cheeks. His narrow eyes focus ahead.

Clarke introduces us by name.

"And this is Devon," Clarke says. "Richard's girlfriend."

"Nice to meet you," he tells me.

I can't speak.

Clarke ushers everyone out of the foyer. The Belmonts file ahead of me into the library, where they fill the sofa. All three lean forward, watching the newcomer hopefully as he pulls out a notebook. I sink into my chair.

"Clarke told me some of what happened," Detective McInnis says. He faces each of us for a fraction of a second. When he looks at me, there's no recognition. He's acting like he's never seen me. Why would he do that unless—*was* he following me? The thought did cross my mind the last time I ran into him. Now, it turns out that he's a detective with ties to the Belmonts. Did Vanessa hire him to investigate *me*? "As a first step, I'd like to talk to everyone individually and get a better idea of the last twenty-four hours. Starting with you, Clarke, if you don't mind."

"Please," Clarke says.

"Then I'll approach the neighbors, in case they saw anything. Assuming the police get involved soon, as they promised, you should expect more interviews with them and an announcement on local news at eight. But like I said, I'll start with Clarke."

"Would you like any coffee?" I ask the detective.

"Sure, thanks."

His expression reveals nothing.

Richard, Oliver, and I stand.

"Don't touch *anything*," Clarke snaps.

I walk on eggshells toward the kitchen.

Don't touch anything. I already made everyone coffee this morning. I ate lunch in the kitchen. If this house is a crime scene, what are we doing here? Ahead of me, Richard puts an arm around his brother and pulls him closer. They take seats at the kitchen island, while I collapse on the sofa. The murmur of Clarke and McInnis's conversation drifts in from the library.

Did the detective ask for coffee? All I remember is that he acted like a stranger. Then again, of course he did. It's his job to be discreet. I'm almost positive that Vanessa hired him, but even if I'm right, what does that change? It's no surprise that she'd invade my privacy. The real mystery is that she's gone.

Richard and Oliver slant toward each other. From this angle, for the first time, they look alike—the same big ears, bright hair—just in different sizes. They're becoming more and more tightly bonded the longer they go without their mom. I can't believe we still haven't learned anything new. All day, we've done nothing but look for her—probed her entire network—and nothing. The eeriest part is that making no progress means things are getting worse. Minute by minute, with no new information, the unsettling situation has become a crisis.

Eventually, Clarke returns and summons Richard by name. He rises, and I follow a beat later. Clarke shows me a cautionary palm.

Right, one by one.

I nod that I understand.

Clarke takes Richard's seat at the island and puts a hand on Oliver's shoulder. Oliver returns the gesture, tying them together. Clarke starts to shake. He wipes his eyes on the collar of his shirt. It's such a raw moment that I have the urge to draw it: the arch of Clarke's neck, his rounded back, and the pots hanging over their heads. It's the most pain I've ever seen in a setting so beautiful. Everything in this room is in order, and they can't even lift their heads.

What happened to her?

The more time passes, the more I come around to believing that maybe this wasn't an accident. Sure, Vanessa didn't mingle with unsavory people, but did she ever anger someone so much that they wanted to hurt her? Needle someone for so long, they snapped?

Richard returns and sends Oliver in his place.

"Dad, can we double-check the list together?" Richard asks.

"Yes." Clarke moves into the dining room.

I don't know what to do except—clean? Would that help? I run a paper towel under the faucet and start to wipe the counter. Immediately, I regret it. Is everything evidence? I throw the wet paper towel away as if it's infectious, going to poison not just me but my relationship with everyone in this house. The bin shuts loudly. I pray that Clarke doesn't stick his head into the kitchen, that he doesn't open the trash, grab the paper towel, and ask what I was erasing.

I wait, heart drumming.

When no one comes, I join Clarke and Richard in the dining room. While they crane over a spreadsheet, I pick up a photo of Vanessa. She's shown here at a black-tie event, surrounded by ladies in updos and sweetheart necklines. Everyone else laughs in the same direction. But Vanessa alone faces the camera. She's calm in the horde, a soft smile teasing her lips. I can see why Clarke chose this photo. It singles her out. It makes her look special.

Oliver appears beside me.

"The detective's waiting."

I go warily through the house on my own.

In the library, Detective McInnis is already on his feet. He holds out his hand while I'm still a few paces away. I don't hurry, even though it's mildly uncomfortable to see him frozen with his arm outstretched. Should I confront him about following me around New York? I doubt he'd admit anything. Besides, focusing on that *now* would be worse than petty. It might be . . . obstructing justice. When we finally do shake hands, he's the first to pull away after a few seconds of up and down. I must be more nervous about this interview than I realized. We sit.

"How are you holding up?" he asks.

"Fine."

He looks impressed.

"I mean, I'm torn up inside, like everyone. But not . . ."

"Not what?"

"I don't know."

He writes something with his left hand. His wrist bends in a way that hides his note. I try to stay calm while he asks a few factual questions about me: how I spell my name, if I've ever gone by any other name, and where I'm from. He should know those answers already. He must be keeping up appearances.

"How long have you been with Richard?" he asks.

"Two years," I say.

He nods as if Richard said the same thing.

"And can you describe what happened last night?" he asks.

"We had dinner together as a family."

"Anything out of the ordinary?"

"No."

"You don't want to think about it?" he asks.

I think about it. It feels so long ago already.

I remember Vanessa was the consummate hostess. During cocktails, she glided between the library and kitchen with her usual agility. When we lined up for dinner, I asked her if a small wedding sounded good. Meanwhile, six-petaled diamond flowers blinked on her ears. I rephrased and asked about her guest list, but she just kept clicking silver tongs, unable to give me a straight answer. It was a toned-down version of the confrontation I'd wanted to have, but I can't bring that up now. It would overstate the importance of the exchange. Was anything else unusual?

"How would you describe your relationship with Vanessa?" he presses.

I feel anxious for some reason.

I clear my throat.

"She's going to be my mother-in-law—was," I correct myself. "Is," I decide.

"Was or is?" he asks.

"I don't know."

I squeeze my neck with one hand.

"Can you shed any more light on your relationship with Vanessa?" he asks. "Not the factual relationship. A few adjectives, maybe."

His pen stalls.

"Well," I go on, "we get along because we both appreciate art." The detective's pen is frozen, as if he's daring me to say something of value. "She loves the greats. You know, artists who have stood the test of time. She couldn't get enough of the Hudson River school." I point to the landscape painting in this room. Detective McInnis looks only briefly. "She really was a gifted observer. She could see mistakes in an abstraction. Do you know what I mean? She could look at a mural by Jackson Pollock and know *that* drop was an accident. *That* was the trickle that haunted him."

"Was there any tension between you and Vanessa?" he asks.

"Tension?"

Did I give him that impression?

Maybe I'm talking too much.

"Sure," I admit. "But it was just . . ."

"Just what?"

I don't know what to say.

"I'm just getting a lay of the land." He shrugs amicably, as if this is a conversation between friends. "I know it's normal to have some tension with your in-laws." He raises his left hand as he says it. His wedding band glints. "I just want to know if there was anything unusual about the relationship, anything at all."

"No. Thanks."

He makes a note.

"Last night, do you recall getting out of bed for any reason?" he asks.

His tone is confident.

Richard must've mentioned that.

"Yes. I went to the bathroom."

"Which one?"

"The one in our room."

He segues into a series of more general questions. No, Vanessa didn't mention any plans she'd made for today. No, there were no arguments last night. No, she didn't get into a fight with anyone. The detective rephrases that in a couple of ways. The questions appear to be routine, but eventually I realize that in this house, the only person on poor terms with Vanessa was me.

I touch my brow, unsettled.

"You all right?" he asks.

He points at my arm.

A few red marks are visible above my sleeve.

"Oh, those," I say.

He eyes them.

"I scratched myself."

"Can I see?" he asks.

I don't like the idea of showing my body on command. Worse, I don't like the implication that this is at all relevant to the case. I'm fingering my sleeve when I realize that I don't have to show him. I could refuse—but that would look suspicious. I set my jaw and roll back my cuff to reveal three long red trails. They're more gruesome than I remember, the dark crusts interrupted by sticky beads, like red dew on the side of the road. Then again, I haven't paid them much attention.

"When did that happen?" he asks.

"Last week."

"They look fresher than that."

"I pick at them. I know I shouldn't."

I smear a drop of blood until it disappears.

"Do you mind if I take a photo?" he asks.

"I do."

He stares at me.

I don't budge.

He scribbles a note.

"When did you scratch yourself exactly?" he asks.

Most likely, it happened during therapy. I remember warning Gretchen *They're desperate to disturb me* before catching an early bus home.

"Last week," I repeat without detail.

"Those look pretty deep."

"The skin on your forearms is very thin. It doesn't take much to . . ." I roll my sleeve back up, hiding the marks. "You know."

He underlines something.

"Right," he says. "Has anyone else seen those?"

I swallow. "No."

"Not even Richard?"

I shake my head. I don't explain that we haven't been intimate since I cut myself, that we've barely slept together since I met his parents. The few times we have, the circumstances have been . . . off. We were either in the middle of a fight or desperate to get out of one.

"Now, is there anything else you want to tell me?" he asks.

"Nothing."

"Before the police get here? After that . . ."

"No, thank you."

I stand up.

He follows after a beat.

"In that case, thank you for your time," he says.

I lead him toward the dining room, where the Belmonts will be waiting. *Has anyone else seen those?* His tone was grave. It feels uncomfortably silent now as we walk. I wonder if I should ask him something, but the only questions that come to mind are too casual—*Do you have any kids? What's your family doing for the holiday?*—or too intrusive—*Do you have any other open cases right now?* Each second feels stiffer than the last.

When the Belmonts see us, they stand.

Detective McInnis asks Clarke for a tour—and Clarke readily agrees—before turning to address the rest of us. "In case I don't see you again today, the next forty-eight hours will be crucial. After that, your memories will fade. So I might come back with a few more questions."

"Whatever you need," Richard says.

Clarke escorts the detective upstairs.

I'm at the head of the table, Richard and Oliver on either side. The wall clocks on my left seem ominous now, as if they're counting down to something. As if they're pulling us toward an end that might not be benign. Clarke shouldn't have made this room the headquarters. The sense of time is too palpable here, too persistent. It makes my heart sound like it's ticking. I try to ignore it and face Richard. The windows behind him are dark, filled with our reflections.

"Richard?" I ask.

He looks at me.

"Do you have a moment?"

He follows me into the hallway leading to the kitchen. A stained glass mosaic colors the ceiling. Richard looks sad, like his spirit is sinking, bringing his body down with it. I know that he's fragile right now, but I have to ask.

"What did you tell the detective about me?" I whisper.

"Why?"

"Because he was treating me like a suspect?" I raise my eyebrows. "There were questions about my *motive*. He didn't say that word, but I could tell he was fishing around it." I study Richard's stare. "What did you say?"

"I told him the truth."

His tone is resigned.

"What truth?" I demand.

"Everything."

"What do you mean 'everything'?"

He shrugs, looking weary.

"Did you tell him . . . we've been fighting?" I ask.

"The good and the bad, Devon."

I try to collect myself. I'm being selfish.

Of course Richard didn't have an agenda when he talked to McInnis. It was a brain dump in the hope that something might stick, that anything might help. He did speak to the detective for a long time, now that I'm thinking about it. But he was probably just spilling every anecdote that came to mind, not knowing which one might hold the key to where she is. His mother is missing. He's worried. Who am I to care for a second about how he described me in a moment like this? He knows I had nothing to do with this. Everyone knows I had nothing to do with this.

"I'm sorry for asking," I say.

He shrugs again, looking so heartbroken that I throw my arms around his neck and hug him. I hold on even when he doesn't hug me back immediately.

"Devon, also . . . ," Richard says.

"What?" I pull away.

"I need to stay here and help."

"Of course."

"For as long as it takes."

I'll stay too. My next show starts tomorrow in the city. Richard and I were going to be there for opening night. I should tell Marc—

"Don't," Richard says, as if he's read my mind. "This show is important for you."

"But your mom—"

He covers his eyes and breaks down. I don't think I've seen him cry before. He teared up when we got engaged. He's gotten misty at weddings, watching lifelong friends say "I do." But I've never seen him *cry* like this, with so much of his body involved. I hug Richard and squeeze—to comfort him as much as myself.

EIGHTEEN

I make dinner while the Belmonts crowd around the TV, watching local news on the cusp of eight p.m. Clarke sits in the middle of the sofa, leaning toward the flat-screen in the kitchen island. Richard next to him holds an unblinking stare, fiddling with the strings of his Columbia hoodie. Oliver, on the other side, is limp.

The police left two hours ago with our answers, didn't give us anything in return. There have been no leads: no activity on Vanessa's credit cards, no withdrawals from her bank account. According to Detective McInnis, the neighbors didn't notice anything suspicious over the past twenty-four hours: no unusual noises at night, no one they'd never seen before. None of the Belmonts' relatives or acquaintances have heard a peep from her. She didn't tell any of them a plan to leave.

It's as if she just . . .

Free-fell into oblivion.

I'm cooking spaghetti with red sauce. We'd planned to have Thanksgiving dinner at their country club, so I'm improvising with what's here. I took care to avoid more emotionally charged foods—none of the seasonal treats in the fridge, the special cheeses Vanessa had bought for tonight—and opted for a simple, satisfying pasta.

"Welcome to *Eyewitness News at Eight*. I'm Lydia Carlson—"

The montage preview of tonight's top stories is hard to endure. I can't see the TV from the stove, but I hear how theatrical it sounds. There's an aspect of entertainment to all TV news, but it feels grotesque right now. Vanessa's disappearance is too somber for these performative voices, the sensational language. Already, it's clear how much noise Vanessa's case has to compete with for any attention.

"—police ask the public for any information that may help them locate Vanessa Belmont, a Greenwich mother last seen by her family at home last night." Lydia's voice is punchy. "Sergeant Mark Jones said that a search of the area using police dogs found no sign of the sixty-five-year-old woman. Searches will continue with aerial support." I stride around the island to see a recent headshot of Vanessa on-screen. "When asked if foul play might be involved, Sergeant Jones said they haven't ruled anything out. Anyone with information should call the number below."

I walk back to the stove and spoon a noodle out of boiling water—perfect. I strain the pasta and mix in sauce. The rising steam smells sweet, not just *tomato* sweet, but deeper. Maybe it's caramelized onions or a wicked teaspoon of sugar. Meanwhile, Lydia has a back-and-forth with another anchor that includes the phrase "Thanksgiving nightmare." The transition to the next story is abrupt.

Clarke mutes the TV.

No one mentioned dinner, but if I didn't make it, they wouldn't have remembered to eat. Instead of asking them any questions, I decide it's best just to offer them a bowl. They can accept it or not. My stomach turns as I carry a red nest to Oliver. I present it between my palms. He shakes his head with a flicker of something nasty across his face—or did I imagine it? I'm being too sensitive. This isn't about me. I offer Richard the bowl, which he takes. Clarke shakes his head preemptively.

I hunch over mine alone at the island.

"That's the whole announcement?" Richard asks quietly.

No one answers.

My first bite is silky smooth. What's in this sauce, exactly? I couldn't read the fancy Italian label on the jar. There must be anchovies in here—or olives, something briny and complex. It balances the sweetness of the vegetables in a terribly pleasant way. I smell my next forkful to suss out the ingredients.

"They're already on the next story." Richard puts his pasta down on the coffee table in front of him. "That's *it*?"

"We need a publicist—" Clarke says with authority.

"Yes," Richard agrees.

"—to get her face out there."

I'm chewing when a silent call from Grace Ferrell illuminates my phone. The photo that appears is from decades ago. I haven't seen it in ages. It captures Mom outside our snowy house in Ohio, with toddler me on her hip. I've always loved this shot. Mom beaded everything dangling in her ears. Her smile shines through a white flurry. This picture makes her look like the most vivacious person alive—but it's not enough to stop a spreading fear.

She never calls.

I reject it. The screen turns black.

I resume chewing, more slowly this time.

Did she pocket-dial me? Was I her last contact, a couple of weeks ago, and she just fell asleep on her phone? I picture her cheek on the glass.

Clarke stands abruptly, phone to his ear.

He strides out of the room.

"McInnis, yes, we saw the news . . ." His voice fades.

I rinse my empty bowl, thinking through it all again. I don't know the first thing about unsolved disappearances. I never read any true crime. Richard won't watch anything angsty, so we never saw investigations like this on TV. The only reference point I have is one murder mystery that Hunter and I watched on HBO. In that show, the detective found his villain *inside* the mind of the victim; he didn't crack the case until he understood her better than anyone.

Does Detective McInnis understand Vanessa?

I really should tell him more about my relationship with her. No one else in this room will describe her like I can. Oliver will only tell the detective how doting she was. He'll say that she cooked him dinner every night, an endless queue of fine meats in sauce—an industrial amount of sauce, really. It was so generous how she always made more than anyone could reasonably eat. He'll say that Vanessa was affectionate. She was always preening her boys, grooming them with her hands. She was so tactile she almost never let them go.

But the detective should know how judgmental she was, how meddling. He already knows she invaded my personal privacy. I should tell him how she interfered with my relationship too—starting with the time she told Richard that he deserves a healthy partner. She easily could've provoked someone into such a terrorized state they actually sought revenge.

But—is it wise to tell the detective that? To describe the ways she attacked me right before she went missing? I don't think anyone would legitimately suspect I'm involved. Still, opening up to the detective doesn't feel right. I'd be condemning her on an official record at the worst possible time. What if the detective cross-checked my theories with Richard? Richard would be shaken that I'd talked about her like *that* at a moment like *this*. When Vanessa isn't around to defend herself, there's something violent about the idea of tampering with her memory.

NINETEEN

When I wake up the next morning, our bed is empty. Richard sits at his desk in boxers, hunched over his laptop. He looks like Rodin's *The Thinker*, thinking not just with his mind but with every muscle, down to his curled toes.

"Any news?" I ask.

"Not yet."

I rub the sleep out of my eyes.

After dinner, Clarke hired a publicist to get the word out. He put together an agenda for the call with her this morning. Whenever a new errand came up—find Vanessa's planner, make a list of everyone she spoke to this week, and track them down—it never went to me. I spent the night racking my brain on my own. I did have the idea to contact morgues or jails in the area, though I couldn't bring myself to say it out loud. I was too afraid of how they'd react to the thought that she was dead or guilty of something. So I felt useless except for the role I played in staying there, inhabiting the tragedy alongside them and acknowledging their pain.

Then I started to have trouble staying awake.

The Belmonts were still crowded around the dining room table at 1:00 a.m. when I finally asked Richard if I could get some sleep. He didn't say anything—just nodded. Everyone was too overwhelmed with work to pay much attention to my exit. Still, I felt like a traitor as I crept away by myself. Even Woolf stayed downstairs, perched on the windowsill, as if he were part of the search team.

Were the Belmonts up all night?

"I can't go to my show today."

"You have to." His voice is defeated.

"But—"

"Please," he says softly. "We need some good news."

It's hard to argue with someone so downhearted, someone who's clearly trying to do what's best for me. But I want to stay. I know what this feels like. I've spent my life sorting through the emotions of needing someone who isn't there. Isn't that helpful? Someone who's been where you are, who understands what you're feeling?

He clears his throat.

"Also . . . ," he starts slowly, lowering his gaze. "Dad wants to have a family meeting this morning—just the kids. He said that last night when you were asleep. He wants privacy . . . I told him that you and I are the same person, for all intents and purposes, but he's falling apart. He wouldn't listen. I'd fight him on this, but it's not the time. We don't have time." When he lifts his eyes, they're pink and innocent.

So, I should leave—now. The suggestion is clear. I toss the covers aside, hurt but helpless that Clarke would actually kick me out. Why is he treating me like an intruder? *Through* Richard once again? Engaged isn't married. I know that. We aren't legally united yet, but aren't we committed to be?

"I'm part of this family," I say.

"*I* know that."

He walks toward me and sits on the bed. Feeling starved of him, I sit on his lap and wrap my arms and legs around him.

"I love you," I say.

"I love you too."

He rests his forehead on my chest.

I don't want to let him go. A small part of me is afraid that if I do leave, I may never come all the way back. Last night, the Belmonts were tied more tightly together than I'd ever seen them. They were so connected on their mission I could almost see the strings between them. Richard drank out of Oliver's water glass several times, and his brother never corrected him to say it was his. They're coming together so fast I can't see them leaving space for anyone else.

"I'm just so confused," he says.

His voice cracks.

"You're going to find her," I say.

He nods ferociously. His head rubs my chest.

When I lean back, we look at each other for a split second before he pulls me in for a kiss. He keeps one hand around the back of my neck. I've missed his mouth so much. I've missed how he can be gentle and fully in control. My stomach twirls as he lifts me and then holds me over the bed. Gravity pulls me loose.

Richard kisses me one last time.

Then returns to his laptop.

I pack while he hammers away at the keyboard. Maybe I should insist on staying. But—this isn't about me. This is about him. This is a time to listen. I throw on khakis and a black cardigan before I zip up my suitcase. The metal teeth make a slithering noise as they come together, raising the hairs on my neck. I lug my bag to the first floor.

Clarke and Oliver sit in the dining room.

Their necks snap up as if I'm a harbinger.

Richard lumbers after me in sweatpants, pulling the Columbia hoodie from yesterday over his head. When we're alone in the foyer, I reach for his hands and push my fingers into the slots between his. For as long as I've known him, he's cheered me up whenever I needed it. I feel like I owe him the same duty. For once, *he* is the one who needs encouragement.

"Please let me stay."

My voice is quiet and breathy, like a balloon slowly losing air. I know that I'm imposing. I know that Clarke made himself clear, and I'm asking Richard to fight his dad *now* for *me*. But aren't Richard and I a unit? Aren't we saying vows to that effect next year, to face everything together for the rest of our lives?

Oliver appears on the edge of the foyer. His face has thinned in a single day, his chin sharp in the middle of a small jaw. He crosses his arms, staring me down. Why is he giving me that look? I glance at Richard. Is he seeing this?

"I am part of this family too," I say.

"Not yet," Oliver says.

I gawk at Richard.

"Not the time," Richard says quietly to me.

I hate that he's right.

Richard stays calm, acting like the bigger person. I try to stand tall too. When this is over, we can talk to his family about how wrongfully exclusive this is, but he's right. Now is not that time. I kiss him on the cheek and grab his hand, keeping it as I step toward the door, holding on until our arms are straight. He looks even sadder to see me go than I am to leave. When the door finally closes, I look back. The house is hushed and still.

TWENTY

Our doorman Carson is bright eyed when I return to our building. He must be filling in for Paul during the contentious Florida trip. Carson is midsixties, built solid, and enthusiastic about his jazz trio. Richard and I went to one of his shows downtown, where we stayed until the very end and gave the band a standing ovation.

"How was your Thanksgiving?" Carson asks.

I freeze momentarily.

Richard's mom is missing, I imagine saying. His natural follow-up question would be, *Then what are you doing here?*

I don't know what to say.

Richard and I never talked about this.

"Eventful," I manage. "What about you?"

"Same. We hosted twenty people. Don't ask me how." He flashes a tired but satisfied grin.

Elevator doors close like curtains.

I sink into Richard's and my living room sofa. This apartment doesn't feel like home without him. I moved in last year with almost nothing. Since then, I've hung a few paintings, but otherwise, most of the decor is the same: Persian rugs, backgammon boards on the walls, and exposed overhead beams. Now that I think about it, this place has familiar Tudor touches. We have some of the same rich fabrics and velvet throws that the Belmonts do.

I check emails for the first time in two days. At the top of my inbox is a message I've left unread on purpose, meaning to reply further along in the wedding planning. It's a list of questions from Lucas, Richard's college roommate and our officiant. He wrote that our answers will help him write his remarks. I was looking forward to responding. But right now, wedding planning is on hold. That has to wait until we find Vanessa—just like she would've wanted.

Did she . . . ?

I want to bury the idea. Stash it somewhere so black and deep that no one will know I touched it. The apartment is silent except for clacking radiators. I'm tempted to sit up and look around in case someone saw the thought darken my mind.

I glance left and right, but I'm alone.

Of course I'm alone.

And without any eyes on me, I keep the idea just a little bit longer. I give it a little more room. Did she fake a disappearance to drive Richard and me apart? I remember how bone weary Richard looked all night in his Columbia sweatshirt, with photos of her gleaming like it was her wake. His pain is palpable even here, thirty miles away. No, Vanessa would never hurt her own family. She'd never twist the knife like this, disappear by *design*. I keep coming up with reasons why she'd never do it, but the idea stays. It has a murky sheen, a taboo glimmer.

Could she actually do it?

If I so much as mentioned the theory to Richard, it might convince him that I'm mad. He might even leave me—which is exactly what she'd want. I stand up too fast and feel lightheaded. I lean against the nearest bookshelf, where my hand grazes faded monographs on Diego Rivera and Frida Kahlo, portals into their artistic worlds. Was Vanessa provoking me so I'd lash out and make myself a suspect? Did she plant evidence against me, waiting to be found?

Or am I being paranoid?

I think back to the last day I saw her, summoning every detail. The naked trees in their driveway. Richard's dwindling tank of gas. Birds migrating in dark V shapes. More took flight from the trees ahead of us, as if their branches were dissolving. The three Belmonts waiting on the ledge. She was holding that book—what was it called? *When the Stars Go Dark*. I google it in case there's more to the story because with Vanessa, there's always more.

My phone rings—Mom.

"Hello?" I ask cautiously.

"Happy Thanksgiving."

She sounds clear, but I'm confused. She's never called to wish me a happy holiday. It's always required too many things to go right: knowing the date, its significance, finding my contact, calling at a decent hour, and then speaking coherently. Is this why she was trying to reach me yesterday?

"Thanks, Mom. You too."

"How was the visit?"

I'm silent.

"With the monster?" she adds.

Maybe last week, I would've appreciated the sentiment. Right now, it feels wrong. I can't bash someone who's legally missing.

"Devon?" she asks.

Should I tell Mom what happened?

And my theory?

Then I wouldn't be in control of it anymore. My idea could get out. She might let it slip, trust the wrong person with it, or even get involved. If Richard found out I believe his mom is *that* manipulative, it could destroy us. It wouldn't matter if I'm right. People aren't logical. I can't verbally attack Vanessa when she hasn't been found, when there's a small chance that she's the victim of a freak tragedy.

But I can share the facts.

"Vanessa is missing," I admit.

I tell Mom everything, starting with the moment I saw a copy of my engagement ring on Vanessa's finger. I clarify that it's a rose cut—realizing Mom's never seen it—which is subtle. It's the ring that's most about love and least about itself. I go on to share every detail of the past two days. The whole time, Mom is a beautiful listener, reacting at appropriate times. It takes me back to when she was truly my mom, before I became hers.

"And now, Oliver actually thinks I'm involved," I admit. "He said, 'This is all your fault,' pointing right at me. Clarke kicked me out of their house this morning. He told Richard that he wants 'privacy.' So, here I am in New York City, physically separated from my fiancé in the worst moment of his life."

"What do you think happened?" Mom asks.

"Nobody knows."

"Except you," she says.

I don't know what she means by that.

Is she suggesting that I could figure it out?

Or can she tell I have a theory?

"Can you guess," I go on, unable to control myself after all, "the book she was reading the day before?"

"Tell me."

"*When the Stars Go Dark.*"

Nothing.

"It's about a detective who investigates missing persons," I explain with a "gotcha" tone. "Don't you think that's a little strange? *That's* the book she's reading when *she* goes missing?" I stare at the beams across our ceiling. They look like mammoth ribs, the building's cedar skeleton. "It's inspired by a real case. A twelve-year-old girl was kidnapped out of her own room in the nineties. It happened in the middle of a sleepover. Her parents were down the hall when a man climbed in through her window, picked her up, and left." I pace. "Isn't that strange? Vanessa's reading about something like that, and then it just happens to her?"

"I'm not really following you," Mom says.

I stop at our living room window, which faces another apartment building. It's a brick wall in all directions, punctuated by dark glass.

"I'm saying that—"

"How's Richard?"

I exhale.

"He cried for the first time since we met," I admit. "I don't know if he slept last night. I don't know if he's eating. All I want to do is be there for him. There's nothing worse than feeling what he is and being dead alone."

"Will you see him after the show?"

I imagine my paintings.

Rub my neck.

"I should get going," I lie. "There's a lot to do."

"You're going to be a star."

"Thanks, Mom."

"Call if you need me."

I puzzle at my phone when she's gone.

TWENTY-ONE

I walk shakily to Marc's gallery. My call with Mom is still rattling me but not for the usual reasons. This time, the strangest part was that she was rational. I didn't hear any troubling noises either: no lusting scoop through the ice drawer, no gibberish whispers to herself. It's not often she has prolonged bouts of clarity. She sounded even more grounded than I am.

Maybe she really will recover.

I get closer to the show.

The brick facade is interrupted by a concrete strip, carved with ZELLWEGER. I'm in all black with a touch of makeup: concealer, plum lips. The doorknob almost slips out of my hand. My sweaty palms make it feel like everything is melting. I find Marc in the showroom, his back to me. He's standing in front of my new paintings, both installed this week.

Why is he staring at them now?

I swerve around two massive sculptures by the world-famous Saint Lalanne—neon, angular showstoppers—which will be the focus of the evening. They've already sold, but they add luxury to the atmosphere and panache for Marc. The walls boast dozens more paintings. What's wrong with mine? I make my way over to him.

"Speak of the devil."

He's in his usual: a blazer, T-shirt, and navy slacks. Marc is unfailingly polished and energetic, which he credits to avoiding caffeine. He's always jet-setting from one of his galleries to another but never gives off a hint of jet lag.

We air-kiss.

My feet feel cold, as if I'm literally chilled by the thin ice under me. We both know I don't make him any money, and fine art isn't a charity. It's a highly competitive industry where hopefuls will sacrifice basic comforts for decades if given a minuscule shot at success. It's a dream business filled with gritty dreamers. Plenty of them are ready for my spot, so Marc *must* believe in me. But how long will that last if no one else does? We don't have any long-term contract binding us together. He could drop me at any second, even before tonight's show begins.

"How are you, dear?" he asks.

He cradles one elbow in his hand while the other holds his chin. Every one of his gestures looks well bred. His parents are famous dealers, too, based in San Francisco.

"I'm all right," I lie, bobbing my head.

The power he holds in my life is unfathomable, and every cell in my body knows it. If an exchange with him goes poorly, it will ruin me for days, overshadowing everything else that happens. On the other hand, just a word of validation from him is enough to keep me going for weeks. I've become addicted to his approval.

"The Lalannes are stunning," I say.

"They're not shy," he agrees, speaking in his unhurried way. "But *these* are deadly." He cocks his side part toward my paintings, hidden in my periphery. "When I first saw them, I didn't recognize you. I was intrigued, but they're nothing like you at all. They're all so—dark." His eyes blaze with interest.

"Thank you."

"Can I ask what inspired you?"

"The mystery of the artist's mind," I evade.

He grunts thoughtfully. "Your past couple felt a little bit—stilted, to be honest. In some ways, they were incredibly well done, but they were also a cipher. These"—he points to my latest—"are ripped from life. Are there any holes around the city I should know about? Anyone walking around without a face?"

I laugh deliberately.

"I have to admit, it did make me worry about you, to see these come into the gallery." He pauses long enough to make it a question. I don't answer. "Well done, Devon. I'd buy one myself, but it might kill me in the middle of the night."

He nods approvingly.

My heart's racing as he leaves. He waves to Manuel Sanchez, a rising star in Cuban art, here early in a black shirt and fedora. His paintings are vibrant portraits with cubist influences. Everything he creates has a distinct personal seal, something I have yet to find in my work. My most recent paintings are wild deviations from everything I've ever done, and maybe that's because I'm still a flailing amateur, even after all these years. Manuel was photographed in a *Vogue* spread that came out a couple of weeks ago, profiling the who's who in contemporary Cuban art.

The room fills with artists. I recognize everyone, whether or not we've met. I smile at a new RISD grad who jumps as if I've scared her. Painters tend to be solitary and inward, even at promotional events. Maybe we're busy comparing ourselves to each other, trying to understand where we rank in a field without titles or career paths. The women on either side of me already have work in the MoMA—and their pieces aren't even the best here. Marc's most successful artists won't show up at all. Lalanne is probably in his studio, his goggles on, chainsaw singing.

A line of people forms outside. Some peek through the glass door at the Lalannes. Of course they're here for those. We've all heard of him. I never expected fame to matter so much in the art world. On bad days, I compare it to show business, where viewers just come for the stars—stop it, Devon.

The doors should open soon.

Just a few more minutes.

The line gets longer. No one looks at my work, not even with a casual glance. Why can't I connect with an audience? People need to be outsiders to choose this path—in order to endure the time alone, rejections, and constant demand to *stand out*—but maybe I'm too much of an outsider to thrive within it. I wouldn't be where I am without blinding confidence, but maybe I have so many positive self-delusions that they're hiding a clear message from the market.

I said stop it, Devon.

You deserve to be here.

You are cool and collected.

I nod along to my own pep talk. Even if no one stops in front of my work tonight, they'll pay attention to it eventually. One day, I'll break through the noise. I'm prepared to give everything to my paintings because that's what the arts require. When your work is synonymous with your name—a Lalanne, a Devon Ferrell—it has your blood, sweat, and spirit in it.

One of Marc's assistants walks to the front door in high heels. I take a last look around the gallery. Manuel waits proudly by his gilded frames. He may be the next big thing, but those are a little nineteenth century for my taste. Mine hang without any frames at all, which is the more modern style. I like when my canvases are open and free to affect who they choose.

The first people inside head to the bar. Drinks in hand, they surround the Lalannes and snap photos, as if the statues might disappear. The showroom gets louder. Street noise comes in waves as the doors open and close, but no one walks over to me. I start to feel like a child by her lemonade stand, asking adults if they'd like something overpriced to drink—stop it, Devon.

Eventually, two young women speaking Korean come this way. They stop and give my work their full attention—the first people all night to face it. Fear twists their expressions as they leave. Maybe I should mingle with the other artists, chat with Marc. Last time, I was the only one who stood by their pieces all night. I just feel attached to what I make.

Someone familiar approaches from across the street.

It's—Detective McInnis. He strolls into the gallery with his hands behind his back. Oddly, he looks like the calmest one in the room. Everyone else is buzzing with the energy of the night or something stronger. Meanwhile, he takes measured steps, scanning every painting in a cool circle until he spots mine. His expression stays remarkably even as he takes them in. His feet aim for me. He walks a little faster now, cutting across a group photo by the Lalannes. He might even be in that photo. It's a curious move for someone whose job is to go unseen.

He waves from two feet away.

"Hi, Detective," I manage. "Any news?"

"I'm afraid not."

Then why is he here, neglecting the investigation?

He points at one of my paintings.

"You want to tell me what this is?" he asks.

"It's called *For an Inch of Sleep*."

He cocks his head.

"You don't want to look at it?" He points again.

"I'm superstitious."

"Meaning?"

"I don't look at my work once it's done."

Besides, I know this one cold.

"Huh." He chews on the idea. "So, you want to tell me about it?"

"Right . . ." I picture the piece behind me.

It's in gray scale, except for a bright bob over a skull. The severed head has strong, handsome features. It's beautiful the way that Jodie Foster is, or that Sigourney Weaver is. The only other thing in the frame is a crow the size of the skull, crouching on it and picking at scraps of flesh on the hairline. Its claws grip the eye sockets. Every hole looks infinite: the gap in the nose, the mouth, and one fatal crack in the temple. A piece of skin hangs from the bird's beak.

I clear my throat.

"My work starts with sketching."

The detective's eyes flit to the painting beside it, *If You Die in a Dream*. This one features a swarm of birds in a feeding frenzy. They coalesce into something dense, dark, and spiky with beaks and wingtips. The only clue as to what they're eating is at the bottom of the canvas, where a tuft of yellow hair survives. On closer inspection, a sliver of a mirror shines in the mess of hair, like a lustrous needle snapped in half. Its bloody tip makes the painting seem even more sinister.

I clear my throat again.

"Sketching builds good habits. It loosens the wrist to capture movement. It trains the eye to see the essential." I hear myself go on in a wooden voice, adding that I try to sketch every day. *Stilted*. Marc's critique returns. That's exactly how I sound right now.

"Do these look violent to you?"

Of course they do. I painted them while coping with my lack of control around Richard's family. But that doesn't mean I took her.

"No," I lie.

"How would you describe them?"

The only word that comes to mind is "playful." There's joy in the dancing light, the layered swirls of paint. The buttery patches that savor the deadliest parts. Subject aside, there's pleasure here, traces of dark euphoria.

"If you're at a loss for words, I have one."

"What's that?"

"'Vicious.'"

I repeat it quietly.

"Do these look vicious to you?" he asks.

When I don't reply, he leans forward—his nose just inches from the second piece—and pauses, rapt. My arm tenses, as if I'm about to reach out and stop him from touching the surface, from taking a sample as evidence.

"What kind of paint is that?" he asks.

"You know paint?"

"I'm a quick study. It looks . . . thick."

"It's oil. Lots of oil."

He looks skeptical.

"Is there something else you want to ask me?"

He shakes his head.

"Excuse me," I say, pardoning myself.

I head to the bar, where I pick up a sparkling water and squeeze a lime into the soda. Drops vanish into the fizz, adding an invisible spike of citrus. I take my time walking back. When I arrive, the detective pockets his phone after clearly having just taken photos.

He waves but does not smile goodbye.

~

I leave the gallery around eleven. Not a soul other than Detective McInnis stood for long in front of my paintings. He was the only one who got dangerously close, who listened hard to what they were saying.

I speed walk to the bus stop.

A subway groans under me.

Why would the detective do that now? He must've told the Belmonts where he was going. Why didn't Richard stop him? The detective said the first forty-eight hours are the most important. But—it's a two-hour round trip from Greenwich to New York City. That's a big chunk of the first two days, not to mention the time he spent with my work, getting so close he might've smelled it. I'm not even sure if Vanessa was legitimately kidnapped, but there's a chance that she was and they're wasting valuable time on *me*. As if the key to finding her is in my work.

I call Richard from the bench.

I never thought I'd miss Greenwich this much. I imagine Richard at the dining room table in his Columbia hoodie, the skin under his eyes paper thin. Are photos of Vanessa still on the table? Is there anything more heartbreaking than staring at pictures of her when she's gone? I have to get back into that room, next to my person. He needs me as much as I need him. Even if he let the detective visit my show, of course I'd forgive him. Am I going to voicemail?

"Hello?" His voice is raspy.

"Babe."

"How'd it go?" he asks.

"Detective McInnis showed up."

His side of the line is silent.

"Did you know he was going to come?"

Nothing.

"Richard?"

"Hey, have you seen Carson today?"

I'm blindsided.

"Carson, our doorman? Yes, why?"

"He texted me," Richard says slowly. "He has a jazz show this weekend and wanted to invite us." So? "I called Carson as soon as he texted and told him that Mom's been missing for two days, that we're all desperately trying to find her. He apologized. He said he saw you earlier today and had no idea. He said he even asked you how you're doing, and you said 'Fine' or something. You didn't mention that my mom is missing? When he asked you how you are?"

"I didn't say 'Fine.'"

"That's not the point." He says "point" with a hard *t*. "Sorry, I just don't understand how, when someone we know asks how you're doing, you don't share that your mother-in-law is a missing person. You have a whole exchange with him that's so normal he invites us to a jazz show."

"You asked me to be here, Richard."

"Yes, I did."

Silence.

"But I didn't ask you to cover it up. I find that to be really . . ."

"Really what?"

Silence.

"Don't do this, Richard," I beg. "Don't read into what I said." I can feel how powerless I am from this bus stop, miles away from him in the dead of night. "You know me better than that. Please, let's talk about this."

"Sorry, now's not a good time."

"Why not?"

"I'm with my family."

With your family?

I *am* your family.

"Babe," I almost cry.

"I'll talk to you later."

Is that it?

"Take care of yourself," he adds more softly.

Then, the voice I craved is gone.

TWENTY-TWO

I'm awake in bed that night, convinced Vanessa is behind this. No one kidnaps a sixty-five-year-old woman out of her own home. No one could've done it without waking up Clarke—or me. I was walking on *her* floor. I stood outside *her* door. The idea that she's been kidnapped is so absurd—so clearly manufactured—I'm surprised no one has said it out loud.

Of course I look suspicious, especially after tonight. It's all going according to her plan. Detective McInnis actually visited my show and questioned me like a person of interest. *What kind of paint is that?* As if I smeared parts of her on the canvas? What kind of demon does he think I am? The only way out of this mess is to find her myself.

Who haven't we talked to?

Clarke ordered Oliver to text everyone in the family. Did he get through to Vanessa's parents? I hold the thought, intrigued. Why exactly was she so distant from them? I've only ever heard one side: they don't value arts and culture. But does that even make sense? As an *art*ist, I have a strong opinion on the *arts*, and I believe the heart and soul of them is empathy. Loving the arts requires compassion for all of us fragile human beings. So, how could Vanessa enjoy pieces about complicated, vulnerable people, and then be so cold as to outgrow her own parents? Maybe that's not the real reason. Maybe her parents know something—if not about where she is, then about her. Something about Vanessa that's been overlooked.

They live in Bristol, Connecticut. I know that much from the return address on a card they sent us in July. *Congrats, Richard and Devon!!! We couldn't be happier! We hope all your dreams come true. Love, Grammy and Pops.*

I write them an email in the dark.

I ask if I can visit.

~

I wake up on Richard's side of the bed. Books slant on his nightstand: *Deacon King Kong, A Man in Full,* and *The Lincoln Highway*. He bought these in hardcover to support the authors. We were in our local bookstore last year when he said I'd shown him how much artists sacrifice, and he'd never buy a paperback again. I kissed him quickly in Nonfiction, before he led me to Mystery for a longer one. Richard has a wide circle, but I feel like the only one to see his tender, intellectual side. He's the life of the party to most people, but he's everything to me.

On my phone, there's a new email from Grammy.

Subject: Visit?

Hi to our Devon!

You are welcome anytime!!! We are at home this weekend and always love to see our grandchildren.

Hugs and kisses!!

Grammy and Pops

I respond instantly, telling her that I'll drop by this morning. While I change, I keep checking my messages. There are no new texts waiting for me.

I text Richard anyway.

Thinking about you.

With you always.

I zip up black pants, then throw on a dark long-sleeve shirt. There's not a single color in my outfit, not even a silver thread of lint. I look only briefly in the bathroom mirror. Last night's braid is neat enough.

In the lobby, Paul is back with a slight tan. He waves without asking any questions, just opens the door with a smile. As I step over the threshold, I debate telling him that Vanessa is missing. Is blurting it out even worse than not mentioning it? What would Richard want me to do?

I'm on the street before I decide.

I make my way to Grand Central Station, where I buy a pure white bouquet for Grammy and Pops and hop on a train. The car is half-full. A couple of people glance in my direction and stare too long. What are they looking at? Eventually, I notice the man behind me. He has a birdcage on his lap. His coat spreads over the top, shaped more by its edges than his body. It looks like the cage is part of him, the steel bars his thin and curling ribs.

I feel our train leaving the station.

The image stays with me even as I turn back around. If Richard were here, he'd make a joke about it. *You know you're in New York City when that's not even the weirdest part of your day.* We'd hold hands, laugh about it. And when we got home, I'd paint it. Moments like that always enlist me: when something is so *out there* it practically sticks out of the world at a fourth dimension. Points right at me and demands to be recorded in full color, in full detail. Moments like that need a picture light and an audience. They need space on the wall.

My phone buzzes with a text from Marc.

Good news, lots of interest in your work last night. Talking to potential buyers. I'll keep you updated. XM

My heart leaps.

I text back, Thank you!

For someone in my position, it's a victory for anyone to be seriously interested. If Richard knew, he'd be punching air. He'd want to celebrate as if it were a six-figure sale. He always did believe in me—and still does. Doesn't he? I pull open our idle conversation and will it to move.

~

It's a short Uber ride to Grammy and Pops's place. There are no police cars or news crews here by their one-story house. They're so distant from their daughter they're irrelevant when she's missing. I pay the driver in cash and approach the front door. I pass an oversize puddle in their backyard, where it looks like rainwater has filled a dip in their lawn. Two empty planters guard the entrance. I knock, bracing myself. How distraught are they about the disappearance? Grammy avoided the topic in her email. Are they mourning? Hopeful?

I look left and right, not sure for what. Maybe for a clue as to what's really in Vanessa's mind—I forgot the flowers. I picture the white bouquet on an empty seat, riding the train alone. I had *one* thing to bring with me.

You need to calm down.

You really need to calm down.

The door opens to reveal Grammy in a salmon-colored T-shirt, sweats, and a smile. Richard showed me a few photos of her, but in person, she's even warmer than I expected. She's bosomy with soft arms. Her face is freckled with age spots, brightened with coral blush and lipstick. The cheerful palette is distinct on her pale skin. This is Vanessa's mom? The only resemblance is in their blue eyes. Grammy's have faded, but the color is there, linking them across generations.

"My, my," she says. "You came all this way?"

"Grammy! Of course."

"Welcome home."

She waves me into a hug that smells like over-perfume. I didn't even know how tense I was, but my shoulders are melting. My own grandparents passed away decades ago. Maybe I'm keener to meet Richard's than I realized.

As we pull apart, Grammy invites me inside. There's an excited jitter in the way she moves, doubling everything: two motions to step forward, two pats on my back, two loving pumps on my arm. I know why *I'm* happy to be here, but I'm surprised to see her so upbeat, so unbroken by the mystery around her daughter.

I take my shoes off.

"Is Pops here?"

"He's asleep," she says.

I check my watch. It's only nine.

"Right, sorry for barging in."

"My dear, you're family."

She waves me into her living room, which is filled with family photos and grade school–level art. They cover the walls as thoroughly as a coat of paint. Maybe this is where Vanessa gets the magpie instinct that I observed in her office: the desire to keep, to collect, to fill space. I like knowing that no matter how different she fancies herself to be from her parents, they have an undeniable connection.

I step up to a photo in the mosaic: it's Richard and me outside Colby. We sent them this one over the summer. In it, our hands interlace in the foreground, where our ring catches all the light. I can't believe Richard and I haven't visited here before. I know it's been complicated for him to stay close with his grandparents when Vanessa doesn't do the same. But it's achy to think about this room going empty.

Grammy volunteers an impromptu batch of hot cocoa. Her tone is inspired, with a wholesome zing. I take a seat as she leaves the room. She returns with a tray of two mugs and offers me one. She raises hers in a cheerful toast "to the wedding."

"Is Richard coming?" she asks.

It's an odd question.

Doesn't she know his mom is missing?

"Not today," I say.

"How are you two lovebirds?"

Another odd question.

"I had an art show last night in New York." The sentence feels stranger the longer that it goes. Still, Grammy seems eager to hear more. She's leaning forward, lifting deep wrinkles in her brow. "I had two paintings on display. I think there was some interest." I remember the bloody mirror in the patch of blond hair and feel too uncomfortable to elaborate. "But I didn't come here to talk about my show. I just wanted to make sure you're holding up all right."

"Oh, thank you, sweetheart," she says. "Yes, this whole business is just like Vanessa, isn't it?" Her tone stays pleasant, as if disappearing is one of her daughter's special talents. I lower my mug. "Is the cocoa all right?"

"Yes. Sorry, what's just like her?"

"Running away again."

I control my surprise.

"She's done this before?" I ask.

"Well, I don't know where she went this time."

"When did this happen?" I ask.

Grammy looks pensive.

"In college," she says eventually. "Her first year, she disappeared for a week. But you don't want to hear about that, do you?"

"Actually, I do."

"It was so long ago."

I wait.

"Well, I suppose it's no secret." Her smile wobbles. "The truth is that Vanessa was always—special." Her mood recovers with the slight change in subject. "For her tenth birthday, she asked for tickets to Carnegie Hall. They were going to play Mahler. He was her favorite." She shrugs as if there never was a girl quite like hers. "Even as a kid, nothing mindless ever made her happy. No reruns, she wanted Rachmaninoff. The Impressionists. The New York City Ballet. They were such specific requests, they're hard to forget, even now." Grammy beams softly until something sad creeps into the end of her sentence. It's just a glimmer, then disappears. "She never did make much art, but she wanted to be around it. She wanted to observe."

I remember her blue gaze.

"I think she got frustrated with us," Grammy admits, her smile threatened again. "It's not that she wanted us to be rich. She wanted us to be—complicated." She strokes a small chip in her mug. "As she got older, she spent more and more time at her friends' houses. People who had antiques and master's degrees. Who ate ceviche and took her to Broadway." She makes each item in her list sound mystical.

I have to prompt her.

"But she ran away before?"

Grammy nods. "It wasn't out of nowhere. When she went to college, things got even worse between us. Columbia was full of families she—wanted. It wasn't just the *students* who were stars. It was their parents. From what she told us, they went to Amsterdam just to look at a painting. They could name the piece playing in the background at Starbucks. Vanessa wasn't jealous of their money. She never wanted money. She wanted parents who understood her. Parents who shared her interests. She told us as much on a phone call. She'd only been there a week."

Grammy rests her mug on one knee.

The cocoa slants toward the floor.

"I think that's when she stopped hoping we'd be people we weren't. The more time she spent at school, the less we heard from her. Then winter break started, and she didn't come home like she was supposed to."

"Did you call the police?"

She shakes her head.

"She was a grown-up. And . . ."

"And?"

"We knew she ran away." As Grammy's voice softens, I feel a pang of guilt for prying. "She'd mentioned that she might do it a couple of times. Not directly, but in so many words. You'll see that with your kids—you just know."

"I'm sorry," I admit.

Grammy nods.

I ask what happened next.

"She came home the day before spring semester to pick up her things. She wouldn't tell us where she'd been. The only thing she said was, 'See?' She kept asking, 'See?' I think she was trying to make a point. I think she was trying to show us what it was like to want someone who wasn't there."

It's hard to hear Grammy describe the calculated rejection. It's emotionally violent, strange, and—validating. Because this is the Vanessa I know. Of course she's pretending to disappear. She's done it before to *tweak* people, to make them feel what she wanted. I imagine her hiding now in a well-stocked room as her sons slip into a panic. Grammy seems uncomfortable in the growing silence. She offers me more cocoa, even though I've only taken a few sips.

"I'm all right. Grammy . . ." I try to word this as gently as possible. "Do you think there's anything unusual about Vanessa?"

"Of course."

I lean forward.

"She's just so smart." Grammy's compliment is quick and earnest, tinged with mild awe. "I just wish we could've been what she needed. But when kids are gifted like her, maybe they need gifted parents too."

"It's impossible to be born into the wrong family," I say, repeating the words I used to tell myself back home. I did try hard to believe them.

Grammy looks unconvinced.

174

"For a long time, I didn't understand why she had to be so—hostile about it. We weren't her perfect parents. She was going her own way. But I didn't understand why she had to shut us out. She disappeared once in college, but she's been disappearing all over again ever since. We haven't spent a holiday together in decades. The question followed me around—why did she *ban* us from her life?—until I finally figured it out." She glances down at her slippers.

"Yes?"

"I realized that we must've made her suffer. We gave her a life that didn't fit. We brought her into this world, wanting something she could never have—some*one* she could never have." She doesn't have to say it for me to understand: a different mom. "Maybe you're an orphan when you have parents, but they're not the ones you need." She winces. "Her life might *look* perfect, but something about us must hurt even now, because she still locks us out." Grammy takes a long sip of her drink. She seems eager for the excuse not to talk anymore, embracing the opportunity to put something in her mouth. After she lowers her mug, she looks at me gently.

"Yes?" I prod her on.

"How's wedding planning?" she asks.

"Sorry, you were saying? It might '*look* perfect'?"

If I didn't *need* to keep talking about Vanessa, I'd leave it alone. I wouldn't force Grammy to harp on what's clearly a sensitive subject. It's practically torture—and what would that make me? But my future depends on this. I can't go back to the life I had before I met Richard. It was too pitch black, too spiral.

"I just meant that she lives in the world she always wanted." Grammy's tone is downbeat. "The Belmonts changed everything for her. She didn't just fall for Clarke; she fell for his whole family. They dressed up in fur and went to the opera. To lectures, sculpture parks. It looked like Vanessa had finally found the family of her dreams." Grammy spills some cocoa on her shirt. I rush her a napkin, feeling responsible, and find that I just can't dig any deeper.

She asks me a few questions about the wedding. I don't have the heart to admit that we're not thinking about it at all these days. So I tell her it's coming along nicely, then change the subject. I point to a happier time on her wall, where she and Pops cut the cake on their own big day.

"What flavor?"

"Angel food cake." She grins.

I walk up to a photo of teenage Vanessa. She stands next to Grammy in this room, almost exactly where I am now. Grammy has one arm around her daughter, while Vanessa glares at the camera. Her intensity feels—familiar. I'm uncomfortable with how much I understand the skinny girl looking back at me. I know what it takes to leave home, to build a whole new identity. I know what it's like to avoid questions about the past. But I still call my mom. Part of me is always connected to her, and I hope we only get closer with time.

I keep looking around.

The photos are interspersed with student art, landscapes made with primary colors, signed with fingerprints. In the corner, there's an old photo of Richard, Oliver, and—that girl. It's the same brunette from the photo in Richard's dresser. The one with long hair in smoky angles. In this shot, all three of them stand outside the Louvre. She's leggy in black jeans, coyly twisting an ankle in combat boots. Richard has his arm around her, his kiss frozen on her temple.

"Sorry, who is this?" I ask.

"Who?" Grammy squints. "Oh, you mean Amber?"

"Amber?"

Grammy looks confused.

"Richard didn't mention her?"

"No," I say.

He told me I was the first woman he brought home. Amber went on vacation with his family? How did Vanessa let that happen? I look for any ring, but Amber's left hand is bare.

"Sorry, I just . . ."

I lose my train of thought.

"What happened to her?" I point at Amber.

"Richard would know better. We've done our best to keep up with her since she left. She wasn't like Vanessa, running off without telling anyone. Amber said her goodbyes. Then she left." Grammy sighs. "It took everyone a while to heal from that—especially Richard. Then, of course, he met you."

Did she learn something?

That scared her off?

"Would you like anything to eat?" Grammy asks.

She offers me her specialty: chocolate chip pancakes, the chips extra melted. I tell her I really should get going. The idea lets her down so visibly I promise to come back soon. We chat about the rest of her day as I call an Uber. Pops should be up shortly, and if he has the energy, they'll go for a walk. As we hug goodbye, I face a cuckoo clock on her wall and watch the pendulum swing. The rod looks warped, holding a subtle curve. She waves to me as I slide into the back seat of a black Toyota. She's still waving as she fades in the rearview mirror.

I call Richard. No answer.

When I call again, he sends me to voicemail on the first ring. *Hi, this is Richard. When you hear the beep, please text me instead.* What's he doing now? It's just after ten on a Saturday. I imagine coffees cooling on the dining room table, the dark ponds between silver laptops. I probably shouldn't call three times in a row. He's busy. Of course he's busy, looking for Vanessa. But this is about her too.

"Hello?" he murmurs.

"It's so great to hear your voice."

I mean it.

"I can't really talk," he says.

His tone is low and textured. It's the same one that used to wish me good night, whisper jokes during movies. It's not supposed to push me away.

"Vanessa ran off," I say.

"What?" he snaps.

"In college. Did you know that?"

There's a pause.

"No." The word is cold. "What are you talking about?"

"I just visited Grammy. She said Vanessa did this in college—"

"Where are you?" he asks.

"Bristol."

He goes quiet.

"I wanted to see if they knew anything—"

"Mom barely talks to them."

"But—" I'm frustrated.

"Do you want to tell me about your show last night?" he asks.

My stomach sinks.

Did the detective share his photos?

Even if he didn't, there were a few other photographers in the room. Their camera flashes were stupefying, white-out blips. It wouldn't have taken Richard more than a second to google the gallery and see my new paintings in thousands of glowing pixels. Of course he's seen them by now—and he must know who they're about. He's always been able to identify the emotions behind my work, sometimes down to the second that inspired them.

"How do you think that makes me feel? She's missing, and you're standing next to *those*?" he demands. "In some of the photos, you're smiling."

"I'm sorry."

"And now, you're saying that *she* is behind this? You're going on secret trips to prove that she's *trying* to put us through hell?" As his voice rises, I wonder if anyone else at his house can hear him. It's hopeless. The more I accuse her of being the bad guy, the more I become one in their eyes. "You know, Detective McInnis stopped by this morning. He wanted to know more about you. All about you, actually."

"What did you say?" I ask.

"I told him the truth."

"Which is?"

Silence.

"The truth is I think we need some time apart."

"What?"

"I need to find her—not prove that she needs help."

I'm so incensed I hang up.

As soon as the call ends, though, I regret it. Now I'm never going to get him back on the line. I didn't even get to ask about Amber.

TWENTY-THREE

Back in our apartment, I sit on the living room floor, trying to learn more about Amber. With the curtains shut and lights off, I sink into shadows. They shrink my world down to something I can manage, down to the phone in my hand.

I open Instagram.

My account is small and neglected. I've never gotten into social media, mostly out of artistic pride. I care too much about what I make to post a bad photo, or worse, to waste time on one that disappears in twenty-four hours. When you have no line between *work* and *life*, everything is part of the masterpiece. Still, I have an account and follow Richard's family, including Grammy. Her profile is almost empty: no posts, no profile picture, and no bio other than her name, Donna Becker. I scan through the list of who she's following and find one Amber: Amber Hewitt.

I sit up straight.

Amber's profile is private. Her thumbnail photo doesn't show her face. It's a wide-angle shot of a dark figure overwhelmed by a sunset. The person's body is the size of a comma, surrounded by shades of red. Is this *the* Amber?

I google her name.

Scroll.

Click dozens of links that have nothing to do with—*her*. Amber Hewitt, music photographer. I'm on her professional site. On the infinite internet, I've found *her*. She looks defiant in her black-and-white head-shot: sharp nose, sharp chin, and eyebrows that don't curve at all, just grow straight across the bone. Her expression is strong and perceptive. Her only bio is a mission statement quoting Ansel Adams: "There are no rules for good photographs; there are only good photographs."

I can't help but compare us, and when I do, all I see are similarities. We're both in the arts. She must be a loner at heart to end up working by herself. We both have dark, moody hair. A sleek chunk of it frames her face, while the rest disappears behind her. On a good day, that's how mine would look. We both have the fierce desire to make something original. Does Richard have a type? Or was he looking for another chance with her, in me? I wonder if she taught Richard about different kinds of cameras. If, when they went on dates, he asked her what she saw.

I open her Portfolio tab.

It looks like she spends a lot of time with the rock band Emotica, having shot their past three concerts. Her photos focus on the die-hard crowd, capturing their hair midflip, their mouths midscream. I wonder if she and Richard went to any concerts together, if they ever danced while she was at work. I remember how much time he and I used to spend looking at art, back when we started dating.

If I showed up at the next concert, would I find her weaving through the mob? The more crowded a place is, counterintuitively, the easier it can be to find a moment alone. I click on Amber's Events page. At the top of the list, she's slated to speak at a rock photography workshop in Midtown. Should I go?

I look back at her headshot.

What happened?

Did she learn something about Vanessa, something so unforgivable that it drove her away? Did Vanessa *do* anything to her? Does Amber have proof? I find the address for her workshop in Times Square. The event is on Monday, just two days from now. I imagine showing up, sitting in the back, and then getting in line to ask her a question.

Do you have a moment to talk about Vanessa?

~

I'm sketching in my studio the next morning when my cell phone rings. It's steps away from me on the floor, plugged into the wall and charging. I lay my pencil down and walk over to the bright screen: BLDG FRONT DESK. I answer with a cautious hello.

"Morning." It's Paul. "Detective McInnis is here to see you."

"He is?"

"Should I send him up?"

Pause.

"Devon?"

I give the only answer I can—yes—and navigate out of the room. In the entryway, I give myself a once-over. I'm in painting clothes, which look like a popped parachute around me. At least I'm wearing socks. They might be the most polished part of my outfit: formfitting, their stains hidden on the soles.

Two crisp knocks.

I open the door to find the detective standing closer than I expected. Was he listening in? I picture his ear to the wood, absorbing every faint vibration. If he was eavesdropping, he doesn't look morally conflicted about it. His expression is aggressively clean and mildly impatient: shaved chin, spirited eyes. His short hair is combed back, emphasizing the cape of his widow's peak. He asks if he can come in. Again, I give the only answer I can.

He crosses the threshold with a tight smile. Dimples prick his cheeks like shallow scratches. *Detective McInnis stopped by this morning. He wanted to know more about you.* As we walk, his khakis chafe, and his chin sweeps from side to side. His gaze lingers on the silver mount where Richard's mirror used to hang. What else is he noticing? Is the air stale? I feel even more unkempt now in his sharp line of observation. I tuck flyaways behind my ears.

He pulls out a familiar notepad.

"I never asked," I say. "Do you live in New York or Greenwich?"

"I go between." His tone is flat.

"What brings you to New York?"

"Just having a look around."

In the living room, the curtains are shut. I yank them open, lifting two chairs and a coffee table out of the dark. I scan the area quickly, checking for anything too private left in the open. I wasn't expecting visitors. Then again, I never am.

"Beautiful home," he says.

"Thank you, it was Richard's place first. I think Vanessa did the decorating." The detective nods but doesn't write that down. "I moved in about a year ago and almost didn't a change a thing." Still, no notes. Does he understand my point, though, that I've been living peacefully with her decor for the past twelve months? If I hated Vanessa so much that I took her, why would I let my home *feel* like her?

I lead Detective McInnis into the kitchen, where an overripe banana peel lies on the counter. I must've forgotten it there after breakfast. I grab the stem and throw it away while he opens and closes three drawers in a row.

"It's just a kitchen," I say quietly.

"Richard told me that his parents sent you both to therapy for some of your anger management issues." He looks up. "Is that true?"

"It's true they sent us to therapy."

"How did that go?"

"I graduated."

He doesn't smile.

"You know, not everyone can make jokes in hard times," he says, eyeing the Wüsthof knife block. Ten black handles point at us.

"I wouldn't read into it."

"Why's that?"

"My jokes don't make light of this, Detective. They express how I feel without spelling it out. You know how to do that too. It's like walking into this apartment today and asking about my anger while looking at my knives." He stares at me, momentarily frozen. "Now, would you like to see the bedroom?"

I extend an arm in that direction.

It takes him a second to regain his composure.

He keeps an eye on me as he crosses into the next room. I open the door to our walk-in closet, where Richard's clothes hang on the left, mine on the right. His side is more organized: pressed oxfords in a neat row, pants in plastic dry cleaning bags. Meanwhile, my half is stuffed, borderline explosive. Nothing there looks particularly clean: khakis rehung in a dozen different ways, clipped into positions that only deepen the wrinkles. All my clothes are mixed together, bottoms bleeding into tops and even some outerwear—one parka wedged into the middle.

I don't want to launch preemptively into self-defense. But if I did, I'd tell the detective that my things are normally in better straits. Besides, a few months ago, Richard started a decluttering initiative. Every day, he removed one thing from his wardrobe. The only problem was that I generally wanted whatever he was discarding. His old pants and shirts are perfect for painting. So I moved the hangers he'd decluttered onto my half until the rods were full.

The detective steps inside.

He keeps his back to me as he faces off against my clothes. He's staring as if the stains might be important, as if the rips might have a malevolent secret. Eventually, he pivots to me. "I know you weren't in therapy for long. Richard said you only went to a few sessions, and even then, you left early." He pauses, leaving me a hole to fill. I let it deepen. "Still, he said you resented his parents for sending you. You were so enraged you destroyed parts of this apartment. You even laid a hand on him, on your own fiancé. All you wanted to do was 'confront' them."

"Is that a question?"

"Yes. Is all that true?"

His eyes are steady.

"It's true, but it's not . . ."

"Not what?"

"Relevant."

He takes another look in the closet, stopping to focus on the suitcase in the back. It's the one that I brought to Thanksgiving, open on the floor and barely unpacked. My hose still lie on top, like a black mist over the outfits.

"Do you mind if I take a look?" he asks.

"I'd love it."

He slides the notepad into his pocket and removes rubber gloves. As soon as they're on, he kneels over the suitcase and shines his phone light inside. I don't like watching him probe my things. He's starting to remind me of Gretchen: someone who knows everything about us, while we know nothing about her.

"Mind if I ask *you* something?"

"Go ahead," he says.

"What's your first name?"

"Liam."

"Where'd you grow up?"

"Larchmont." His tone is civil. "My parents were police officers. I guess you could say that I wanted to follow in their footsteps. They're still in Larchmont, retired now." A beat. "What about you? What are your parents up to?" He looks at me as if he already knows the answer. Did he find out from Richard or from his own research?

He returns to the suitcase and feels the inner lining with careful fingers, as if he's wary of what he may find. It's a painfully slow process. Eventually, he stands and cranes over the hamper. "I didn't expect you to answer that. Richard said you wouldn't talk much about your family, that it would be a waste of time to ask."

"I know what Richard thinks."

"Do you?"

After he inspects the closet, I reluctantly show him our bedroom. He looks under the bed, mattress, and through my drawers before following me into the bathroom. As he opens our medicine cabinets, I stare at the painting between the twin sinks. It's an abstract piece I made after Richard and I spent a weekend in Nantucket. Blue and gray waves combine into something like a blurred galaxy. Richard added a brushstroke across the middle.

"How're the scratches doing?" he asks.

I cross my arms.

"So, have you ever found anyone?" I ask. He doesn't turn around. "I mean, in previous cases. I'm just curious. Ever actually found someone?"

"I'm afraid I can't answer that."

"Why not?"

"Confidentiality."

He faces me and then walks away without saying where he's going. It feels like he's taken charge of the tour. He passes the kitchen and then stops in front of the door to my studio. He reaches for the handle.

"What are you doing?" I ask.

"May I?"

I'm unable to answer right away.

Even Richard's never been in there, not really. The closest he's come has been here on the threshold, glimpsing ahead through a hairline crack. It feels wrong to let a stranger see something I keep from my own fiancé. Then again, I wouldn't be showing the detective what I *do* in here. He wouldn't pull up a chair and watch me paint. My process is still my own. This is just the—hardware.

"After me, please."

I open the door halfway. There are too many supplies in here to push it any farther. I watch Detective McInnis closely as he crosses the threshold. He flips on lights and surveys the room with neutral eyes. Seconds pass. He's still inscrutable. Maybe he thinks I'm a hoarding slob. Maybe he thinks I'm strangely amphibious, to find my cave damp and clammy, filled with puddles of paint. The wall tarps are blotched with more wet explosions. He shifts his feet, shoes squelching. He keeps looking around, studying the slick tendrils on the wall. The maroon beads like condensation. The colors spiraling by his toes. Only a dripping stain breaks the silence.

"You mind if I take a photo?" he asks.

"I do."

He takes another step inside.

I remember my session with Mrs. Campbell. She warned my *friend* not to deny her situation for long. It was strange advice, though. As if denial is in anyone's control. It's the opposite of imagination, isn't it? I don't *choose* what I imagine. I've never sat in here and *picked* a strange new thing to see. The flip side must be we can't choose to ignore something either. If it were possible, of course I'd do it. I'd pretend that McInnis isn't standing in front of me, staring at my unfinished work. That he isn't invading the one haven I have, the last place that lets me be myself.

"I was talking to Richard about your painting," he segues calmly. "He said sales had been a little . . . disappointing, that you hadn't found your audience yet. He also said you're a first-rate workaholic, that there isn't another painter in your generation who could've spent more sheer hours at it than you. You've made an enormous bet on yourself and put in the time. It must be difficult to be so talented, and to work so hard, and then for it not to go the way you'd like."

It's not a question.

I don't treat it like one.

"It must be extremely difficult is what I'm saying," he goes on, as if I didn't understand him. "Most people need some kind of validation, or some kind of reward, to keep them sane. Not many can stay committed to a dream for so long when it stays exactly that: a dream." I am dead silent. "I can only imagine how hard it must be to keep waking up early and going to bed late, to keep pushing yourself to your personal limit, to keep pouring your soul into something that . . . leaks."

A bad feeling starts to simmer.

"Richard says he pays the bills—" he goes on.

"My art isn't a hobby."

"I know," he says. "I'm just saying that it can't be good for the mind to be in a position that's a little desperate. I admire the risks you've taken, and in some respects, you're living the fairy tale. But it can't be easy to feel like you're working—and working and working—and not getting heard. It's an unusual amount of pressure. It could lead anyone to do things they wouldn't otherwise."

Is he trying to intimidate me?

Does he want to make me feel weak and cornered, to elicit some kind of confession? Of course it's been a tough road. But the reason I chose this route and the reason I've survived it is because I'm strong.

"Richard mentioned that you stay sober for work." By now, Detective McInnis is standing in the middle of my studio. His right shoe is tinted pink. A black stain behind him drips. "You sacrifice so much for your art, it affects how you treat your body. You devote your life to this, and the world barely bats an eye. Meanwhile, Clarke and Vanessa haven't worked in decades. They drink every night, stock a wine cellar, and bring their own bordeaux on luxurious safaris. Their glass is always full, so to speak. That can't have been easy for you to witness, especially if you thought Vanessa had a vendetta against you. It must have seemed unfair."

"Life's unfair."

"Richard also mentioned that your mom has some problems with alcohol, and that she has pronounced, prolonged mood swings." I tense up even more. "Apparently, sometimes, she talks to people who aren't real. She is paranoid and delusional. Richard also said that your mom has some issues with anger—"

"I've called my mom recently," I say proudly.

"You called her recently."

"It went great."

"So, you two understand each other now?"

"Look, Liam, I didn't have anything to do with this."

"I never said that."

"You're not saying anything. You're just hiding behind other people's words. And you're hiding the truth of how you know so much about me."

"Are you accusing me of doing my job?"

"Not *this* job . . ."

But what if they're connected?

Maybe Vanessa hired Detective McInnis knowing that, one day, he'd investigate her disappearance. Maybe she poisoned him against me before the search even began. If that's true, he won't believe a word I say. And what could I do about it? Tell the Belmonts that McInnis is part of a conspiracy against me? That he was following me *before* Vanessa went missing? My sanity is already in question. The only choice I have is to stick to my plan: I have to find her myself.

"Devon, did you know the Belmonts outfitted their house with Nest cameras?" He interrupts my thoughts. "The one that captures the hallway outside Vanessa and Clarke's room was removed, somehow. But there is other footage of you walking around that house in the middle of the night. The next morning, Vanessa was missing. Do you want to tell me what you were doing?" I bite my lip. "The last time we spoke, you said you got up to use the bathroom, the one *in* your room. So I'm hoping you can help me understand: What brought you *out*?"

"Nest cameras," I repeat.

"That's right."

Silence.

"Did you lie to me?" he asks.

"This is the end of the tour, Detective. I wish I could be more helpful, but that's all I can offer right now. I've talked to you, and I've talked to the police. At this point, if there are more questions, I'll have to insist on a lawyer."

TWENTY-FOUR

The next day, I'm across the street from Amber's rock photography workshop. The sun's setting behind neon billboards. I take my seat in a coffee shop, next to the window. There are still two hours before her event, but this gives me a chance to catch her early.

Amber feels like my last hope.

I don't have a firm plan. I'm here on a feeling. She *must* know something that can help me. She must be able to validate my perspective. Amber has seen the strange Belmont ecosystem up close. I imagine telling her my theory that Vanessa is hiding by choice, sabotaging my relationship as we speak. I'll tell her everything right here in Times Square if I need to, over the roar of theater crowds and tourists. Maybe Amber knows where Vanessa is now.

Maybe this has happened before.

I rip the top off my black coffee without looking at it, keeping my eyes peeled for her dark hair. When someone asks for the second chair at my table, I give it away freely and glance around the shop. People gather around baguette sandwiches and snack bags. Pretzels crack, chips split. I didn't even notice the food by the cash register. It was just a tawny blur.

"Should I have a bite?" I ask no one.

My phone rings on the table—Richard.

"Hello?" I answer.

"She's back."

His voice is wet.

Vanessa?

"Is she—okay?" I ask.

It sounds like he's crying.

"Richard?" I press.

"She's alive, but she isn't . . ."

My stomach sinks.

Did something really happen to her?

I glance left and right, feeling a plunge of shame for being here. I toss my coffee and leave. The street is loud.

"What happened?" I ask.

"I was in the kitchen when . . ." He starts again: "I was in the kitchen when she came back. She was outside, hitting the window . . ." He chokes on a sob, leaving the details for me to imagine: Vanessa bone white with sunken cheeks, bruises like dark bracelets on her wrists. "She's at the hospital now."

I tell Richard I'm on my way.

~

My taxi passes between news crews on Waverley Road. Reporters glow in spotlights next to vans branded with channel numbers. As we pull into the Belmonts' driveway, their estate is dark except for the dining room where Richard and Oliver sit side by side. Their backs are turned to me.

"You sure this is the address?" the driver asks.

"Yes, thank you."

"God bless." His tone is solemn.

I ring the bell. It echoes inside.

Nearly a minute rolls by before Richard opens the front door. He looks hollowed out. His eyes are glassy, lids puffy. His whiskers are long and chaotic, pointing in every direction. He's wearing the same Columbia hoodie from days ago and now, black jeans over mismatched socks. His gaze drifts over my shoulder as he ushers me inside.

I throw my arms around his neck and hug him as the door shuts behind us. His body is more lifeless than I've ever seen it, but still, it's reassuring—his height and hard shoulders, the roughness of his cheek. I haven't been myself without him. I breathe him in and let out a sob I didn't know I had in me.

"Richard, I'm so sorry."

"Thanks for coming."

When he finally does hug me back, there's almost no muscle in it. It feels like his body is merely arranged around mine. *The truth is I think we need some time apart.* He doesn't still think that, right? *He* was the one who called *me* with the news. Aren't we going to help each other through this disaster? Lean on each other the way we always have?

And then, move on from it together?

Richard waves me into the dining room, where Oliver remains. He's sitting with his feet on the cushion, forehead on his knees. He barely lifts his head as I walk in, revealing pink eyes and raw cheeks. The skin on his brow looks tender, as if he's been forcibly wiping tears. When someone in a tight-knit group goes through hell, it appears the rest of them do too.

"I'm so sorry," I tell him.

I feel Richard's big hand on my back. He's leading me forward into the kitchen, where dishes fill the sink. Coffee-stained mugs crowd the counter. An empty soup can rests on its side, mouth open. Richard guides me to the sofa. I sit first, and instead of sitting next to me, he takes the armchair a foot away.

"What happened?" I beg.

"She was on her walk when they grabbed her." His voice is tired and quiet. "They pushed her into a van. Tied her up. Drove around for an hour, she said. When they stopped, they moved her into a basement. They were going to hold her for ransom—two men—but they kept arguing over the amount. Kept pushing each other around, losing their heads over it. Today, they left her in the middle of a fight and forgot to lock the door. So she ran for it. She didn't know where she was. She just bolted for her life until—she started to recognize the houses. All this happened in our own neighborhood. She kept running home, and then—"

He covers his eyes.

"I saw her." He keeps his eyes pinched shut a moment longer. "We took her to the emergency room. Dad told Oliver and me to go home right after she was admitted. I think he was trying to protect us from hearing the doctor's questions. Or maybe, from her answers."

I just listen.

"She was locked in their basement," he emphasizes. "Can you imagine what goes through your mind in a situation like that? No windows. No idea where you are. Just four walls and zero control. I feel powerless just thinking about it, like there's nothing I can do except—pray. Can you believe that? I haven't prayed in years, but I've been talking to God all afternoon. When one of your parents is in that much pain, all that helps is remembering they have a soul." His forehead shrinks into creases. "It will be easier when she's home, when I can help her recover."

"How can I help?" I ask.

The silence is too thick.

"Mom's coming back tonight," he says eventually. "We think it'd be best if it's just family when she comes home." The sentences are remarkably clear. There's nothing ambiguous about them, except his reason.

"But, Richard . . ."

He looks at his knees.

"I'm sorry. I know you took a train here. Honestly, I wasn't sure you would after everything that's happened. It's really nice of you to show up like this, but . . . we think it'd be best if it's just family when she comes home."

The sentence is repeated with the exact same intonation. The words don't feel like his own. I want to debate him. This isn't right. We've spent two years in each other's heads. No matter how bad it got, we never shut the other person out. I want to be here for him, the way a wife is for her husband. We haven't said our vows yet, but the commit-ment remains, doesn't it?

"Richard, I want to stay."

"It's not about what you want—"

"But—"

"It's about what's best for her." He interlaces his fingers and tugs his hands in two directions. "Devon, I'm sorry, and I love you. I'm just very confused by everything you did while she was missing. Dad and Oliver saw photos from your show too. We just want Mom to feel supported right now. We don't want there to be angst in the house. This morning, she was tied up in a basement. She was . . ."

He glances over my shoulder, then down fast. I turn around as if there's someone behind me, but there's only the Belmonts' backyard. Headlights illuminate the covered pool in the distance. This must be the window that Vanessa knocked on earlier today. This is the view that elated and terrified him. I look for any smudge of her knuckle, but the panes are clean.

"Richard?" Oliver calls.

Richard looks at me apologetically, as if there's only one choice to make. Of course he has to answer his brother. Of course he has to stay here. He has to do everything that he possibly can—for Mom.

TWENTY-FIVE

I dry my hands in the Belmonts' powder room before heading back to New York. Their disposable napkins are monogrammed with a palm-size *B*. Ivy twists through it, turning the letter into a labyrinth. How do I stand up for myself in the middle of someone else's tragedy? How do I defend my own wants and needs when he's suffering more than I am?

I should ask Hunter.

When I open our thread on my phone, I see I'm overdue to respond to her last couple of messages.

Hunter: I know this must be an extremely emotional and exhausting time for you and Richard. Please let me know if there is any way at all I can be helpful or supportive. Sending all my love to your family.

Hunter: I'm thinking you probably have a lot going on right now and wanted to reach out and offer to help with any housework/meals. I don't want to impose but let me know if I can help. Sending love.

She must've seen it on the news. The publicist Clarke hired got Vanessa's story on Today.com, in a feature reposted by a dozen other major sites.

I ask Hunter if she's around to talk tonight.

Hunter: Yes! Any time, you name it.

Hunter: I could come over?

I tell her that I'll be home in an hour, and I'd really appreciate seeing her.

Hunter: I'll be there.
Hunter: Soon.

~

On the train, I cry more than I expected.

It's stupid to think about the wedding at this point, but I can't help it. Are we still going to get married? Why do I feel uncertain about our whole relationship now? Maybe it's because I can't talk directly to Richard anymore. Whenever I try, I feel the rest of his family in our conversation. They rallied around Vanessa's disappearance, and now, they're rallying around her recovery. It makes sense, of course, but how long will this last? He's no longer thinking about what's best for us. He's thinking about what's best for her.

I imagine Vanessa knocking on the window. For some reason, it calms me to picture the scene in detail. I see her slim wrists even slimmer, drawn into the bones. I see red hair on her crown, the color spreading. I try to trace her path to the window. Where did she—but the Belmonts' backyard is contained. They have a fence around the whole lawn, which connects to a gate at the top of the driveway. She knocked on the kitchen window but from *inside* their fence? How did she get there? Why didn't she go down the driveway and up to the front door?

The doubt returns like fog.

I imagine asking Richard, *Why did she choose the kitchen window?* In my mind, the question physically repels him. How could I be anything but happy? How could I cling to skepticism, now that she's returned with horror stories? Hasn't she been through enough?

But the question stays. It nips.

I find Hunter in my lobby. Her white chiffon blouse is tucked into high-waisted black pants. She's carrying a portfolio under one arm, as if she's just come from work. I picture her chatting with sophisticated buyers, people who have cultivated such understatement that they only show personality in a pair of painstakingly chosen glasses. Meanwhile, I haven't showered in days. She wraps me in a hug that lasts the elevator ride up to my apartment. I thank her for coming so many times the sentence almost loses its meaning. The words verge on nonsense.

At the door, I use the wrong key. She rests a hand on my back as I try again. We cross the threshold, and I feel a flicker of embarrassment when I turn on the lights. My apartment has become a portrait of chaos. Even since Detective McInnis was here, things have gone downhill. Multiple trash bags line the front hallway—I've been meaning to take those out. A clog in the kitchen sink prevents three inches of gray water from draining. For some reason, I'd normalized it, but Hunter's presence reminds me it's not normal.

She holds my hand as we make our way to the sofa. I download everything, starting with Thanksgiving. I go on to describe my trip to Bristol, where I learned that Vanessa had run away before. Hunter's mouth parts slightly, as if she's tempted to interject. But I plow ahead, breaking the news that now, Vanessa's back. She knocked on the Belmonts' kitchen window earlier today, and Richard was the one to spot her. She's with Clarke in the hospital.

"But it doesn't make sense that she went to the *kitchen* window," I say. "If she really came in the driveway, why didn't she go to the front door?"

Hunter rests her fingertips on her lips.

"Where's Richard now?" she asks.

"He wanted to stay in Greenwich. Apparently, it's best for Vanessa if it's just her family there when she gets back from the hospital."

I shrug callously.

"Is everything all right between you?" she asks.

"I don't know."

"You don't know?"

"I think he might break up with me."

Do I really believe that? "Break up" sounds so juvenile, but what other term could I use? We're not married. Going our separate ways wouldn't technically be "divorce," even though that's what it would feel like.

"She did this." I'm firm. "Vanessa did this. She's behind all of this." Hunter winces. "No, I can prove it. I found out Richard used to have this ex-girlfriend, Amber. She got to know the Belmonts, and then, something happened. I just *know* something weird and terrible happened because she left, and Richard's never mentioned her." My hands fly. "Vanessa must've gotten to her too. If I could just *find* her, then she'd back what I'm saying." Meanwhile, Hunter stiffens. Her composure makes me realize how frazzled I am.

"Even if you *can* prove it," she says slowly, "do you really want to?"

I puzzle.

Of course I do.

"I'm just saying that it can't be easy for you to put that burden on yourself. This fight to prove that Vanessa's manipulating you—"

"*Everyone.* She's manipulating *everyone.*"

"Ok*ay*," she says, "but proving that won't be easy. Do you really want to go down that road?" Her tone is worried, as if I'm toeing a dangerous threshold. As if I'm one step away from an impossible maze, where the walls and doors rearrange. "I'm just saying that it might not be worth it in the end. You might drive yourself over the edge trying to prove someone else is insane." She bites her lip. "Maybe it's a good idea to rest for a second. You've been through a lot this week."

"But it's not just about me. It's about—justice. Not to sound grandiose about it, but she can't get away with this." My face is wet. I wipe my cheeks with one sleeve. "She has to be held accountable for what she's done."

~

The next morning, I leave the apartment to pick up breakfast for Hunter. She was so worried last night, she slept over. She's still on Richard's side of the bed, curled into a protective big spoon. I pay for a fresh croissant at the bakery across the street and carry it out in an elegant brown bag. The only time I can spend money without feeling guilty is when I'm buying something for someone else.

On my way home, steam and butter corrode the bag in black patches. It looks like I'm carrying a handful of shadows. Paul opens the lobby door while holding up a "one second" finger. He shares that something arrived for me, then disappears into the mail room. I wait until he emerges with a small box. He keeps it between his hands, the shipping label facing his chest.

"Who's it—"

"I'm so glad she's back."

I nod, staring at the box.

"When Richard told me what happened, I swear, I started looking for her myself." Paul is wide eyed, every wrinkle deeper. "It was a cloud over my wife and me since I heard, and yesterday, the sun came out."

He hands the package to me.

I'd pass the message to Richard, but now, it appears that Paul talks to him more than I do. I stare at the box from SecondChanceClothes. It's not until I'm in my kitchen that I remember ordering from here. Painting my birds, I ruined some khakis beyond redemption. One hem ripped clean off. Another was stiff and maroon even after rounds in the wash. So I ordered replacements. I open the box and lift two pairs of heavy black cords. Not khakis? I check the name on the packing slip and then, the order below it. According to this, I hold khakis in my hands.

What do you see?

Richard's old prompt comes back like a challenge. I run my fingers warily over the cords and feel the ridges push back. *I know what I see.* I call customer service. After I explain the problem and email Sandra photos of the pants, she asks me to stay on the line.

At that moment, Hunter walks fresh faced into the kitchen in her clothes from last night. I smile and point to the bag in front of me, shaped around the curling bulge of her croissant. I point next to the

Keurig, then the cabinet filled with mugs. Hunter seems to understand my signing and gives me a thumbs-up in return.

"Thanks for holding," Sandra says. "We'd be happy to send you a return slip. You'll get a full refund as soon as we receive your return."

"No, I don't want to return them. I'd like a refund."

"Happy to help, ma'am. We'll just need the items back first."

"Sorry, I don't want to create a problem here, but I didn't buy these. So how can I *return* them?" Over by the Keurig, Hunter appears to be listening. "Do you understand what I'm saying?" Sandra tells me she doesn't. The pants below me are arranged in a looping dark nest. "Again, I don't want to create a problem, but this isn't a return. This is technically *you* asking *me* to send back your lost merchandise, and I don't consent to that. I'd like my money back for the items I never received."

"Ma'am—"

"Do you understand what I'm saying?"

"We can't refund you until we have the items back."

"Do you have a manager?"

"Let me check. Do you mind if I put you on a brief hold?"

"It'd better be quick."

The acid in my voice surprises me.

Violins play through the receiver. I cross over to the nearest window. Eventually, Sandra returns with the news that no one is available.

"Okay, but *when* will your manager be available?"

"It's hard to give a precise answer—"

"Please ballpark it."

"That's hard to say exactly—"

"Closer to five minutes or an hour?"

I ruffle an eyebrow with stiff fingers. I've never been this gladiatorial with customer service. Why am I starting now? I say goodbye, hang up, and call back, reaching a different rep. After restating my problem, I look over at Hunter to find that she's finished her croissant. Only a few brassy flakes remain on her plate. She's scrolling through her phone at the island, stealing glances at me. Once again, I'm given the choice: keep the merchandise or return it for a refund.

"Please, it's not a *return*," I insist. "If you give me a return slip, what items will you list? You don't know what you sent me."

"I'm sorry, but those are the rules."

"Do you see they don't make sense?"

Something warm shocks my elbow. I jolt until I see Hunter holding my arm. Her pressure is light, but there's authority in it. She wants me to end the call. I nod that she's right. Of course she's right. I'm not getting anywhere with SecondChanceClothes. I need ThirdChanceClothes. FourthTime'sACharm. I turn back to the window. From this angle, the brick facade next door looks infinite.

"Okay, thanks for your time," I say before hanging up. I was trying to be sincere, but the words come out hard. "Sorry"—I face Hunter—"I know it's not a big deal, but it's just not right. They're calling it a 'return,' but . . ."

"Sometimes, you have to let things go to be happy."

Her eyes are firm.

I rub where she held me, my arm cradled to my chest. As she walks back to the island, I feel something shift. When did she stop taking my side?

TWENTY-SIX

That afternoon, I hurry up Grammy and Pops's driveway. It's a bright, cold Tuesday. Maybe I should feel more hesitant about showing up again so soon. But Grammy emailed me this morning, saying that our time together was a dream. That I was such a beautiful, curious girl. And I should come back when Pops is up because he'd love to meet me too. I replied the minute I read it, offering to visit again today. I was already starting to change by the time I pressed send.

I made an effort to clean myself up for them. I brushed my teeth so thoroughly that my gums started to bleed. I knock and glance over my shoulder. No one else in this neighborhood is out and about. None of the clouds drift. There's not even wind rustling through the lawns. If I were in another frame of mind, this might be a peaceful scene. But it feels more like the world is holding its breath, waiting silently to release it. When the front door opens, I turn to see Grammy's hand flying back and forth in an excited flurry. Today, her lipstick is hot pink.

"Sweetheart."

"Grammy!"

She takes my hand and leads me into the living room, where Pops sits in the closest armchair. He can't be more than ninety pounds. His argyle sweater swamps him, the extra fabric bunched into accordion folds.

"This is our new granddaughter, *Devon*," she says loudly. "She's going to marry *Richard*." But Pops doesn't react. His thick glasses enlarge a tired stare. Does he remember our phone call after Richard and I got engaged?

I shake his hand and sit on the sofa.

Does Richard know what kind of state Pops is in? I doubt it. He would've spent more time here. He would've done the grocery shopping every week and handled every pharmacy run himself. He would've invented reasons to celebrate, filled this house for half-birthday parties. Richard should know his grandfather is this frail—but of course, I can't be the one to tell him. Then he'd know I was back in Bristol.

Grammy excuses herself, disappearing into the kitchen. I feel lost without her. What can I ask Pops? What's he thinking? I remember being with my mom, back when I couldn't get through to her. She'd go through periods of paranoia, convinced someone was spying on us—listening through our phones, watching through our TV. I'd try to reassure her in vain. I forgot how silent it feels when you can't reach the only one who's there.

Grammy emerges with hot cocoa on a tray of pressed daisies. Their yellow centers eye the room. She sits next to me while I take a long, deep sip. The sugar is mildly intoxicating. When I lower my mug, the air tastes like chocolate. Have I eaten yet today? I can't remember having anything, not even coffee. I must've had *water* after Hunter left. Or did I go straight to my studio? I spent the morning trying to conjure the perfect green, trying so many different shades it felt like I was inside a lime. Grammy interrupts to ask how I am.

"You first," I evade.

"Well, we're just so happy Vanessa finally came home."

I wasn't sure they'd heard.

"Who told you?" I ask.

"Oliver." She sips her cocoa. "I wasn't expecting any news when I called him. I just like hearing his voice, and he's nice enough to put up with us." She beams through the self-deprecating remark. "He's taught us so much about pickleball."

"You talk to Oliver often?"

"We try, but we don't want to be nosy."

I was so focused on learning about Vanessa that I never asked Grammy about Oliver. "I'd thought he might move out soon, but now with his mom home, he'll probably stay for a while . . . Did he ever tell you why he moved in?"

"Of course. He was dating that woman . . ." Grammy snaps her fingers. "But it didn't end well. I think he caught her stealing from Vanessa."

"Stealing?"

Grammy nods. "After he brought her home for the first time, he found a pair of Vanessa's earrings in her purse." Grammy shakes her head. "They were living together too. To end their lease early, he had to pay six months of rent at *once*." Her head shaking gains speed. "After that, he moved back home to save money. And I think he just got cozy."

It seems like a dream come true for Vanessa: Oliver's girlfriend was out of the picture, and her son came home. Was Vanessa—involved? It wouldn't have been difficult. All she would've had to do was drop her earrings in the girl's bag. I remember hearing about this ex-girlfriend a couple of times. She was in medical school; she taught Oliver how to bake bread. It sounded like she was earnest and motivated to make a difference in the world. *Steal* earrings?

"Poor Oliver," she adds. "The week before, he'd told his parents that he wanted to marry this woman. Then he catches her stealing."

Her expression disappears as she takes a sip. I wonder if she suspects Vanessa the way I do. Then again, she doesn't suspect me of anything either—not that I've done anything wrong. But she's been more than happy to open her door and share family secrets. She's been quick to assume this is an innocent visit, that nothing in *my* life's out of place.

When she asks me about the wedding, her eyes brighten. She has such relentless good-heartedness. It's like an inner light coming out through her red fingernails and orange bracelets. It's as if she believes no one has a dark side, and I feel guilty for knowing that people do. Of course she doesn't suspect Vanessa. No one does except me.

"What wedding?" I ask distractedly.

"*Your* wedding, sweetheart."

"Right, that one."

Where did we leave off planning? I picture the emails on Vanessa's desk and improvise a story about cake tasting. Grammy's smile is so wide I keep going. I tell her we must've tried at least ten different flavors. I describe a candied lemon option topped with glazed lemon peels. I describe a black sesame in such detail that my own knack for lying astounds me. Maybe it's an extension of painting, the ability to concoct a world on the spot. I smile, even though I doubt Richard would answer a text from me today, much less lock arms and feed me dessert.

I drain my cocoa.

"One more thing," I segue. There's no seamless way to broach the subject, but I have to mention it, in case there's any more Grammy can tell me. "That woman you mentioned the other day, Amber—"

Pops lifts his head.

Did I imagine it?

"She's a photographer now, isn't she?" I ask, my tone harmless. "She spends a lot of time shooting rock bands . . ." Pops pushes his hands into his seat. He opens his mouth—twice, three times. It looks like he's trying to *say* something, like he's using his whole body to muscle out the words. Grammy walks over to examine him. His lips keep tracing the same two syllables. Is he trying to say "Amber"?

"Let's go rest, sweetheart," Grammy whispers.

"Can I help?"

She says she has him, strangely firm.

She lifts him up, holding just one arm. He's still agitated as she guides him into their bedroom. I wait in the doorway. Was Amber too sensitive a subject for some reason? Did I push my luck too far? Grammy lays him down on their bed, then pulls a blanket up to his waist. It's done with as much tenderness as if he were fully aware. Is she going to ask me to leave? These people feel like my last two connections. If I alienate them, who will be left to listen to me?

~

I get a call from Richard when I'm in my Uber, about to leave his grand-parents' house. I answer on speakerphone.

"Where are you?" he asks.

Grammy waves goodbye on her doorstep.

Should I lie to him? I'm not sure how much he knows.

After Grammy put Pops to bed, she wasn't quite the same. She kept glancing toward their room, her smile slanted. I wanted to win back her good mood, restore her faith in my visits. So, I did what I had to do: I talked about the wedding. For half an hour, I built castles in the air about it: about the three-piece band of former Broadway performers, our weekly lessons for the first dance, my bridal bouquet of white roses, and the floral crown I'll wear down the aisle. If I tell any more lies today, I'm going to lose track of them. I might even start to believe them.

"I'm in Bristol."

"*What?*"

"Why? Where are you?"

"I'm getting lunch for everyone." He sounds exasperated. With me? With his own circumstances? "Why are you in Bristol?"

The car reverses out of the driveway.

Grammy stays on the front steps until she's a pink dot.

"Are you still trying to prove that Mom's somehow behind all this?" He waits, but every honest reply would hurt him. "You know what, Devon?" he says at last. "I'm sorry, but this has been a nightmare on its own, and for you to run a campaign against my mom at the same time, it's shown me . . ." He exhales for a long few seconds. "If you're not on my side when it counts, then you're not on my side at all. I tried to say something when you were here last night, but I . . . couldn't. The truth is that we can't move forward with a wedding right now."

I don't understand.

I know how people get engaged: Two people meet. They date. They live together. One of them buys a ring and gets down on one knee. But the story of how people *dis*engage is less clear. I don't even know the word for it. "*Un*engage"? How does *that* story go? It's so unfamiliar I can't tell if it's just happened to me. When people undo their engagement, are they still dating?

"Richard—"

"I'm sorry, but I'm not calm enough to talk about it right now. I'm trying to take care of the exact same people you want to undermine."

He hangs up.

We can't move forward.

I look at my engagement ring. The stone is grayer than I remember. I should clean it—even though it doesn't really matter if the diamond fades. This ring is a symbol more than anything else. It's a commitment to stay with each other. *We can't move forward*—but we *can* because he told me we always would. This ring is his word, and it's so loud I can almost hear it.

TWENTY-SEVEN

A week later, I haven't heard from Richard. I'm on our sofa alone, where I've spent the past few hours watching *Succession*. Logan won't give his kids any control.

Our living room windows are violet, gray, and pale blue. Our neighbors across the street are absent or cropped into pieces—upper bodies, profiles. A room temperature bowl of popcorn is tucked into my arm. Every now and then, I pinch one of the kernels and feel it collapse between my fingers. I pause the show to check my phone.

Nothing.

I've drafted a dozen texts to Richard this week, each one searching for different answers. Does he have a problem with *marrying* me, or just with planning a party now, while his mom recovers? Does he want to stay together, or was this the beginning of an even tougher conversation? Why can't we talk to each other like we used to? In one draft, I swear that I'm committed to working through this rough patch. Our kind of connection happens once in a lifetime. Doesn't he remember what it was like to feel at home with each other? I'm not even talking about our grandest moments, just our small ones. Holding him in bed used to be everything to me.

But I never hit send. In every message, I sensed that I was begging, and when you have to beg someone to stay, they've already left.

I didn't even tell Richard that I sold my first painting. One of Marc's longtime patrons bought *For an Inch of Sleep*. The sale is more than a milestone. It's a jump-up-and-down-screaming victory. But how could I break the news to him now? Vanessa's health is everyone's primary concern. Some tragedies are so loud they mute everything around them. Joy feels like a betrayal to whoever's in pain. Besides, Richard doesn't want to hear another word about that painting, much less learn it has a future on display in someone's home. Maybe it will end up in a museum, immortalizing violence to someone with a striking resemblance to his mom.

I hate the silence between us.

Still, I've been managing to get out of bed every day and spend time in the studio. I make myself sandwiches for lunch, not that I have the desire to finish them or the energy to clean up. So, dishes mushroom. The bed gets messier. The only part of our apartment that stays the same is our closet, since I wear the same clothes on repeat.

I don't want to lose him. We weren't just in love. We were companions, best friends. We had our own private world, where everything was different, down to basic physics and natural laws. Winter was warm with him. Even in the dead of night, it was never fully dark. If this is the end of us, it's agonizingly indirect. Why can't anyone in his family speak their mind? Even Vanessa never confronted me. She never sat me down and told me what she really believes.

I'm turning my phone over when it illuminates with Richard's name. I stand up, heart racing. What time is it? Seven a.m. Usually, this is the best time to reach me, before I disappear into work. But these days, my internal clock is broken. It's all but stopped, leaving me with no reliable sense of morning or night. I have to keep my phone nearby to tell me *when* I am.

"Richard." I'm almost breathless.

"I hope you're doing all right," he says.

I'm not.

He clears his throat. It sounds like he's shaking the silence, a few ripples cracking through it. "I really was just checking in . . . Last time, we talked about the wedding. Did you happen to call Blue Hill?"

I sit back down and shield my eyes.

"If you're too busy," he says, "I'm happy to call them myself. I'll say we're looking for another date. But it needs to happen."

I'm mute.

"All right, I'll take care of it," he says.

"*Are we* looking for another date?"

"I don't know."

So I'm supposed to wait while you figure it out?

All I can see is Vanessa's subtle smile. The way she was stroking Richard in the library the day before she went missing. Her ankles were crossed under the sofa, paw prints woven on her velvet flats. These days, does she stay in bed whispering about her night terrors? Murmuring that she can't be left alone? Why doesn't anyone else doubt her?

"How is she?" I ask.

He sighs. "Every day is hard. When you go through something like that, it changes you. She's in therapy. There's no long-term physical damage, thank God, but the mental part . . . we're all chipping in."

How did she get to the kitchen window? The question is on my tongue, creeping, dangerous. *Why didn't she knock on the front door?* I'm so close to asking it that my lips shift with the intention. I can almost see his face change on hearing it.

"Are you seeing anyone?" he asks.

A beat.

"Therapy, I mean."

"No."

"You should reach out to Gretchen, maybe get a few sessions just for yourself. You've been through a lot too. This kind of thing affects everyone."

"When are you coming home?" I ask.

A pause grows.

Is he shocked? Angry? Sad?

"I am home," he whispers.

"No, you're not."

"Sorry, Mom is calling."

~

I'm in bed that afternoon when I refresh my inbox and find the subject line: Ferrell/Belmont Wedding Update. My stomach drops. The message uninvites me from my own wedding, telling Blue Hill that in light of recent family events, "we" are working to find a new date.

I run to the bathroom—desperate to throw up, end the nausea—but nothing comes out except a hacking cough. I sit on the cold tile floor. Maybe if I had a manager, coworker, or client, I'd have a reason to get back on my feet, but there's no one else here. I've never struggled with my invisible days before. But right now, with no one watching, there's no one around to help. Richard is gone, and I'm alone, without even a tick from my internal clock.

TWENTY-EIGHT

Two weeks later, Richard and I are meeting at the Joe & the Juice next to our building. I'm here first, at a table by the window.

I didn't choose this place.

Richard was the one who texted last night, Do you have time for a coffee soon? At that moment, I was working in the living room. My studio has overflowed into the rest of the apartment. Now, tarps cover the floor from the front door to the bedroom. The drying rack in the kitchen is filled with brushes. They poke out of tubs for silverware like single-pronged forks, blunt knives. When Richard texted, I was painting the storm that's been drenching our windows. So far, the painting is severe: hard angles, slanting rain, and a blue-gray mood. Of course, I told Richard that I'd meet him anywhere, anytime. He suggested here, now.

This Joe & the Juice is almost empty, a few minutes after opening. Raw vegetables chill on the counter: skinned carrots, sprawling ginger roots. A couple of New Yorkers pay five dollars for bitter green shots. I fidget slowly. I have a feeling that Richard's coming with bad news: he's going to move out. This will be a logistical meeting to handle the apartment, his things, mine. Our lease will end in two months. Knowing him, he'll probably leave it to me for those two. Then it will be up to me to find my own place, to make my own life.

I am sad down to my bones. My whole life, I've met one Richard. It's been a blessing and a curse to stay in our apartment for the past few weeks, surrounded by his DILL WITH IT tie, his charismatic footwear, his bag of treats for the no-kill shelter, and photos of us together, framing the best moments of my life. I've moved lots of those photos into our bedroom, onto my nightstand. I go to bed with them, wake up with them, and then paint.

I've prepared myself to beg. I have nothing left to lose. I want there to be an *us* again, but—is it possible? He'd need to see Vanessa for who she really is in order to forgive me. And does anyone change at our age?

Richard arrives looking surprisingly kempt. He's in a collared cashmere sweater over jeans. His new beard has been groomed since the last time I saw him. His haircut is different, too, surprisingly lush on top. It's almost like a professional started to style him—like someone started to choose his clothes, lay them out on his bed—but still, *he's* familiar. His expression is solemn and sensitive, showing the side of him I know better than anyone.

I stand, wishing I'd spent more time getting ready. I'm in splattered jeans and biker boots, the laces undone. There's wet paint on one toe in an unraveling spiral. I should've at least brushed my hair, but it's hard to neaten up when you feel like you're in free fall.

I hug him, resisting the urge to kiss his cheek.

He takes the straight-backed chair opposite mine and sits on the edge. His mouth opens and closes without making a sound. He looks as sad as I feel. It starts to rain again, spraying the window beside me. I've been looking at rain so much this week the crooked rivers on the glass are familiar. It's almost as if they've all come out to support me.

"I'm sorry," he says eventually.

The words are too small. I know what he means, but he owes me the decency of articulating it. After all that we've been through together—years of *us*, seeping into each other—he can do better than that.

"Sorry for what?" I ask.

"We can't . . ."

"What is it, Richard?"

"I'm sorry, but we can't do this anymore."

I tell him evenly that we can.

"I don't see how. You weren't there for me when I needed you. You went on a wild-goose chase to prove my mom's insane." He pulls his own hair, the strands tight in his fist. As if the idea is so feral it's attacking his mind. "She was beaten, Devon. Her arms are still blue. So, I see that, and the next thing I know, you're interviewing her parents, trying to dig something up on her? I mean, are you fucking kidding me?" He cuts himself off, covering his mouth with one hand. "I'm sorry. If you saw her right now, you'd know why I'm like this."

"I can't see her, because you kicked me out."

"She's too fragile for anyone but family."

He looks grave.

"I understand that I could've been a better partner while she was missing," I admit. "But now that she's back, can't we . . . ?"

He doesn't understand.

"Put this behind us?" he tries.

I nod vigorously.

"I don't think that's possible. I needed you to be on my side, and you weren't. When I was looking for her, it's like you were—playing for the other team, to use a crude analogy. Every night, I went to sleep without her and without being able to talk to you. If you're not there when I'm drowning, then . . ."

"I'm sorry."

I mean it.

"I'm sorry, I'll change," I go on. "I'll never do this again."

"I'm sorry too. But I don't think you understand how much you hurt me. And I don't see how we can get married if I don't trust you to support me when it counts." He bows his head. The high-pitched whir of a blender cuts briefly through the air. "And honestly, it did make me worry about you . . . You know, we've talked about some of your family history—"

"What family history?"

He looks up.

"Your mom being schizophrenic."

I recoil.

"Sorry, isn't she?" he asks, exceedingly gentle. "I've never heard you label it, but I just thought, with all the paranoia, talking to furniture . . ."

"She's a recovering alcoholic," I say, defending her with an edge. "She gets loopy when she's drunk, but she doesn't have *schizophrenia*." I make the word sound as ridiculous as the idea, turning it into a clunky jumble. "*I'm* the one who's spent my life with her. How dare you? How dare you, when you're breaking up with me, insult my mom?" The teen behind the counter glances over at us, then back quickly.

"I'm sorry," he says.

The rain picks up.

Umbrellas bloom.

"Our apartment is yours until the lease ends," he says, still quiet. "I'll be working from Greenwich." I notice now that he doesn't even have a bag with him. He doesn't plan to stay. He's going to turn right around when this is done and head back to the suburbs without me. I can almost smell the Belmonts' detergent on him, the one that soaks all their towels and sheets.

"You fuck her too?" I ask.

"*What?*"

"You live together, eat together, tuck her into bed. I'm just curious if you fuck her too."

He stands up, shaking his head.

Outside, he cries into his hands.

"Don't let that be the last thing we say!" I howl.

TWENTY-NINE

Over the next few weeks, I sell *If You Die in a Dream* and move out of our apartment. I leave behind everything that we shared: the ocean painting, all our books, towels, and dishes. They'd only hurt to keep, and I won't have the space. I say a few last words to each room on my way out, then channel Richard's charisma as I say goodbye to Paul. He tells me not to forget him when I'm a star.

I move into a six-hundred-square-foot studio downtown. The window overlooks Eighth Avenue—loud, busy—but I'm on the sixth floor, which softens some of the noise. The best feature of this apartment is its distance from where Richard and I used to live, so I won't happen on any of our old haunts. There's no chance I'll pass our favorite restaurants: Elio's, the old-school Italian joint, or Antonucci's, a similar place where we were always the youngest ones there and held hands under the white tablecloths. I won't run into him eating burgers with his friends at JG Melon or toasting beers with his coworkers at the Penrose. Downtown is a blank canvas.

My studio is to the point: mattress in one corner, easel in another, kitchenette in the third, and my door in the fourth. Hunter has been texting me, eager to visit. But we still haven't seen each other since she slept over. We only texted after Richard and I broke up because—I'm embarrassed. My life has shrunk down to its essentials. Maybe there *is* something wrong with me, to wind up on a path that's so absolutely solitary, so astoundingly alone. I only have the company of my work and intermittent calls with Mom. I criticized the Belmont boys for an unhealthy attachment to *their* mom, and here I am, with no one on my Recents except mine.

～

I'm kneeling over a canvas, painting a pelvic bone, when my phone rings. I follow the sound to my window. The sun is starting to set, splitting into vibrant blues. It's a FaceTime request from Mom—I reject it. For once, I'm worried about how it would look on *my* side. I don't want her to see how chaotic my new place is, the palettes of oil paint surrounding my mattress on the floor. With the streaks on my face and in my hair, I'm living in my art now.

I call her back, audio only.

"Happy birthday to you," she sings. "Happy birthday to you. Happy birthday to my mini Matisse. Happy birthday to you."

I'm smiling.

"Thanks for reminding me." February, already. "Is there anything fun about turning thirty?"

"It's like turning twenty-one. But with more experience."

I laugh. "Since when are you so funny?"

"Since you turned thirty. So, what are you up to?"

"Just working." I face the canvas upside down. Marc requested more paintings in my new style for a show next month. At first, I was hesitant to agree, because those portraits came from such a dark place. Then I realized I don't have much choice. Those are the only paintings I've ever sold. I tilt my head to align with the skeleton, flowers growing out of its fingers.

"Living your dream," she says.

"In some ways. I still miss . . ."

"I know."

I feel that she understands.

"I keep thinking about everything that happened," I admit. "Did you ever have any issues with Dad's mom? Sorry." We haven't talked about Dad in longer than I can remember. "My mind wanders more now that I live alone." I don't just wonder about myself. I wonder about all women, all couples. Why do people *wait* to introduce their partners to their parents? Isn't that misleading? As if parents will stay in the background, content to be unseen?

"Mom?" I probe.

"It's your birthday."

"So can I choose the topic?"

"Clever girl," she says. "Lynn and I actually got along . . . fine. In her day, things were different: no cell phones, no internet. Kids left the house at eight, came home at five. Letting go was part of being a mom. But it doesn't sound like Vanessa was willing to do that." Meanwhile, I walk back to the window. My view of the sunset is better here in the West Village than it ever was on the Upper East Side. "If you ask me, you're lucky you got out of that family now instead of ten years down the line: no divorce, no custody battles. Now, you're young. Your art is getting attention. I mean, how wild and free are you? Why not date yourself?"

I don't want to talk about me anymore.

When I ask how she's doing, she says she's started beading again. She found some gorgeous quartz beads in town this morning, and apparently, they just blush in her hands. She's going to use them in rope necklaces, forty-inch strands she can double or triple loop. As she goes on, I wish Richard were here. *See?* I'd ask him. *See?* When she's sober, she's perfectly sane—better than that; she's lively and interesting. She appreciates beauty and inspires you to see it.

"Seeing anyone this weekend?" I ask.

"Just my projects."

"Me too." I smile.

After we hang up, I let myself dream about what it might be like when Mom gets better—not cured, of course, but really better. I picture her with a year or more of sobriety under her belt, steady employment. Maybe she could visit my place, or I could make the trip to hers. I haven't been home since high school.

I return to my canvas.

Maybe I could see her this summer, and we could paint together. When she was in event planning, she had a gift for floral artistry—arranging colors, textures, and ideas. I remember photos of her arrangements: elaborate canopies of green foliage, wild daisy bouquets, and bowls of succulents with dark roses. If she could make art with flowers, I'm sure she could with paint. I feel like we'd work well together. Our oily fingerprints might even look similar around the studio, or on the soap dispenser by the sink, with the same tiny swirls in the thumbs.

THIRTY

I pay for a matcha latte the next day at Muse Coffee on West Tenth. Mine is thick and green with an extra shake of matcha powder on top. Chewing the green tea crumbs is a small luxury that I'll savor all the way home. I'm snapping the lid on my to-go cup when I glimpse a familiar face in the mirror—Amber's behind me.

She's in line to order.

I'm positive that it's her. Her dark hair fills a messy knot on top of her head. Smoky liner blurs her eyes. She wears her leather jacket with perfect posture, patiently waiting her turn. It's not often that I see anyone fierce *and* collected at once, but here she is. Here she finally is.

She orders a black coffee.

"And what time do you close?" she asks.

"Five," the barista says.

"That early?"

I make room for her at the counter. I keep fidgeting with my drink, as if there's something left to do here. She slides her cup into a cardboard sleeve before stepping onto the street. I trail her into a bookstore and pretend to look at new paperbacks. I pick up a soft copy without reading the title, barely feeling it in my hand, trying to decide if I'm going to approach her.

Does she know who I am?

I follow her back outside.

Clouds tint the sidewalk. I slow my pace so she won't notice me. We pass heaped trash bags outside a high-end Italian restaurant. More line a row of brick town houses, one pile for every front door. Now, I'm a block behind her, watching the slim back of her neck. The more I think about it, the more I doubt she knows anything about me. If she did, she would've reacted in the coffee shop. She would've sensed me in her periphery and done a double take.

I want to meet her. Have to.

I imagine speeding up to join her. When we make eye contact, maybe I'll act unsure. Maybe I'll even shake my head, as if I don't believe it myself. *Sorry, I know this is a long shot. But do you by any chance know Richard Belmont?*

She's across the street when I make it to the curb. The pedestrian sign turns red. I ignore the warning and sprint toward her. I'm halfway there when a yellow cab swerves around me, its horn blaring. The noise sounds like it's bending as it comes toward me, then tapers off. I make it across as Amber turns into an apartment building. It has a quiet entrance, just a slice of old brick between a diner and a dry cleaner. By the time I'm there, the door's shut.

As I catch my breath, I notice names by the call buttons. 4B: A. HEWITT is the only one written in Sharpie over a printed label. The letters beneath peek through in formal corners, crisp curves. They look broken, but I try to *unbreak* them, piece them back together. I'm positive the original last name starts with a *B*. The twin peaks of an *M* rise out of the middle. I put the word together, edge by edge, but—that can't be right. Can it?

The printed label reads A. BELMONT.

I gaze up to the fourth floor, but the windows are mirrors. They reflect the neighborhood with a silver glaze and offer no views inside. I wander into Abingdon Square Park across the street, googling *Amber Belmont* on my phone. Did she and Richard get married? The first link is an article from Greenwich Academy's student newspaper. Apparently, Amber Belmont graduated in 2009, just a few years after Richard graduated from its brother school. There's no mention of her since. All articles about Amber Belmont are from decades ago.

She wasn't like Vanessa, running off without telling anyone. Amber said her goodbyes. Then she left . . . Maybe Richard wasn't lying when he said he'd never brought a woman home. Maybe Amber wasn't an ex who broke his heart.

Was she his . . . sister?

I gaze up to the fourth floor.

Hunter's voice drifts into my mind. *Even if you* can *prove it, do you really want to?* If she were here, she'd tell me there's no way to win this anymore. Richard is gone. The only other people in this park—a quarter-acre slice of the city, one of the smallest parks in Manhattan—are in various states of disturbance. No one here, in the middle of a weekday, appears to be on stable ground. Maybe I should walk away. Maybe I should focus on rebuilding my life.

But I can't stop scanning for 4B.

THIRTY-ONE

Men are simpler than you imagine, my sweet child. But what goes on in the twisted, tortuous minds of women would baffle anyone . . .

I'm listening to the audiobook for *Rebecca*, waiting in Abingdon Square. My bench faces the front door to Amber's building. The trees between us branch like gray lungs. My phone tells me that it's almost four, a couple of hours since she went in with her coffee.

What if she doesn't leave until tomorrow?

Did you know, you did not look a bit like yourself just now? . . .

I don't usually listen to audiobooks. I'm a visual person who enjoys the aesthetic experience of a hard copy. But last week, reading up on *When the Stars Go Dark*, I saw that I could listen to it for free with a trial of Audible. So I did, ears piqued for clues. I stayed up all night to finish it, curled up on my mattress, wondering if the novel could be a smoking gun for Vanessa's deception. Did she rip off the plotline in staging her own drama? Did she fabricate the men who took her based on characters in this book? But I couldn't make any connections. Since then, villains from the story have crawled into my nightmares. Maybe that was her intention.

Until my trial ends, I'm listening to more of the books I saw in Vanessa's office. I haven't lost hope that I'll win Richard back. The better I understand his mom, the better chance I'll have against her. *Rebecca* is of course the classic about a second wife who can't escape the lingering presence of the first. It takes place at Manderley, an estate as magnificent as it is haunting. The setting is so rich and textured it's almost a character in the story. With its own relationships and secrets.

The more I hear about Manderley, the more I feel like I'm back on Waverley Road. I can almost see the Belmonts' estate again. Just like the de Winters', it has its own caretaker: Oliver. He's the resident devotee, shuttered in and obsessed with its mistress. I still remember his texts to Vanessa, coordinating their daily rituals. The only difference is that Manderley's haunted by a woman who's gone. Waverley is haunted by a woman who's still there.

I'm getting cold, sitting here in one layer. I should be painting—my skeleton waits for me at home, eager for its eye sockets—but this feels important. I rewind my audiobook thirty seconds. My mind was so loud it blared over the story. When I look up again from my phone, Amber is leaving her building with a camera around her neck.

I have to follow her.

She turns left on a cobblestone road. It's a short stretch between busier streets, lined with dark bars and restaurants. They're places that will come alive at night, but right now, we're the only two here. I step on a cellar door that sinks an inch.

"Amber!" I call.

She spins around.

I wave, rushing to close the gap until we're just a foot apart. Up close, her hairline is blond; she must've dyed her hair black. She's strung a metal chain through her belt loops. More dangle from her combat boots. Still, there's something elegant in the way she carries herself. As if she took years of cotillion classes and can't unlearn them. As if she grew up dancing ballet, and the poise has stayed in her bones.

"Yes?" Her low voice is handsome.

"I'm Devon. I used to date your brother Richard." She stiffens, and regret stings. Should I have admitted that so soon? I didn't practice anything in the park. It was too nerve racking to imagine this moment. Here I am with my chance, unprepared. "Then something happened to Vanessa. I'm not with Richard anymore. I'm sorry to catch you like this. I'm just—having a hard time." The ice in her expression thaws. "If you can find it in your heart to meet with me, I'd just really appreciate talking to you."

We stare at each other.

"I'm sorry," I flounder. "I know this sounds desperate. I don't usually flag people down on the street. But I didn't know what else to do."

She glances at her watch.

"I'm headed to a job," she says.

"Right." The normalcy of it feels sharp. I haven't had a meeting in weeks.

"But I can meet you for coffee tomorrow. Maybe noon? At Musc?"

"Thank you."

"Nice to meet you . . . ?"

"Devon," I repeat.

"Whatever happened, Devon, I'm sorry."

THIRTY-TWO

The next day, I wake up to my 11:30 a.m. alarm.

I barely slept after meeting Amber. She doesn't just have the power to change my future—she could change my past. She could change how I understand everything. My excitement fueled eight hours of work on my skeleton. I splashed red on its teeth, while the rest of the block lay dreaming. Maybe I was, too, but I never closed my eyes. Only when the sun rose—while I was washing brushes, rubbing greasy colors off the bristles—did my eyelids finally droop.

I put on my cleanest, sleekest outfit and head outside for Muse. I turn left into a curving alley. The city grid breaks down in this area. Uptown is a matrix with streets in numerical order. But here, the roads wind with unpredictable names. I pass a cracked watch on the pavement. Views of the Hudson River leak between buildings. Soon, I'm at Muse with my back to the store, and Amber is nowhere in sight. Two separate couples arrive and leave with steaming drinks.

At seven past, I wonder if she's still—

"Devon!"

Amber waves.

"Thank you for coming," I gush.

"I have a duty to help my mom's victims."

She's relaxed, though her word choice is alarming.

We head into Muse, where I let her order first. She pays for her black coffee with a scratched debit card—nothing like Richard's glossy

Chase Sapphire. Amber has four cartilage piercings in her left ear. One snake earring weaves through them all. I wonder if Vanessa's seen these, if they made her bristle. If Amber liked putting her mother on edge.

We take our coffees to Abingdon Square and find seats on a bench. I notice a tattoo on the inside of her wrist. It appears to be an aperture, the essential form of a camera lens. If I weren't so desperate to know about her family, I'd waste time on technicals: What kind of camera does she use? What kind of sensors? But I don't have a second to lose.

"What did she do to you?"

I'm not going to hide anything. The more honest I am with Amber, the more honest she'll be with me. Besides, I just feel like she's on my side. She's a Belmont, but only when you look at her closely and see the polish she can't scrape off. Now, she and I are in similar artistic worlds, on the same spiraling pavement. Drinking the same coffee.

I tell her everything, starting with the engagement. I tell her that Vanessa waged war on my sanity. The worse I got, the more my relationship broke down. "And then she went 'missing.'" I sense that I'm on shaky ground as I mock the word. "But when she came back, she knocked on the *kitchen* window. Why would she do that unless she was on the property the whole time? When I tried to prove something wasn't right, Richard called off the wedding. He said my vendetta against his mom was insane." I wipe my eyes with the back of my hand.

Amber touches my shoulder.

It's brief but reassuring.

"Vanessa wanted me out of the picture." I encapsulate everything I've been trying to say. "And instead of getting rid of me, she made me get rid of myself." I catch my breath after the monologue. By now, I'm leaning forward over my knees, as if I've physically purged the stories. Meanwhile, Amber is upright with her shoulders relaxed. She's so collected that none of the chains on her outfit even vibrate. They just glint in place.

"I'm sorry," Amber says. "That all sounds . . . like her."

She sounds touched but not—surprised.

She takes a long sip of coffee. Her raisin-colored lipstick stays dark. I thought Amber would know *something* about Vanessa, but now, I'm starting to feel wary about what that might be. My stories barely disturbed her. I just gave a detailed description of her mom's malice, and Amber barely moved on this bench.

"What happened to you?" I dare.

"You don't want to hear that."

I tell her that I do. I really do.

"You don't have somewhere to be?"

Her tone is unjudgmental.

"I'm a painter. So I'm . . . flexible."

"I'm a photographer. So I understand."

She nods as if we share a secret.

"I was never that close with my mom," she says quietly. Before continuing, she recrosses her legs. She does it the same way with her ankles to one side, her shins at a ladylike slant. "The irony is, all this started because she wanted us to be a *tight* family." She says "tight" showing teeth. "It wasn't just that she wanted the five of us to be together. She wanted to keep everyone else out. So she never hosted dinners at home. There was never anyone in our guest room. No matter how many friends we had, she had more reasons why they couldn't come over.

"But it was more insular than that." Her blue gaze dips to the path. "We couldn't just *do* things as a family. We had to *like* them. The truth is she never cared if you were interested in another exhibit, because 'don't we adore Van Gogh?'" I can almost hear Vanessa asking with her vise of suggestion. "The concept of 'we' was so important to her. We were supposed to be united, undifferentiated. Love *The Nutcracker* and the Metropolitan Opera House. Be the polite, well-spoken Belmonts, who preferred each other to everyone else.

"My brothers didn't seem to mind," she admits. "Richard was always popular—and by 'popular,' I don't just mean people loved *him* the most. I mean he loved *people* the most. He needed to be in a group. Oliver went along with it because he was always hungry for approval, hers most of all. And me . . ." She shrugs. "I was different. I wanted my own *thing*—it almost didn't matter what, but it had to be mine."

She taps long fingers on her cup.

"I started visiting my grandparents more. At first, it was to get out of Waverley, but we got close." If I weren't riveted, I'd tell Amber they still hang photos of her at home. Her name was the one word that seemed to get through to Pops. "I'd visit them every weekend I could, and they'd spend hours with me. I'd paint with my little red brush, make paper flowers. But that only put more distance between Mom and me. She didn't like my visits to Bristol." She finishes her coffee with a long sip, looking no more energized when she's done.

"My brothers would say they had a dream childhood. And maybe they did. All I know is Mom guarded what they had. They were her precious family. They were her boys, even when they became men." Amber keeps her pace steady, slow. I sense her working up to a more difficult topic, taking the long way. "Then in high school, I had to write an essay on someone in my family. I chose to do it on my dad's mom. All I knew about Agnes was that she'd died in a car accident before I was born. Mom was in the car too." She twists her cup. "I thought the essay would be a tribute to her. A chance to learn about the one grandparent I'd never met.

"So I asked my dad if he wouldn't mind talking about her. I didn't ask my mom because that felt—insensitive. But she insisted on being there. When my dad and I were supposed to meet, she was the first one ready in the library. I thought she might contribute something, but she just sat there, listening. And it felt . . . off. It felt like she didn't want to *join* the conversation.

"She just wanted to watch it.

"When I asked Mom about Agnes a little later, she kept dodging my questions. It made me *dig*." She squints her cool blue eyes. "I kept asking. The questions only got deeper under her skin. She looked at me with more ice. And then eventually, she snapped at me to 'stop it.' It was a voice I'd never heard her use, low, intent." She throws her coffee away. "That's when Mom told me that she and Agnes didn't get along, if I had to know. Agnes didn't like Mom, didn't want her to marry Dad. It sounded like the truth, but it didn't sound like the full story."

Amber twists a chunky ring. It looks like a silver knuckle spinning around the bone. "I couldn't let it go. Part of me wanted to figure it out. A bigger part of me was . . . baited. I'm not proud of it, but I wanted to provoke her a little bit.

"I wanted to stir things."

She twirls the ring.

"So I started to bring Agnes up at the dinner table. I started putting photos of her around the house. Why weren't there any on display, anyway? But they kept getting taken down, moved. Then Mom caught me hanging a photo of Agnes in the front hall. She grabbed me by the arm and told me to 'stop it.'" Amber impersonates the eerie voice. "I asked what would happen if I didn't. She said, 'Then I'll take you for a drive too.'" Amber enunciates the threat with cold clarity. "It wasn't a hard confession, but I knew. I just knew what she'd done."

"Did you tell anyone?" I ask.

She nods. "I told the family, but . . ."

"But?"

"Out of nowhere, I was claiming that Mom had killed someone twenty years ago. And I didn't have any proof." Her tone is deadened. "None of them really listened. I told them she'd threatened me, and that got just as far." A strand falls from her updo, cutting a black slash across her cheek. "I went to Grammy and Pops, but they didn't hear me either. They only saw their daughter in one perfect light. It was my word against hers. And at home, Oliver kept calling me 'insane.'

"Do you know what 'insane' really means?"

I shake my head.

"Everything is a battle of perspective. There's always a winner, and when you lose—when you decisively lose—then your view becomes the crazy one. So when people call you 'insane,' they're letting you know who won." She tucks hair behind one ear, flashing the aperture.

"After that, I didn't feel safe at home anymore. When you don't trust your mom, the spine of your whole life . . . It's not paranoia, but it's close. I started hiding from her, spending most of my time in the storm room—it's by the pool," she adds, as if she can read my confusion. "But staying in that house wasn't good for me. When no one treats you like you're sane, it nearly drives you out of your mind. As soon as I turned eighteen, I hit the road and never looked back."

"I can't believe Richard didn't tell me."

Amber looks unsurprised.

"Mom turned herself into the victim. It started before I left. She acted so fragile, like the whole thing was so painful just my name would undo her. My brothers probably had to remove all signs of me from the house. Maybe they promised never to mention me again." It's unsettling now to remember the Belmonts' world-class art: landscapes on every wall, no traces of their daughter. "Moms really do shape how their sons view people. Most, I assume, use the power unconsciously. But my mom knew she had them, and she turned them against me."

Amber reaches inside her jacket for a pack of cigarettes and offers me one. I shake my head. She lights hers with hard flicks on a lighter. The longer we pause, the more she looks visibly wounded. I feel like I understand a version of what happened to her: I left my mom with some hope, but Amber left hers without it.

"What exactly do you need from me?" she asks.

"I guess I just wanted someone to believe me."

"I do, but . . ." She looks skeptical. "There's something else."

"It's Richard," I admit. "I don't know what it was about him, or us, but . . . I still have the engagement ring at home. Once you love someone—really love them—I don't think you can stop. Right?" Amber doesn't react. "Our lives are different, but *we* haven't changed. Maybe there's a way for us to get back together." Something develops in Amber's stare. I clasp my hands together as if I'm about to pray. "I just wish there was something we could do?"

THIRTY-THREE

Later that day, I craft the text: I just met Amber. I'm sitting on my mattress, feet on the floor, debating whether to send it to Richard. My toes brush a fresh pink stain on the tarp.

The shallow pool drifts toward the door.

I still don't understand why he kept her a secret. I thought he and I told each other everything. Even if Vanessa *was* too fragile to talk about her, why wasn't he honest when we were alone? It must've weighed on him. Did he personally replace every photo of Amber in Greenwich? He must've thought about her on her birthday, on holidays, and when we visited the house where they'd lived. I can't imagine going through that and keeping it all to myself.

Maybe this was the source of his depth. I never understood how he'd come out of his charmed life with a soft heart. Now, his empathy makes sense. He was carrying around this loss. Even *I* think it sounds painful and bizarre. My mom might've imagined people, but she never erased anyone. Why didn't Richard discuss this with *me*? He must've put his family's wishes above his own. Will he always? If I ask him point-blank about Amber, will he lie?

There's only one way to find out.

I send the text.

Where will it find him? My phone tells me it's just after five. Are the Belmonts in the library, cutting buttery wedges of cheese? They always revered that centerpiece: the veiny roquefort, bricks of cheddar, brie that seemed to melt in slow motion, and of course, Oliver's favorite, smoked gouda. It was their most necessary luxury. Their mother's milk. Thank God she's home. Will they go to church this Sunday and show Him gratitude? Meanwhile, my splattered skeleton stares back at me from the wall. Its toes dangle above the bottom of the canvas.

Will Richard reply?

I know what I *want* him to say—that he happens to be in the city, so why don't we meet tonight at Antonucci's? It's a wild fantasy, but I've never let the odds determine my dreams. Richard and I always got their zucchini flowers, deep fried and stuffed with buffalo ricotta. Their martinis were enormous buckets with five olives each. Richard never drank much at home, but when we went out with a group, he always kept up with his friends. If someone else ordered two oversize martinis, an espresso martini, and then an after-dinner shot, he would follow suit.

Two sharp knocks shake the door. My feet slide an inch across the pink. I'm not expecting anyone. I rise slowly, looking for something to grab in case I need to defend myself. There are vases of paintbrushes, but nothing heavier than that. The window leads to a fire escape—running away would be my best option. I tread toward the peephole. On the other side, Hunter waits with a grocery bag. I rush to unlock my door and practically throw my hug onto her.

"Easy now." She laughs.

"What are you doing here?"

"I wasn't sure how you were holding up. You haven't answered any of my calls or texts in weeks. I finally decided just to come over." Before I can apologize, she adds, "Plus, I have a very practical, very overdue housewarming gift for you." She lifts the grocery bag. I glimpse all my staples and favorites, including bananas. It's enough to make me tear up.

I invite her inside.

She takes one step forward before stopping on the threshold. I realize the lights are off. Of course she's stopped. She can't see much of what's ahead. After I turn them on, though, she still won't budge. I try to see the apartment through her eyes. It's smaller than my last one. It's messy. My unmade bed is surrounded by concentric circles of palettes, brushes, and splotches diffusing over plastic. The trash overflows with crumpled pages from my sketchbook.

She sniffs.

"Devon." Her tone is severe. "You can't be in here."

She points at the air.

I inhale deeply.

"What?"

"The *paint*."

She strides inside, setting the groceries down on her way to the window. She opens it fast and takes thirsty gulps through the screen. I sniff the air again. It does smell a *little* like paint, but neither of us is at risk. I've spent my life around this stuff. *This* is what most of my memories smell like. *This* makes me feel at home. Icy wind rushes in through the window.

"We have to get out of here."

I don't want to fight her.

I grab a parka and follow her outside. Only when we're on the sidewalk do her shoulders finally drop. The air does smell crisper out here, cleaner.

We find seats in the park. Her low bun is sleek, with a sharp middle part. She's at an angle to me, so the line of her nose curves seamlessly into her eyebrow. Her mouth is small, drawn in on the brink of saying something.

"I'm sorry," she says eventually, "but I'm really worried about you."

"Me?"

"Are you safe with yourself?"

I didn't expect this from Hunter.

Am I *safe* with myself? This isn't something you ask a healthy person. This is something you ask when you think the answer is no. Her suspicion is so dense I can almost see it. It's almost as dark as the smoke around Amber this afternoon, sinuous by her cheekbones. She and I sat right here. By the time we left, she felt familiar, like someone I'd known for much longer than a couple of hours. I wonder who I feel closer to now. Amber, at least, trusts me.

Am I safe with *myself*?

What's the point of answering? When someone has to ask you about your sanity, aren't they inclined to doubt what you say? What does she think I'm going to do, realistically? Destroy my sense of smell with paint fumes? I'm too angry to look her in the eye.

"Devon?"

"What."

"What's going on?"

"We're sitting on benches."

"Are you kidding me? I mean, in your life?" She waits, but I don't fill the gap. I let the blur of city noise do the talking: the growl of buses and brakes, beeping crosswalk signal, spontaneous laughter, and hum of other conversations, but not ours. "I feel like I don't know you anymore. I'm sorry, that was harsh. I know the breakup was hard. But *this*"—she gestures to me as she uses the pronoun—"is not how you get better. *This* is how you lose everything."

This.

Maybe she thinks that severity is appropriate for a pep talk. Maybe she's trying to shake me out of whatever trance is ruining my life. But no matter how hard she tries to make her point, my reaction isn't going to change. I wouldn't be very artistic if I folded every time I met resistance. Force won't be the magic that gets through to me. It's just going to hurt.

"Are you doing this for work?" she says, gesturing at me.

"No, Hunter." I click the *t* sound.

She throws up her hands.

"*This*"—I point at myself—"is not a stunt."

"Do you need help? I'm asking you honestly." She softens her voice, apparently changing tactics. The streetlamp over her head glows like a sinking star. "Help me help you, okay? Do you need to . . . talk to someone? Take time off? Go on a vacation with me? I'll go anywhere you want." She seems desperate.

"The problem isn't that there's something wrong with me. It's that everyone *thinks* there's something wrong with me." Her forehead breaks into a dozen lines. "Well, actually that's not true. There is someone who thinks I'm making sense. Did you know he has a sister he never told me about?" I raise my eyebrows victoriously.

"Who?" she asks.

"Richard."

"I don't care! I don't give a shit about Richard anymore, and neither should you. I'm saying this as your friend. You are not together." She claps her hands after "you," "not," and "together," giving the declaration a beat. "You need to move on. You need to start thinking about the future, start building instead of dissecting."

"You don't think it matters that he has a sister?"

"No! Move *on*. This is destroying you. You're not even making sense to me. I'm sorry." She pinches her nose for a moment. "But even if you *can* show Vanessa was behind everything, you still lose. At this point, winning is moving on. I wouldn't be a good friend if I let you live and stew in the past like this. You need to start looking ahead."

"Are you going to unfriend me?" I ask sardonically.

"I'm not going to stick around while you destroy yourself."

A young couple passes us, absorbed in conversation. They're so wrapped up in each other that they see nothing else—not the jogger sprinting by them, the dog walker branching into five breeds, or me, sitting here staring.

"Do you know what marriage means?" I ask.

"Um, yes?"

"Do you?"

"What are you talking about?"

"Marriage"—I look back at Hunter—"is about committing to someone for richer or poorer, in sickness and in health, until death do you part. *Marriage* is about committing to someone no matter what freak torture life throws at them or at you. Did you know that?" Before

she can answer, I go on: "No, you didn't. No one does. Not you. Not Richard. Not my dad. No one gets it except me."

"Why are you yelling at *me*?"

"Because *you* are just like the rest of them, cherry-picking your life. I'm the only one who seems to know what it means to *commit*. I painted in the dark for a decade before anyone called me a painter. I told Richard I'd spend the rest of my life with him—I gave him my word—and I'm going to keep my promise, whether or not he's going to keep his."

"Devon—"

"I commit, and the rest of you leave when things get hard."

"I'm here, Devon."

"To tell me that you're leaving."

"Just because your parents let you down doesn't mean everyone else will."

Her voice is gentle, but the message is alarming. There is suddenly too much pain. It's like raw skin in my body, an open emotional wound. How did she just reach so deep inside me?

I leave without saying goodbye and walk until I don't recognize the street cafés. Fairy lights glow on narrow roads. I keep going a few more blocks, still feeling like I've swallowed something corrosive. I want to cry it out, hack at it. Kill the feeling however I can. Eventually, I head home. Alone, where no one can hurt me, I do what I've always done.

THIRTY-FOUR

I wake up the next morning to blue light. Across the room, my skeleton piece appears to be waiting for me. I notice pressure on my shoulder.

Is something on top of me?

It's one of my paintings, covering my body like a sheet. I lift it up: this is the portrait I was working on last night. But now, it's a smeared pinwheel. A hazy imprint of the picture sticks to me, dyeing my clothes different shades of purple. It looks like the fabric itself is bruised. Is the painting ruined or just not what I intended? Did it fall apart or just mature? I stare until it looks like a mirror—or until *I* look like a mirror. There'd be no difference either way.

I strip naked and remember what happened. My studio is so crammed I had to hang this piece by my bed. It must've fallen overnight. I find my phone on the floor with a new voicemail—from Richard. My hands are too oily to press play. I run into the bathroom and wash them hard, but I'm not patient enough to clean them completely. I dry them while they're tinted and hurry into clothes, as if listening to the voicemail is a social engagement, and I need to be decent.

"Hi, Devon," he says.

I press pause and hold the phone to my forehead. This is the closest I've been to him in months. I want to savor it, slow it down. These words will only be new once, and I don't know if I'll ever get another message from him.

I start it over.

"Hi, Devon. I'm sorry to tell you like this, but Amber isn't well. She was almost committed in high school. She had a breakdown and stopped making sense. Listening to her . . . it was like reading alphabet soup. She thought there was a plot against her. My parents tried to send her to an institution, but before they could, she cut ties with everyone and ran away. She changed her name. I don't know how she got in touch with you, but I'd be careful. She's very sick."

There's a beat of silence.

"I'm sorry you found out this way. I wanted to tell you sooner, but . . . Mom couldn't handle the grief. It's hard to explain, but I was trying to help her. Besides, I'd reached out to Amber dozens of times, and she never responded. A part of me felt like she'd died." Another pause lengthens. "I'm sorry you were surprised. If you need anything at all, please let me know.

"And please take care of yourself."

I hit replay. I know him so well I can picture how his lips would move with every word. "Alphabet soup"? But Amber made perfect sense to me. No one had made that much sense in a very long time.

~

I can't keep listening to the voicemail.

That afternoon, I force myself to put my phone down.

Finished pieces for my next show surround me. In places, paint bleeds through the weave, whispering about the other side. I glance back at my phone by the sink. It's not right that this message is all I have left of him. This short, static clip. I've played it so many times it doesn't even surprise me anymore: the measured tempo, bordering on formal. The one slight register shift, creeping higher when he says, *A part of me felt like she'd died.* The undercurrent of his breathing, gently rocking back and forth. He was always so gentle. Tender and kind.

He and I only ever had one problem.

One petite, elegant problem.

She's on my mind like glare from the sun as I walk up to the nearest canvas. My fingers touch the stapled corner. I can identify this painting just from the drips on the edge. It's a close-up of a pelvic arch. Bones tend to be hard to paint because we don't know what live ones look like. Most of us only see them in cold white pieces. But I managed to give this one an inner glow. I rub the drizzled canvas, dragging my thumb over bumps in the grid. One mark is still wet. I smear it, my thumb moving forward, getting dangerously close to the work. My thumb's right on the line now, grazing the front, smudging the thinnest streak across the top.

And—I have an idea for my next project.

It's perfect, terrible.

Maybe too dark, even for me.

Then again, maybe I want to lean into the darkness. Maybe I want to dance with the devil. Maybe I want to go deep into my shadows and use everything I have—all the twisted thorns, sunken ships. Because maybe I'm ready to meet my own evil. Then, even if the world scares me, at least I won't scare myself.

I stand over the painting, thumb stained.

The idea lingers.

I must have some morbid curiosity, too, the urge to look under the rock. And doesn't truly great work require you to risk everything? I rub my thumb on my pants, watching the color until it disappears. In a way, this wouldn't be too different from what I've always done. When things matter, I commit. Would I be going through with this for my art or my life? I don't know, but committing is the only way to get it right. The only way to make it—a masterpiece.

Invigorated, I carry my old paintings to the street. I leave them against a tree on the sidewalk, arranged like the start of a bonfire. Soggy brown leaves around the trunk muddy the bottom of each canvas. When I'm finally back in my apartment, I feel a sense of relief. My studio is wide open, ready for something even better.

I text Marc: You're going to love the new ones.

He's typing.

He replies with a photo of *The Scream*, by Edvard Munch. Staring at the open mouth—its empty yellow pit—I realize that my relationship with Marc isn't quite what I thought. All this time, there was a nuance I missed: he doesn't represent *me*. He represents my *art*. If I'm destroyed in the process, that may only raise the value of what he wishes to sell. Tragedy could transform a decent work into a dark spectacular. The thought stays as I draw curtains and turn on tripod lights.

It haunts the room as I paint.

THIRTY-FIVE

The next night, I'm in bed googling tips to cope with anxiety. Is that the right term, "anxiety"? The word feels too mild. Too much like a general cloud, not like this sharp attack to the head. My thoughts race so fast they hurt. I scroll through my phone, the only light in my room. The most common advice is to journal: write your thoughts, slow the mind.

I buy a composition book and pens from the nearest CVS. Back in my apartment, I sit on my mattress and open the notebook.

I write.

I start at the beginning, when Richard and I met. I describe our first date, his first "I love you." Then the moment he asked me to move in. I remember it down to the colors in the snow: gray scale with hints of blue. We were in Telluride, where I turned out to be a great skier— because I had no fear. Hearing my skis scream down a mountain just didn't scare me. Richard and I were on top of a peak, at the start of another steep run, when I mentioned my lease was ending. He asked, "Would you like to live with me more formally?" I smiled, thinking of my clothes in his bureau, my paintbrushes in his dishwasher. "Yes, please."

Even more important than the milestones, though, were the ordinary days when he made me feel understood. His compliments were specific and unique. I write down my favorites. The first time we went to the Met together, he said I was a rare blend of opposites: sensual and structured. He said that as if I were magical, able to pick blue flowers out of the sky. I write about his body, the way he'd thrust his hands into his pockets with a thumb hanging loose. The angle between his thumb and forefinger was unusually wide. And he could wink better than anyone else, his face perfectly still while his eye sent a private message.

But then, we got engaged.

I detail the slights that followed, starting with Vanessa's reference to Richard's ex from Colby. It's almost impressive how quickly, how casually she desecrated my most precious spot. How she wedged another woman into my proposal. I describe the day she warned Richard I might not be a healthy partner. The way she treated my body like some-*thing* she could stuff. I transcribe so much I can almost feel her in the room with me, coming off the words like smoke.

Finally, I write about Vanessa's disappearance with such precision that I list what was in the refrigerator on the day she went missing. I recite the weeks that followed through to this lonely night. I'm not sure what day it is anymore. I'm not sure if the writing has brought me any peace, but at least I finally feel tired.

Exhausted, really.

THIRTY-SIX

Monday, February 14
8:30 p.m.

I went to CVS this afternoon (81 8th Avenue, the building that used to be a 19th century five-story bank). I don't know what time I got there, but it was bright enough to shock me when I left my apartment. I don't know how long I stayed, but I just needed milk (64oz Horizon 2%, it came with the warning: contains milk). What I know for sure is there was only one other customer in the store. We never crossed paths, but I saw them a few times, from opposite ends of the same aisle.

I didn't think much of it.

I just went outside to pick up dinner. On the bench across the street, it's the same person from this afternoon. They're in the same Barbour jacket and baseball cap. The cap was too low over their face for me to get a good look. Man or woman, I don't know. I couldn't see any of their hair either. They weren't doing anything. They were just sitting alone in the dark—even though it's Valentine's Day, the one night you don't spend alone.

Of course they're not following me. Why would they? Still, it makes me uneasy to see the same person twice in one day. I don't see anyone consistently, except for the barista at Muse. Everyone else rotates.

I shouldn't be afraid.

I just wanted to write that down.

THIRTY-SEVEN

Tuesday, February 15
3:00 p.m.

I just saw them again at Muse (236 West 10th). When I turned around with my drink, they were standing across the street: hands in their pockets, facing me, not moving at all, a still life. They wore the same Barbour jacket and baseball cap. The cap was dark pine green with a white crest: a shield with mantling and wings on either side. They wore it the same way as last time, low enough to hide their face.

But I could tell they were staring at me.

Then they just walked away.

I wished they ran, though, showed nerves. Their pace was too confident. It was how someone walks when they're one step ahead. It scared me into staying at Muse. I hovered by the straws and packets of sugar, needing nothing. My hands shook. I kept wondering, What do they want? Are they going to hurt me? But if they plan to do that, I wouldn't have seen them—right? They would've kept surprise on their side. This person must want me to notice them. Are they trying to intimidate me? Or do they have more in store, and this is just the beginning? . . .

THIRTY-EIGHT

I keep track of the sightings in my journal.

The person following me is a man, I write on Friday, February 18. *He was just outside the grocery store (Westside Market, 77 7th Avenue) when I was checking out. I saw him on the sidewalk, and for the first time, he didn't have his head bowed. I saw the bottom half of his face: wide jaw, brown veil of stubble. I only saw his chin, but I know I've never seen it before. I've never met this man in my life.*

I buy an extra lock for my door.

I buy a Taser and sleep with it under my mattress.

Who are you?

I scribble the question.

Again and again.

The only clues I have are his clothes. The Barbour jacket must mean something. I'd never seen a coat like that before I met Richard.

Is this man from Greenwich?

I can't sleep for long anymore. I have no problem falling asleep, but every night, I wake up terrified a couple of hours later. I buy a handful of things that might help from CVS: melatonin, Benadryl. The woman who bags them doesn't seem entirely sober. Even with sleep aids, the night terrors are relentless. *I don't care!* Hunter's voice returns in my dreams. *This is destroying you. You're not even making sense to me.* Richard speaks up too. *Listening to her . . . it was like reading alphabet soup.* My worst nightmares only rehash things that actually happened. Waking up doesn't make me feel any better. My art looks more sinister in moonlight.

THIRTY-NINE

I take a seat in Gretchen's office a couple of weeks later. *Are you happy I'm back?* I almost ask. Her expression is impassive, her blue jumper neat over tights. Even her shoes are clean: black clogs that reflect soft lights. I cross one of my biker boots over the other. Both are crusted with rock salt, but this position hides some of the grime.

Gretchen: It's been a while.

Me: Yes. Thanks for making the time today, kind of last minute. I didn't know who else to ask. I just—really need some help.

Gretchen: Help with what?

Me: Someone's following me. I don't know who, but whenever I leave my apartment, I see him. He gets just close enough that I spot him. I want to go to the police, but I don't have evidence yet. I've been keeping track of everywhere he shows up—which is something—but I need more. I've been trying to take photos of him, but he never faces me for long. As soon as I notice him, he turns around and leaves. Like he has all the time in the world.

Gretchen: Why would he do that?

Me: I don't know.

Gretchen: Have you done any drugs recently?

Me: He's not a delusion.

Gretchen: I hear you, Devon, I'm just trying to get a fuller picture of your life these days. It's been a while since we talked, and I notice you're here now without Richard, without your engagement ring.

Me: I'm not here to talk about him. We're not together anymore. The most urgent problem I have is the person who's following me. He knows where I live, and my building barely has any security. There's a front door that locks, but some people leave it open. This man could be dangerous.

Gretchen: Right. Before I hear more about that, just a question about your family history. Is there any mental illness on either side?

Me:

Gretchen: I know you want to talk about this man, and we will. Like I said, though, I'm just getting a better picture of your life first.

Me: There's some . . . alcoholism down the line? Really far down the line. But this has nothing to do with an addiction. I'm talking about being followed by someone in real life, not in my mind.

Gretchen: Alcoholism isn't just "an addiction." Sometimes, people use alcohol to self-medicate another disorder. In other words, people can drink to cope with all kinds of disturbances: bipolar, depression, and—

Me: That's irrelevant. I'm telling you that someone is following me, and I can't sleep. I am asking for your help. Do you hear me?

Gretchen: What I'm hearing is that you see someone following you around your neighborhood, but you don't have any evidence of him yet.

So, there are two roads ahead of us. One is the road we take before you have any proof. On this road, I can help you be more mindful of your daily habits, especially sleep, diet, and exercise. These are the building blocks for internal stability. Then, once we agree that those are in a positive place, I can help you draw connections between your thoughts and behavior. We can tease out which thoughts aren't serving you well. That alone can work wonders.

The second road begins once there's proof: a photo, video, something concrete. That's when we would get other authorities involved.

Me: Do you know what it's like for no one to believe you?

Gretchen:

Me: That's not rhetorical. Do you know what it's like?

Gretchen:

Me: You know, if I were to do my life over, I wouldn't have been a painter.

Gretchen: Why is that?

Me: Because life is about power. And when you have power, you have a voice. When you don't have power, you're mute. There's no power in painting. A few people get it, but most don't. My decision to paint was an act of faith. I put my trust in the world, saying, "Will you take care of me if I do what I love?" And the world didn't give anything back. Now, I have no power left, and no one hears a word I say. I have to come crawling here to you, someone I pay, to tell you that my life is on the line—that a strange man is following me around where I live—and even here, you don't believe me.

Gretchen: Are you still painting?

Me: [laughs]

Gretchen: What's so funny?

Me: Yes, I'm still painting. I have a few six-by-four pieces of the world, where I can direct my truth as a human being. And no one ever has to look at them, much less understand them, much less believe them.

Someone is following me.

FORTY

Home after the session, I sit on my mattress and lean against the wall. My apartment looks as empty as I feel. All my paintings were moved to the Zellweger Gallery this morning. Two will hang in the new show tomorrow night.

My outstretched legs point at nothing.

When I spent more time in museums, I wouldn't just look at the paintings. I'd watch the security guards too. I've always believed that art changes people. So I studied the ones who spent most of their waking lives in the Impressionism exhibit at the Met, for example. How exactly did the masterworks affect them? I never found anything obvious—no one was floating—but I kept looking, believing they were different for living with iconic haystacks and water lilies. On the other side of the spectrum, living with*out* art must have an equally profound effect, and right now, I feel it. In this lonely room, with lonely walls, something in me aches.

I'm not one to blame other people, but tonight is an exception. I am here at my limit, tired and unable to sleep, because of Vanessa. Why did she do this to me? She had everything, and she took what little I had for myself.

I should confront her.

Hear it from *her* why I'm here.

I sit up straight.

Of course. That's exactly what I should do.

I don't know how she spends her days now. But if she's healthy enough to get out of bed, she must be taking her morning walks. That's when I'll find her. I'll ask why she did this to me, and—I'll tape it. I'll bring my phone and record it all from my pocket. If Vanessa admits something, I'll have the evidence I've always wanted. If she goes so far as to hurt me, I'll have proof of that too. I can't believe I didn't think of this sooner. Things didn't need to spiral out of control.

I plan it meticulously, as if it's an underdrawing, a charcoal guide for the paint to come. I'll rent a car at Enterprise in Midtown. It's only a one-hour drive to Greenwich. She used to finish her walks by seven, so I should leave around five thirty. Naturally, if Vanessa *were* kidnapped on a walk, I doubt she'd resume the habit. It would be too unnerving to return to the exact place where she was taken. But she and I both know that didn't happen.

My phone rings—Marc.

"Devon, hi."

He sounds distracted—or, fascinated.

"Do you know what I'm looking at?" he asks.

I don't. What time is it?

I pull the curtain aside to check.

"Your work scares me more every time," he says.

I imagine him at the gallery, squinting at my canvases. Meanwhile, the world burns outside my window. A red sunset fills the cracks between brick buildings. I feel lightheaded and drop my head between my knees.

"Do you know the story of how Friedrich Nietzsche died?" he asks.

"No."

"Sometime in his forties, he was walking around Italy when he saw a horse getting whipped." Marc's tone is legato. "The horse's owner was unleashing his fury. Apparently, Nietzsche was so affected by it, he charged ahead and threw his arms around the horse's neck. He tried to save the animal. According to some people, he sank to his knees and wept uncontrollably. He was almost arrested for disturbing the peace until his friend walked him home.

"Nietzsche spent the next two days in a vegetative state. Two weeks later, he was enrolled in a mental asylum. In the decade that followed, the last years of his life, he was considered mad." I imagine Marc saying this as he stands in the exact middle of my painting, as though he's just emerged from its world. "When people look back on Nietzsche's life, they point to his encounter with the horse as a turning point, the exact moment when he lost his mind."

Why is he telling me this?

"So, Devon?" he asks.

"Yes?"

"What was your horse?"

PART FOUR

FORTY-ONE

I turn the key, bringing my rental car to life. It's a smooth drive out of Enterprise into Midtown. Dark streets glow yellow and red with traffic signals. My mission gives me a calming sense of peace as taxis cut me off, as a silhouette jaywalks in front of me.

The sun rises slowly.

The interstate is wide.

I'm comfortable even though I'm in the minority, opposing the flow of the morning commute. The other side is packed, while I'm on my own. I don't turn on any music. It's so quiet it feels like the silence is inside everything, even in the ground and short green sprouts on either side of the road. I love silence like this more than I've ever loved a song. It's more than peaceful; it's like staring at Robert Rauschenberg's *White Painting*, three panels of plain, solid white.

My exit approaches.

The roads narrow.

My heartbeat picks up as the lawns expand. I can almost feel the gravity of Richard's house pulling me closer. I pass two outdoor riding rings. A pair of bronze eagles perch on gateposts, their wings wide as if the statues are about to lift. I reach the Belmonts' neighbors and stop. There's no one around, nothing but a few clouds' shadows drifting over grass.

I squeeze my phone.

It's slick. I'm sweating.

Maybe Mom could calm me down. I call her, but as it rings, I'm finding it harder to breathe. The air feels thin, as if Richard and I are back in Telluride, at nine thousand feet, and he's only just asked me to move in with him.

No answer.

Mom's voicemail is full.

I call again.

It rings itself to death.

Her voicemail is full.

I stare at my phone.

Are you okay?

If you're not, who would know?

Mom and I have been so close recently, but she's never mentioned anyone else by name. Has she mentioned anyone at *all?* It's hard to think here on Waverley, within sight of the Belmonts' front gate. The pickets look like teeth. An unhinged bottom jaw. I close my eyes. Mom doesn't belong to any clubs or groups. The only person who I *know* she's seen in the past few months was the neighbor who complained about her dandelions. Mom's an—individual, not that I blame her. I am too. But when you live in your own world, there's no one around to help.

I call again. And again.

What else can I do? I could call the event planning company where she works as a temp, but it's not open yet. Do I still have her AA sponsor's number? I never met Teresa, but years ago, Mom gave me her contact just in case. She never said in case of *what*. Here it is: Teresa Lamont. This isn't a great option, but it feels like my only one. I dial Teresa.

The ringing stops abruptly.

"Hello? Teresa?"

"Who is this?" she asks sleepily.

"It's Devon, Grace's daughter. Grace Ferrell?"

"What's going on?"

"I was hoping you could tell me. I can't get through to my mom. I don't know if you've talked to her recently?" I wipe one hand on my khakis.

"Grace hasn't been to a meeting in months."

"She was doing all right. Honestly, we've been calling each other a lot, and she's been clear every time. I just—have a bad feeling." It's like ink in my stomach, full of tendrils, spreading. "I know this is a big ask. I'm not even sure if you're in the same neighborhood. But is there any chance you might be able to check on her? Just to make sure she's . . . ?"

It sounds like Teresa's sitting up in bed: creaking headboard, rustling sheets. But I still can't picture her. I've never met Teresa. I've never even seen a photo of her. She's just a name, a voice. A silence grows, and I press my phone into my ear in case I might miss something. In case she's going to whisper her answer. The sound of her breathing gets louder.

"I'll drive by, but I'm afraid there's not much more I can do."

"Thank you. Also . . ."

My knees bob.

"Did Mom ever . . . ," I find myself saying. "Did she ever talk about self-medicating for a disorder? I don't want to—"

Vanessa strides onto the road in black leggings and a zip-up. She turns away from me and maintains a brisk, heart-thumping pace. I thank Teresa and hang up, vaguely hearing my phone hit the floor mat.

I step out of the car.

Vanessa moves confidently ahead, not even looking over her shoulder. Her bob is still a crisp yellow stripe. It's the brightest thing on the street, ending with a sharp cut across the neck. It's so familiar I can almost hear her humming again, the way she used to set her life to music. It was her own unique vibration, never louder than a hushed conversation. As the gates close to 654 Waverley, I glance inside. The long driveway leads to a front door so far away it's practically invisible. As if the estate doesn't have a way in or out.

Vanessa turns a corner.

I pick up speed until we're on the same road. There's no one else here, not even passing cars. The properties on either side are tucked away. I'm just a few paces behind her now. She keeps a slight spring in her step, favoring the balls of her feet.

"Vanessa!" I call.

She stops and turns around.

Looks left and right.

"I just want to talk," I say, holding up my hands.

"About what?"

We hold our places, ten feet apart.

She looks just like I remember. This is how I see her when I'm alone, my mental picture accurate down to the point of her nose. She has the same clarity in her skin—no freckles, nothing but gloss. Her kidnappers were kind to spare her face, to keep so much of her intact. Or is she going to tell me the truth? She glances sideways again, but there are only shaking trees.

"Why did you do this?" My voice breaks.

"Do you really want to know?"

My phone's in the car.

I glance back, feeling the weight of my mistake. We're in an unseen crack of space, on unrecorded time. I can't believe I've left it behind, that extra eye, the ear that I desperately need. There's no use to my visit now except my own peace of mind. I face Vanessa again, feeling like I've ambushed us both, surprised myself as much as her. I'm still out of breath from the jog, but I rise to my full height. I ask again why she did it—and she smiles.

"I'm glad it's just the two of us now. I always felt like we didn't get enough time together, didn't you?" Her tone is polite and unnervingly calm. Her poise makes me feel like she has the upper hand. I keep my mouth shut, pant through my nose. "There were so many distractions before. But here we finally are.

"You see, Devon, believe it or not, I have a lot of respect for you. Did you know I never could make art myself?" She grins as if this is an amusing, relevant question. "I always *appreciated* art, but when you handed me a brush, I was useless." She flaps one arm in an unsettling demonstration of someone with no elbow, no wrist. "That didn't stop me from loving the greats. If anything, it made me love them more.

"And I admire that you hold on to your roughness." She continues to answer her own question without sharing why it's important. I feel like she's leading me deeper and deeper into a dark room. "It irks me, but I admire it: you'll never be fully civilized. You're in the world of fine art, one of the poshest circles there is, and you still have an animal in you." She says "animal" with some intrigue. "You're smart enough to know how to blend in. But you're just not interested in other people's rules." Wind slides through branches.

"The thing is, I know you respect me too. If you didn't, I wouldn't have been able to get to you. I wouldn't have been the voice in your head. You can't be tormented by someone unless you're a little desperate for them to love you." Before I can disagree, she continues: "So, this doesn't have to be an unpleasant conversation. We can talk to each other with mutual respect. You don't have to corner me. And I don't have to lie. It can be . . . enjoyable."

"I *respect* you?"

By now, I've caught my breath.

"Yes, much more than that." She sounds gracefully convinced. "You might've thought you were with my son, but we were in an intimate relationship too." I show my distaste, which only seems to please her. "Richard is part of me, Devon. I taught him how to walk without holding the coffee table. I taught him how to say his name. I answered every question he had and made him who he is. You can't draw a line where *he* stops and *I* begin." I wish I could argue, but she's staring at me with Richard's eyes. His are the same hot blue in the same bright ring of lashes.

"Of course I was going to matter to you," she says, "but I didn't expect how *much*. You must've felt it too: I had strange power in your life. An oddly central role in your world. I wasn't sure why, but it was nothing a detective couldn't find out for me." I stay perfectly still. "The day after we met, I hired Liam to take a closer look. I was standing here, actually, when I made the call." She points at her feet. The road is the same color as the sky. "He told me Grace got fired from her last job for . . . calling everyone there an actor? They were impersonating her colleagues?"

"She's better now."

"How optimistic." Her smile is playful. "So, that explained our connection. You weren't just in love with my son. I was the mom you never had." She speaks slowly, as if she likes the way her words taste. "Grace wasn't strong enough for you. She wasn't even strong enough for herself. Schizo—"

"Stop it."

She shrugs. "Don't tell me you didn't crave a mother. Once I understood that, our relationship made sense. I understood why you—someone who doesn't seek approval—wanted mine even more than I expected. You can pretend that you only cared about my opinion when it came between you and Richard. But the truth is that you cared about me. You were desperate for me to be the woman that life never gave you. For me to love and understand you in the way you never were." Her voice is gently sympathetic. "I know what that's like. The truth is we have that in common: we weren't just looking for a partner; we were looking for our real family. Everyone wants a home, but you and I needed one. We had a ferocious desire to nest.

"The trouble was . . . I couldn't let you stay. Because when you've felt homeless your whole life, you'll do anything to protect the place that welcomes you. If you'd gotten comfortable on Waverley, you would've dug in your heels. Defended your spot with a primal vengeance." Two crows land on the tree behind her. "If you spent too long with us, and then I got in your way, I knew firsthand what you'd do."

"Which was?"

"Treat me the way I treated Agnes."

Her posture doesn't waver. She's a straight line from her forehead to her ankles, her limbs evenly balanced. *The way I treated Agnes.* There's no anxiety in her fingers, no twitch in her knees. No physical sign of remorse.

"I hate to admit how easy it was to get rid of you." She looks mildly disappointed. "Just a few questions about your food, your mind. A few tiny personal invasions." The crows are still, their eyes like dark glass. "Then I warned Liam you might try to hurt me. I told Clarke to hire him if anything happened. I made myself scarce for a few days. It really was that simple." She interlaces her hands on one thigh, linking her arms in a relaxed but triumphant V. "I am sorry I couldn't let you into our lives. I did want more time with you. But people like us are too dangerous."

I suddenly feel too close to her.

I step back, unsure which part of her confession is most alarming. *The way I treated Agnes.* Her tone was morally absolved. I can imagine how she must've felt meeting the Belmonts, finding people who understood her. But she twisted it into a vicious excuse, justified the unthinkable with her need for family. And then, every mention of *you and I.* As if we're similarly violent. As if there's a dark lineage running through us, staining us in the same terrible ways.

Maybe the most haunting part is that she thinks I wanted her to *mother* me. Wanted her to be that intimately twisted into my life. Presuming that role is more than invasive. It feels like an unholy kind of trespassing.

Part of me wants to argue with her. I'd tell her that I don't wish her motherhood on anyone—I've met Amber. I know how Vanessa treats her own daughter, and I want none of that. I'd tell her that my mom and I get closer every year. That *real* family isn't about how much you have in common; it's about how much you forgive. How much you let happen and hold on because *that's* how much they matter. I could debate her, but the bigger part of me wants distance from her.

I never needed Vanessa to raise me, love me. And I don't need that from her now.

I take another step back. One more.

The farther I get, the calmer I feel.

This is what I should've done at the beginning: put space between us. Refuse to give her power over me. She deflates more with every step I take, as if she doesn't just believe she's my maternal missing piece—it's as if she likes it that way.

I turn my back on her.

"Richard doesn't mention you," she says.

I pivot halfway.

"I just thought you should know that he never brings you up." She steps toward me, reclosing the gap. "You know, I told you that I couldn't make art, but I did make something else. I made a beautiful family, didn't I? You can almost see them from here." She points to the blur of their estate through the trees. "Richard, Oliver, Clarke, and I eat together every night. We talk about Richard Serra and the oak aging of the day's wine. I have the family I always wanted. I wasn't born with it, but I made it, Devon. I made it with my bare hands." I imagine those hands turning the steering wheel in Agnes's car. "So let me be clear: there's plenty that I like about you. But I didn't spend my life on this so you could take it away from me.

"You'll have to kill me first."

"I won't have to," I say.

"They're not tied up. They want to be at home." A part of her looks conflicted, maybe even apologetic, as she turns around. "Thanks for stopping by," she calls over her shoulder. "But if I see you again, I'm afraid I'll have to call the police. And I'm rather close with them these days."

I watch the bright back of her head, feeling at peace as she fades.

Never more at peace than when she's gone.

～

I return the car to Enterprise and cut through the nearest park. It's a crowded green sharing one edge with the New York Public Library. There are so many landscape painters here that they paint each other into their scenes. I sneak through the sidewalk traffic. The only part of Greenwich that I miss is the privacy. On Waverley Road, I didn't see a soul except Vanessa. I didn't leave any footprints in the grass, didn't even disturb the worms. Only she knows I was there.

I should focus on my new show tonight, but I can't stop . . . enjoying the peace. I never should've doubted myself. Of course Vanessa was trying to get rid of me. She was trying to provoke me all along. If I'd been this sure months ago, she never could've gotten to me. I would've been cool as a stone as she tried to dismantle my life.

I slip past countless men in overcoats, countless backs of heads.

My phone rings—Mom.

"Why did I wake up to Teresa knocking on my window?"

Her voice is eerily calm.

"I'm sorry, I thought—"

I reject an incoming call from Teresa.

"You thought what?" she asks.

"I don't know," I lie.

"I think you do."

"I was just trying to help."

My stomach twists.

"I'm sorry, Mom."

"If you want to *help* me, then *trust* me." She hangs up.

I stare at my phone, ashamed. This is the first setback in our relationship that's been *my* fault. What was I thinking? It couldn't have been six a.m. her time when I called Teresa in a frenzy. Mom's always been an early riser—like me—but still, missing calls *that* early isn't a reason to panic.

I call Teresa back, fragile.

"Hi, Teresa. I'm sorry."

"Don't be." She sounds out of breath.

"What happened?"

Her breathing slows.

A car door opens and shuts.

"Sorry, I didn't mean for any of that," she says, more recovered. "I tried, Devon. I drove to Grace's. I thought I would just look through the window—but I couldn't tell if she was okay. She was crawling on the floor in a circle . . ." When her voice drops, I plug one ear with an index finger. "I wasn't sure if she'd dropped something. I rubbed the fog off the glass to get a better look. She must've seen me. She stood up and started shouting."

"She just called. She sounded clear."

I feel Teresa's lingering doubt.

"I'm sorry to blow up your morning," I go on. "I was just anxious about something else. I shouldn't have asked that of you. I won't do it again."

"People can only be helped when they want to be."

"I know."

"Until then, nothing will change."

FORTY-TWO

Saturday, March 5

6:00 p.m.

My new show starts soon.

I didn't see the man today. But I wish I did.

This could be the biggest night of my career. The gallery will swarm with collectors, photographers, and journalists. And for once, I feel optimistic about my work. Marc loves this new direction more than anything I've ever done. He said yesterday that he's eager to show more of my paintings. He has a new space in Chinatown, where he'd like to hang twenty of my pieces this year.

Twenty—it's a dream.

I've been to opening nights before, but never feeling so supported by Marc. I always got the sense that he was ultimately indifferent—that he thought I had talent, but he wouldn't force the world to agree. Now, I feel like he's a real advocate. He wants to fight for my work. He went on about how these new pieces chilled him. He said they gave him nightmares, not knowing they came from mine.

The man must know all of this. He's trailed me for weeks. He must know that tonight is the culmination of everything I've ever worked for, every painting I've ever made. All the dark nights, the doubts. The cross-country move, people lost, and art no one will see. Going deeper than anyone should for their work. Going through all of that for decades and still showing up to work alone. He must know it's time for the finale. And maybe he was absent today because he was getting prepared.

I get dressed for the show. None of my clothes fit anymore—except for a pair of black biker boots, though they feel heavier than ever. I've been too nervous to eat well for weeks. I pull the belt tight around loose black jeans.

Richard always called me his Dev, but only now do I appreciate the name. I am his fork-tongued Dev. I'm a destroyer and a tormentor, not even sparing myself. Without Richard, there's been no one to stop me from becoming my own victim. In just one season, my body's collapsed like a needled balloon. I look more like Amber than ever—dark makeup, dark clothes, sheer skin—but with sadder eyes. I have all of her punk and none of her defenses: no anger, no barbs. I feel like I have nothing left to protect myself, not even that brief, hopeful connection with my mom.

I open my front door a crack and peer down the hallway. There's no one in sight between the chipping gray walls. Nothing waits for me on the scuffed brown carpet. As far as I can tell, the way forward is safe. I hurry downstairs, and when I'm finally outside, I do a full spin on the street, checking every angle.

It's a half-hour walk to the show. Each step is quicker than the last until I commit to running. When I finally cross the threshold to the Zellweger Gallery, my lungs burn. I feel like I'm being torn in half. I double over and catch my breath.

Marc's loafers waltz into view.

"Running from your horse?" he asks.

FORTY-THREE

The next morning, I wake up to the most beautiful beige beam of sun. My sheets are the color of steeped tea, rippling to my toes. This studio may be small, but it gets the same sun as the nicest places in the world. I savor it before grabbing my phone.

No new messages. I check the news.

It's not long before I find the headline: **Greenwich Mom Found Dead in Hit-and-Run.** My heartbeat picks up, softly clapping.

I'm not sure I want to read it.

But of course I do.

The article claims that Vanessa Belmont was killed outside her home. She was apparently hit by a car and then discovered at the scene today by one of her children. Was it Oliver? Or Richard? I imagine him at the end of their driveway—or wherever it happened—and raising a horrified hand to his mouth. The *New York Post* runs the same story under a different headline: **Connecticut Mom Murdered on Family Lawn.** Included with that article is a bird's-eye view of the Belmonts' estate on a glorious day. In the photo, their pool is uncovered—I've never seen it open before. It's a dazzling aquamarine in the shape of a capital letter *T*. Stripes in the lawn show where it was recently mowed. Overall, the house has never looked better. It feels a little strange that they paired her story with such a magnificent shot.

FORTY-FOUR

I'm sketching the next morning when my buzzer rings. I figure it was a mistake, so I stay put in my spot on the floor. I'm drawing the skinny middle of an apple core, while a real one rests on the corner of my sketchbook. It curves like an hourglass, red on both ends. My buzzer beeps again, loud, insistent, leading me over to the intercom.

"Devon, it's Detective McInnis. Do you have a moment?"

"Hi, uh—yes, sure."

I buzz him in and listen. There's no one else on the stairwell, no sounds other than his nearing steps. When they reach my floor, I check the peephole—and it's him, scanning each door as he passes it. He looks somber in a gray polo shirt.

I unlock my door three times.

We greet each other with guarded nods.

Once he's inside, I check the hallway for anyone who might've followed him into the building. All I find are silent apartments. I shut my front door, lock it again, then turn to face the detective. He's moving ahead, surveying my space, with his back to me. In the middle of the room, one of the black seeds falls off my apple. It hits the page without a sound.

"Did you hear the news?" he asks.

"Which news?"

"About Vanessa."

"Oh, right. Yes."

He stops short and sniffs audibly.

"Sorry." I gesture to open buckets of paint. "Occupational hazard."

After I crack the window, he beelines to the screen. I return to the front door while he stays, taking greedy swallows of fresh air. As if the room is filled with invisible smoke. It takes him a moment to settle. When he turns back around, his gaze briefly registers the stack of journals. He pulls out his own pad and clicks a pen to life.

"Clarke hired me to find who did this." His tone is flat, his mood appropriately grim. "So, I'm talking to everyone who was close to Vanessa over the past year. If you don't mind me asking, how'd you hear the news?"

I point to my bed. The mattress cover has slipped off to expose a bare blue corner. The comforter rests in a tangle on top.

"I read it there on my phone."

"When was the last time you talked to Vanessa?"

My cheeks feel warm.

"Months ago. Before Richard and I broke up."

He stares at me.

"All right," he declares.

The trust in his tone is relieving.

"And where were you two nights ago?" he asks.

"I had a new show." He nods as if he isn't surprised. "I got to the gallery by seven. It went until eleven, and then, everyone went to the NoMad for drinks. I was there until . . . maybe four? I'd sold both my paintings that night and wanted to celebrate."

"How'd you feel when you got the news?"

"The way everyone felt."

A beat.

"Horrified, of course," I add.

He looks at me for almost too long.

"I believe you," he says eventually. "One more thing."

As he reaches for his phone, I remember how much I used to resent this man for digging into my personal life. Now, I appreciate it. He knows all my secrets, and he's come to the conclusion that I'm innocent. He shared some things about his parents too. It's almost like he's my friend, this Mr. Liam McInnis.

When he turns his phone to me, my newest painting gleams on-screen. In *Veiled Watcher*, a lone figure in a Barbour jacket sits on a park bench. It's mostly a peaceful scene: grass in dappled light, touches of the cityscape beyond the park. There's the smooth blur of people moving around him. Almost everything is unsurprising and pastel. But under this man's baseball cap, a smoky knot replaces his face. It's a violent, scratched-out mess of shadows.

"You want to tell me about this one?" he asks.

"He's been following me for weeks."

"Who?"

"I don't know. A man in a Barbour jacket and a baseball cap." I walk over to the wall and stand beside the journals. "Here," I say, pointing at them. "I kept track of every place I saw him and when. I added as much detail as I could." I pick them up. "Honestly, I haven't slept in weeks. I got an extra lock for my door." I point to it emphatically. Detective McInnis turns and sees the lock for himself. "I saw a therapist about it. I had no idea what he wanted."

"You ever get any photos?" he asks.

I shake my head.

"Videos? Any proof?" he presses.

"He never stuck around for long. He must've just wanted me to *see* him, because as soon as I did, he was gone." I hold the journals out to him. Detective McInnis opens the top one and skims an entry. His light eyes skip down the page. "Two days ago, I didn't see him at all. I thought he was preparing for something to do with *me*. I never thought his victim would be . . ."

"Vanessa."

He asks for my permission to photograph the journals, then takes a series of shots. He tells me he'll call if he has more questions. Once the journals are back on the floor, we make our way to the door. We're on the threshold when my phone vibrates in my pocket.

I check the name—Amber.

"Who is it?" he asks.

"Spam." I pocket my phone again.

He lingers as if he has one more thing to ask.

Instead, he says a crisp goodbye, and I'm almost sad to see him go. It wasn't long ago that I counted on him to look at me when no one else would. Come closer when everyone else stepped back. At my last opening, he was the only one to stand in front of my work and give it the dignity of his attention. Now, he's the only person I've ever hosted in this studio for more than a couple of minutes. He may know more about me than anyone.

I watch his red flare disappear, still holding the door open when I'm alone.

FORTY-FIVE

I'm painting the apple core a few days later when my phone rings. The canvas before me is supersize, towering over me on the stepladder. I'm stretched at my tallest with my arm raised, brush gliding, trying to ignore the sound.

Amber has called me six times this week. I haven't seen her since that afternoon on the bench, about a month ago. I'm not sure what she wants, but the prospect of reconnecting with her makes me uneasy. I stay on the top rungs of my ladder, facing the fruit. The red skin is scalloped with bite marks. I drag my hand in a massive arc, spreading a shadow on the stem, while my phone continues to toll. Eventually, I get curious enough to glance over—it's Richard.

"Richard!"

"Hi, Devon."

His voice is wet, low.

I regret sounding excited.

"I saw the news." I'm so disoriented that I slap my paintbrush on the windowsill. It leaves its black signature on the ledge. "I'm so sorry for your loss. I thought about reaching out, but I didn't want to impose."

"Thank you."

He's being gracious, but I know my words are inadequate. There's nothing I could say that would make a difference. When I lost Richard, no one came close to mending the hole. Condolences were noise.

"Where are you?" I ask.

"I never left."

He must mean Waverley. He's been there since November?

I imagine him lying down on his bed, staring between the clock and the desk. Hearing just a little bit from him now, I desperately want more. I don't want to be having this conversation by phone. We should be in the same room, face to face. I wander to my own bed and sit down. It's something, maybe, that we're both on beds, even though they're in different rooms. It's a small connection.

A pause grows.

Is he having trouble saying something in particular? Does he have anything to say at all? Maybe he's just reached out to hear my voice, to be with me by phone. He may have been cut off from people for a while now, tending to his mom. I don't know who he's kept up with since he moved back to Greenwich.

"How's Clarke? Oliver?" I ask.

"In shock."

Another silence.

"Do they have any idea who did this?" I ask.

He tells me that McInnis interviewed a dozen people. Apparently, a few noticed someone matching the same description. "This guy was watching you, Dad, and one of our neighbors—Chris Landeau, a family friend. Dad and Chris only saw him a couple of times, but the point is that you all saw the same man. He wasn't just stalking; he was . . . *triangulating.*" His voice sounds pained. "Ever since . . . that day, no one's seen him. He has to be connected, but we don't know how. We don't know *who.*" I tell Richard that sounds terrible, my tone dripping with sincerity. "McInnis says this man could be someone from Mom's past seeking revenge. So he's investigating that angle . . . All I really know is we have to find him."

"You will."

I want to reach out and touch him.

Ahead of me, there's one bite left on the painted apple. Most of the flesh is gone, gnawed down to a skinny middle. A few black seeds poke loose. But there's one sweetly sour bit left. I tell Richard that if he needs help with anything—funeral arrangements, chores—I'm here.

"Thanks, Dev. You know . . ."

He leaves a thought unsaid.

"What is it?" I ask.

"In that case, there is one thing."

FORTY-SIX

On the day of Vanessa's funeral, I step out of the Uber toward Christ Church of Greenwich. The asphalt is warm under my dark heels.

Richard and Oliver stand on both sides of the front door. Richard is handing out programs, thanking people solemnly for coming. I hadn't seen him in so long my heart forgot what it's like. He looks slimmer, especially around the arms, as if he hasn't been to a gym since he moved here. I don't recognize his suit and wonder if it's new, bought specially for today. His eyes connect with everyone who drifts inside—and while his details may be different, those eyes are the same. Those are the round blues that stare back in all my best memories.

I walk toward him.

He stands under a stained glass window. It must showcase a religious scene, but I don't recognize anyone in it. They're just beautiful strangers to me, sparkling like a box of spilled jewels. As I get closer, the organ music gets louder, a little sweeter.

Richard hugs a gray-haired woman. He doesn't tear up, even as she wipes her eyes. Maybe he's beyond sad. Maybe he's moved past the place where people go after devastating news—past that purgatory of resistance, past grief—on to somewhere new.

He sees me.

In that case, he said on the phone last week, *there is one thing. Would you be able to come to her funeral?* Just because he asked me to be here doesn't mean I expect a warm welcome. I'm prepared for anything. I run my hands through my hair, smooth as water. This morning, I blew it dry for the first time in months, maybe years. I rubbed pale blush on my cheeks, painted on two layers of mascara. It felt curious, putting on makeup. Before leaving my apartment, I took one last look in the mirror and thought, *I've never looked more like my mom.*

I hold my breath.

When I'm a step away, Richard opens his arms. I walk into his hug, wide, warm, and familiar. He kisses my cheek, and I never want this moment to end. I've been dreaming of this, but my dreams were never this thrilling, this firm. I really didn't expect him to kiss me. Maybe he's been in so much pain he doesn't have the energy to hold back.

"Annika," Oliver says.

A stunning, dark-haired woman walks up the steps behind me. An unassuming black dress hugs her curving waist. She's shaped just like the apple painting I left in New York. It's startling to see such a modest outfit look so sultry. Her lips and cheeks are full, glossy. Her eyes look smart. Her nose is wide and interesting. She smiles in a sad but eager way.

She hugs Oliver, whispering things I can't hear.

Eventually, she faces us.

"Hi, Richard." Her voice is husky.

"Annika, thanks for coming."

She touches the side of his arm, then strolls into the church, leaving the electricity behind her changed.

∼

I am the second-to-last guest at the Belmonts' home.

After the funeral today, the first floor filled with people paying their condolences: family and friends from their country club, Vanessa's boards, her charities, and more. I spent most of the time talking to the head of contemporary auctions at Sotheby's, a short and thoughtful man with round glasses. As it turned out, he knows Marc Zellweger. Maybe I'll invite him to the next show.

Now, it's just five of us left.

Richard and Clarke are in the kitchen, wrapping up leftover food. Oliver is with Annika, holding hands on the library sofa. I've deduced that she must be his ex-girlfriend, the doctor who allegedly stole Vanessa's earrings. When they're together, she makes Oliver look stronger. Her back is to me now, dark hair shining by a stained glass lamp.

I don't want to leave, but I've run out of excuses to stay. I walk slowly into the foyer, which feels sunnier than I remember. Maybe it's the start of spring that's brightening the room. I grab my purse from the closet.

"Wait," Richard says.

I turn around.

He's standing on the edge of the dining room without his jacket. His eyebrows pull into a sincere cinch. I walk closer.

"Do you want to . . . ?"

He gets choked up and swallows the rest of his question. I know him well enough to understand that he's asking me to stay. I nod yes and throw my arms around his neck. It feels like too much too soon. I lean back, running one hand down his chest. There's a spark in my fingers that feels inappropriate. Richard doesn't look strong enough to resist it. There's something so dangerously weak about him now I almost expect him to wobble.

Over his shoulder, I notice a forgotten serving bowl in the dining room. I hurry toward it, to find a fruit salad with notable variety—not just melons but tropical wedges and unexpected slices of pear. It looks freed from constraint, almost anarchic. I carry the dish into the kitchen and cover it with plastic next to Clarke. He's so blinded by his own grief that he barely pays me attention. I slide the bowl into the refrigerator under a platter of rare beef.

Back in the foyer, Richard reaches for my hand and leads me upstairs. His fingers are calloused and warm. I know these calluses—from rowing crew all through college, from moving his friends into their apartments, and from dog walking for the shelter, tugging on leashes. I have an urge to drag my thumb across his knuckles, to feel everything about him all over again.

He leads me into his room and shuts the door. I can't hear anything except his breath. He grabs my other hand. His lips part just enough for me to see the straight edge of his teeth, the pink of his tongue. He's always had full lips. I wonder what they feel like now with the faint crust of his stubble. I've almost forgotten that uniquely Richard combination of soft and hard. I miss him, and it must be all over my face. He looks at me as if we're still together.

I nod.

When he kisses me, I don't just feel it on my mouth. It's everywhere inside me, teasing every tender place. We guide each other to the bed and lie down an inch apart. Neither of us moves—not one shoulder, not one hip. Every few seconds, he blows heat onto my bottom lip. I feel us on the edge of something a little wrong, a little wicked.

I glance around the room and notice he's erected two large monitors on his desk. That must be where he's been working for the past few months. There are more photos of Vanessa here than last time, crowded around his keyboard like a frozen audience.

"We'll never forget her," I say.

"I can't talk about it right now."

"That's okay."

"Tell me about you."

I describe my move downtown, never raising my voice above a hush. I detail my studio and the neighborhood: the cobblestone streets, the park just steps from my apartment. It feels seamless, talking to him again, as if we're at home on the Upper East Side and rehashing our days. This is exactly what I'd hoped for in my wildest dreams, that deep down, neither of us had really changed. I tell him that I've sold four paintings, and now, Marc wants to show twenty of my pieces.

"That's fantastic," he says, lifting his head.

A pause follows.

"What about you?" I ask.

"I've been here."

I hug him.

"I haven't slept well without you," he admits. "Not once."

Is this going in the direction I think?

My breathing feels uneven.

He sits up. I follow.

"The day Oliver found her, all I wanted to do was talk to you." We face each other cross-legged on the bed. He touches both my knees. "I didn't want anyone else. Then I saw there *was* no one else. I'd been living without my friends. I'd been so focused on Mom, I wasn't even noticing myself, if that makes sense. I realized that I hadn't been thinking clearly. I can't believe I broke up with you. I look back on that moment and feel like I was a different person, like someone else was speaking through me." He squeezes my knees. "I'm so sorry. There's no excuse for what I did. All I can say is that it was an impossible and strange time." A long pause follows. "Do you think you could . . . find it in your heart to try again?"

I kiss him on the lips.

"Yes," I almost cry. "Yes."

"I love you," he says.

"I love you too."

Our foreheads touch.

"We're on the same side," I say.

"Yes."

"No matter what happens."

"No matter what."

We lie back down and curl around each other. It can't be later than four in the afternoon, but for the first time in too long, I fall into a bottomless sleep.

~

I wake up while Richard is still dreaming next to me. The red quilt over him looks like a mantle from a coronation ceremony. He looks too peaceful to disturb.

I slip into my dark dress from yesterday and creep into the hallway. Halfway downstairs, I find Woolf on the windowsill. He retreats into the stained glass, arching his spine. As soon as I pass, he relaxes. A yawn prics his jaw open, revealing fangs like tiny, sabertooth-style pricks. I wonder if house cats have anything in common with lions. Do the males serve females too?

Who will Woolf serve without Vanessa?

I walk across the first floor under gothic box beams and find myself dragging one hand along the wall. I pass glossy family photos and pause in front of one. Amber was right. There aren't any photos of the Belmonts before college. Vanessa really did erase her daughter from this house. I pick up one picture of Vanessa with her sons. They're at someone else's outdoor wedding, where she hugs Richard and Oliver under the floral arch.

I replace the photo upside down and wander into the kitchen. The sun has just started to rise, turning the white marble counters pink. I run a hand over them. They feel like blocks of melted ice cream, so terribly smooth they might drip onto the floor. I drag my fingers across the stove and fiddle with one knob, making it burn for a bright few seconds. New light peeks through trees by the pool. *I started hiding from her, spending most of my time in the storm room.*

I was enjoying this moment with the house, but now, I feel myself drawn outside. Wet grass sticks to my bare feet. As I approach the covered pool, it lengthens into something truly grand. It's surrounded by chaises without their cushions, stands without their umbrellas. But where's the storm room? Behind the pool house, two wooden doors wait at ground level, illuminated around the edges.

I thought I was the first one up.

I pull one door open to find a concrete staircase. It's such a vertical descent that the stairs blend like a slide. I test out the first one, the second.

At the bottom, I get my bearings. The right wall is stuffed with old board games, the boxes soft, their corners split. I imagine missing tokens and lost dice. Shelves continue onto the far wall, where they hold art supplies: child-size palettes and brushes. One reading nook has a rainbow pillow. A short putting mat begins at my feet. This feels like a playroom that was never reimagined as the kids grew. I picture the Belmonts here as toddlers. Then again, Oliver has been living at home for years. Maybe he still comes here to relax.

I walk down the wall of games, feeling the frayed edges of Trouble. On the opposite wall, there are two closed doors. I step up to the nearest one and touch the brass handle. When I push it open, lights flicker on to reveal a cramped but sophisticated study. This part of the storm room feels decidedly adult: one tufted leather sofa, a black mini fridge, and floor-to-ceiling bookshelves. Only one title is out of place. It balances on the far arm of the sofa. I pick it up: *When the Stars Go Dark*. I stare at the familiar cover, the ring of treetops that evoke an open mouth.

This must be where Vanessa hid. I'm so convinced I can almost see her in here, sitting on the sofa with her legs beside her. Did she stay in this study the whole time, or did she waltz around the playroom? I picture her surrounded by games as people pored over the neighborhood. As Richard cried into his Columbia sweatshirt and Clarke red-lined her planner. But the Belmonts searched the property. Someone must have lied for her.

A toilet flushes. I walk out of the room in time to see the second door opening. Oliver emerges in a golf polo and shorts.

"What are you doing here?" he asks, putter in hand.

"I-I was just going for a walk."

"Underground?"

He strides toward his bag of clubs and slides his putter inside. He now stands between the staircase and me. Should I be afraid? He doesn't *look* like a threat, but I don't like to see the exit blocked. I don't like that Richard doesn't know where I am. If Vanessa could disappear down here, what could happen to me?

"I'm sorry, Oliver." I soften my tone. "I know this must be a hard time for you—for everyone, but especially for you. You two were so close—"

His stare locks on the book in my hands.

Then drifts up to me.

He must know that I know.

The longer we stand here, the less fearful I am. He doesn't get any closer. He doesn't reach for any of his clubs, doesn't even eye them with ideas. And the more secure I feel, the more curious I am. It feels safe enough to ask.

"Why?"

He shakes his head.

"I won't tell anyone," I almost whisper. "I just need to know."

He shakes his head again, his eyes starting to melt. I feel his will breaking down. Maybe he does have a bit of Richard in him after all. Oliver can't withhold the answer that I want forever. Like his brother, he's driven to please—but in his case, he focused on Vanessa. He became the son of her dreams, so devoted to her family, so enamored with his mom, he refused to leave their home.

"Why?" I ask.

"Because she asked."

I suddenly feel like I've been here before. Because I've gone to strange lengths for Mom too. When she thought we were being spied on, I unplugged every electronic in the house and lived without them for weeks—just because she asked. It never mattered if she was right. It only mattered that she could sleep.

"Oliver?" a female voice calls.

Slender legs appear on the steps.

Annika descends in her dress from yesterday. She holds a coffee mug in each hand, treading in Oliver's slippers. All morning, I haven't felt out of place—until now. Seeing someone else in similar circumstances holds a mirror up to me. Maybe she and I shouldn't still be here, lounging in our funeral clothes.

"What's wrong?" she asks Oliver.

"It's over now," he says.

He seems to recover in her presence and suggests we go back to the house. Annika agrees with a solemn nod, her dark eyes sparkling.

~

Annika and I stand side by side in the kitchen. She's scrambling a dozen eggs, and I'm toasting frozen bagels to life. The men are in the library. Right before Richard left, in a private moment, he assured me that I'm more than welcome here—I'm family. When we're ready, we'll head back to New York together.

"So, what kind of doctor are you?" I venture.

"Ob-gyn." She smiles. "I always felt like it was my calling."

"That's how I feel about my work."

"What do you do?"

"I paint. Not exactly saving lives."

"Just giving them meaning."

It's generous, but I appreciate it.

Annika tilts the frying pan over a platter, and the yolky mass slides as a loosely connected whole. She picks the dish up as I lift the tray of cream cheese–slathered bagels. I survey the feast in my hands. Maybe I was too liberal with the spread. The white layers are thick and meringue-like, almost too indulgent.

Annika and I walk in sync toward the library.

"Oliver seems happier with you around," I admit.

She bites a smile. "We hadn't talked in years. Then he called me last week. I lost my mom a long time ago, and he wanted to hear how I dealt with it. We just kept talking and talking . . ." Her expression lifts more, lips fighting her teeth, as if she's remembering how their conversation must've shifted. Tiptoed around what they were holding back. And then, caved into confessions of a love that had never stopped. "It's heartbreaking that sometimes, it takes a tragedy to say how we feel."

I ask where she lives, and she tells me that she's in Manhattan. As it turns out, her apartment is just two blocks south of mine, right across from the Whitney. She suggests we go together with gentle enthusiasm.

"I don't know much about art," she says, "but I hear that guy Renaissance is amazing." I find myself laughing and . . . liking her, this smart woman with a heart big enough to love Oliver. I wonder what he was like when they met, before he moved back to Waverley. Living with Vanessa—smelling nothing but her detergent and perfume—must've taken its toll. Did he used to be more outgoing? Will Annika revive him back to the person he was?

In the library, the men sit in their usual places. Fresh air flows through an open window. A robin hops toward us on the lawn, pausing in a puddle. A sparrow joins her, frisking. Soon, they're pecking their way through the grass again, clean and ravenous.

Annika and I put the platters down. She takes the chair that used to be mine. I remember when I sat there, thinking that I'd found my second-chance family. What do you call a second chance at a second chance? Meanwhile, Richard pats the spot next to him. I remember when Vanessa used to sit there, one hand on each son.

I take the seat, lean back, and look around.

Annika's smiling at Oliver. She's shining, really—rather, her earlobes are. They dazzle as if they contain all my brightest moments: playing with Mom in thick Ohio snow; skiing with Richard between pine trees, their branches lined with icicles that became prisms every afternoon; and when Richard asked me to marry him, holding up the ring that's still in my apartment. Everyone reaches for a plate and starts to serve themselves. I'm a beat behind because I can't stop staring at Annika. She's wearing just the most gorgeous six-petaled diamond earrings.

FORTY-SEVEN

A week later, I take the subway downtown while Richard heads to his—*our*—old place. He renewed the lease months ago, but this is his first time back. I'm going to meet him there after I gather a few basics from my apartment.

I jog up the steps of the Fourteenth Street station, then weave between pedestrians. There's new life in the flower beds. Restaurants have expanded onto the sidewalk. It looks like they've been turned inside out, their tables and chairs now in full view. Birds sing on branches without weighing them down.

My phone buzzes.

Richard: Did you know that next week is our third year?

Me: Maybe

Richard: That's longer than a master's degree

Richard: I guess I have a degree in you

I pocket my phone, smiling.

Grief is strange up close. It looks more like love than I expected. It comes for Richard in waves, and when it overtakes him, he's powerfully connected to her. He's suddenly ruminating over her details, telling me about the way she used to wake him up for school—running one hand through his hair, sitting on his bed. Maybe it's no surprise then that his grief has brought us back together, if grief is a kind of love.

He's still on my mind when I collide with someone by my building—Amber.

We step back, recover.

The black fringe on her jacket continues to shake. She removes her cigarette, blowing smoke. "Welcome back," she says.

"What are you doing here?"

"I think you know."

My stomach drops. What's she talking about?

She flicks her cigarette onto the street and jerks her head assertively toward the park. I start scanning for anyone who might recognize us, but she's already on the move. I follow her nervously over the crosswalk, wishing she hadn't chosen this place. It's too public, too close to where we both live. It's too obvious to meet in the middle of the day.

"I've been trying to reach you," she says.

We sit on a bench.

My throat is dry.

"I was at home when you called." She takes her time setting the scene. She tells me that she'd just come back from a concert, and her ears felt like they were bleeding. "You said it was all over, then hung up. I didn't know what you meant until I saw the news. At first, I wasn't . . ." She shakes her head. "But once I got past my own—" She touches her chest. "I understand why you did it. Twisted as it sounds, I'm grateful. Otherwise, she wouldn't have stopped. I've been trying to call you. I even started waiting for you." She nods toward my building. "Just to say that I know it couldn't have been easy. But sometimes, the right thing to do is the wrong one."

"What are you talking about?"

She raises an eyebrow.

"I didn't *do* anything!"

"I don't know why you're lying to me."

I'm breathing fast. "The last time we talked, we were here. We sat right here and *vented* about her. But that was as far as it went."

Amber looks genuinely lost.

"The last time I saw you, we decided that you'd fake journal entries." She speaks with exacting slowness, as if I might not understand her otherwise. "We both knew the police would never find the two men Vanessa made up, so there'd always be a cloud of suspicion over you. I forget which one of us suggested the journal entries. But we decided you'd create a suspect, the kind of person Clarke or Richard would notice naturally in their own neighborhood. It would give the police a lead while making you look like a victim. You thought it would get rid of the doubt—"

"That's not true!"

"What's not—?"

"Someone *was* following me!"

He was right here. I remember walking home and *seeing* him on this bench. He sat perfectly still. Even as I kept going, his chin didn't turn. He just stared straight ahead, his feet frozen on the winding path. He wore old tennis shoes with grimy toe boxes, creased tongues. It was as if he'd walked all the way from Greenwich, just to sit and look at me.

"Why are you saying this?" I beg.

She cocks her head.

"Someone was following me!"

"You don't actually believe that, do you?" she whispers.

"You said you wanted to help me—but you were setting me up." I put it together. "You're trying to make me think that *I* killed her." I glance up to the fourth floor of her building. "How long have you lived here, exactly?" I remember her name A. BELMONT crossed out, A. HEWITT scrawled on top. As if she'd only just moved in, just seen the mistake and hadn't had time for a formal correction. I remember how Amber asked Muse for their hours, like she was new to the neighborhood. "Did you follow me here? To keep an eye on me, while I starred in your master plan?"

"Devon, please."

"You're only here now to get in my head."

"Devon—"

"This is exactly what your mom did."

"You want to talk about crazy moms?"

For a moment, I'm speechless.

"What do you know about my mom?" I ask.

"Only what everyone knows—well, everyone who cares to look." Her voice softens. "She was arrested for a crime against public order. She wouldn't stop shouting that she was—remind me, a reincarnated Leonardo da Vinci?" I don't confirm or deny it. "If I were a painter like you, that would haunt me. How could you ever be confident again? Wouldn't it feel like a delusion of grandeur?"

I don't answer.

"It wasn't hard to learn more about you too," she adds. "All it took was a trip to your gallery." I grip the bench. Did she talk to Marc? One of the assistants? "I didn't hear anything incriminating, just a few things that made me—nervous. Maybe I should've paid more attention to them." She shrugs with heavy resignation. "Apparently, you shut yourself in a room for days when you're inspired? Painting things only you can see? And when you come out, you describe it as a trance?" My fingers feel cold even in the sun. "That doesn't *sound* like diligent hard work. It sounds more like an episode, doesn't it? Or does it help you to give it a glamorous name?"

I still refuse to answer.

"Also, I heard that you never look at your paintings again after they're done. Isn't that interesting?" Her updo slants as she tilts her head. "It's almost as if you're afraid they might trigger you back into that state. Afraid they might pull you back into the same nonstop fit of delusions. If I were you, I'd avoid them too."

"I'm superstitious."

Her eyes blaze with doubt.

"In light of all that," she says, "I wouldn't try to convince anyone that I 'set you up.' Because really, who would believe you?" She gives me a sympathetic expression. "Besides, you have to admit the whole thing looks like your idea. You were the one who wrote the journal entries. You were the one with a clear motive to kill Vanessa. You still wanted to be with Richard. And now, you have everything that you want." She stands. "I feel for you, Devon. I really do. Maybe just . . . try to enjoy what you have now. You don't have much credibility as a serious person."

She leaves me in the park.

When she's gone, the bench still smells like smoke. I cradle my head, unable to believe that Amber used me. She followed me here. She lured me in. And now, she's trying to pin the crime on me. Of course I didn't do anything to Vanessa. I've never done anything violent, never splattered anything other than paint.

So why am I doubting myself?

I massage my temples.

Pigeons watch.

The whole thing looks like your idea . . . And now, you have everything that you want. There's only one another explanation, but it's ridiculous. Almost too ridiculous to think. The only other possibility is that she preyed on me—and I liked it. *Wanted* to be part of her plan.

Wouldn't that be mad?

I let the idea sink in.

No one would believe that after we met, she reminded me a little too much of Vanessa. That I guessed her true motive when she offered a solution. And then, I still wanted to comply. More than comply, I wanted to lean into the role she'd given me. Wanted to see that man and pushed myself to do it. Turned a weakness of mine into a strength. Triggered a fit—as she called it—that didn't just change my art; it changed the rest of my life. That wouldn't just be insane; it would be—superhuman, godly. No one can create something that vivid on demand. It would be absurd, impossible.

It would be a masterpiece.

EPILOGUE

My hands are an unusual shade of blue. It's a witchy navy, almost black at the fingers. I admire the color, the Belmonts' sunny lawn in the background.

It's the first time Richard and I have been back since the funeral. He's golfing with his dad, and it's such a dazzling June day that I'm barefoot outside. Everything here is green and gloriously alive—the trees explosive, the grass taut and energetic. I'm on the phone with my mom, staring at my stained hand.

"You want to share what's really on your mind?" she asks.

Of course she can tell.

Mom beads as she waits for my answer. The gemstones clink in a faint sparkle. She's been clear since the day I called Teresa to check on her—more than clear; she forgave me. That requires *enhanced* mental clarity, doesn't it? Even I don't know if I'm there yet. If I've forgiven myself for . . . what happened. I never expected to have second thoughts, but the doubt drifted in slowly. I should just tell Mom what's on my mind, what's been on my mind for months.

"Can you be guilty of something if you didn't do it?" I ask. "I mean, what if you *knew* someone was going to do something terrible—something warped and unnatural—and you let them? More than that, you tried to help them get away with it? Would that make you . . . ?" I rub my dark fingers together. They're smoother than usual, some of the oil still there, filling the dips in my fingerprints.

"I think you know the answer."

Do I?

"Is it *your* painting if you watched someone else make it?" Her beads tip-tap. "You could be an inch behind them the whole time, breathing on the backs of their ears, and at the end of the day, it would still be theirs." I picture standing behind Amber as she paints, my eyes on the rise and fall of her brush.

I never did tell Mom the full story.

Right now, I'm tempted to tell her what I can do.

The trances used to torment me. I was always relieved when one would end, when I could put down my brush and stop recording the visual assault. Then I'd be so afraid of triggering another fit that I'd avoid my finished work. But I want to tell Mom I'm past that now. That when I dare to face my art—when I finally turn my paintings around—I don't just draw the images back into my life; I control the thing that used to control me. Recruit all the ghosts who used to haunt me, to help me. And I want to tell Mom that it feels so *good*, like breaking through the wall that's kept me inside for decades. I don't feel omnipotent but . . . unafraid. Like I can face anything. Like my deepest, darkest crack was actually the way out to this rapturous, white-light day.

How could I tell her?

Did you ever think that what scares you the most is the key out of the room? I lie down on the grass, and it's even softer than I expected. My hair spreads over the lawn, the grass poking through it like a green comb. *And all you needed to do was face it? All you ever needed to do was dare to look it in the eye?*

"I made something," I start. "A masterpiece . . ." I feel a twitch of excitement like a black flame. "I think you could make something like it too."

"Darling, I already made my masterpiece."

"You did?"

"You. It was always you."

Her beads are tinkling. Lapis lazuli, she tells me. I imagine the deep-blue beads in her hand while staring at my navy palm. And no matter the distance between Mom and me, feeling permanently, powerfully connected.

ACKNOWLEDGMENTS

First, thank you to my agent, Eve Attermann, who has been my guiding light ever since my first novel. Thank you for your sage advice, bold visions, sense of humor, and, most of all, your faith. I'm grateful to the whole team at WME—Rivka Bergman, Nicole Weinroth, and Caitlin Mahony—who are second to none.

Thank you to my editor, Carmen Johnson, for leading me deeper into Vanessa's mind and toward a more cunning finale. For grounding this story while making it wilder. Thank you to Faith Black Ross for your thought-provoking insights and fine-toothed comb. To everyone at Amazon Publishing, especially Nicole Burns-Ascue.

Devon's world wouldn't have come to life without Carrie Feron, whose passionate early reads and daily texting helped me bring depth to Devon and Richard. Your zeal for the project was transformative and personally meaningful.

I couldn't have nurtured Devon's artistic identity without the expertise of others. Thank you to Bill Valerio, director of the Woodmere Art Museum in Philadelphia, for your generous consult in addition to an extraordinary tour through the Jasper Johns exhibit at the Philadelphia Museum of Art. Thank you to Alexander Berggruen, owner of the gallery based on the Upper East Side by the same name, for sharing your highly sought time and unique perspective on all things art.

Dan Brown, your guidance over the years has fueled tremendous creative growth. Your belief has been a source of strength.

Blake Crouch, thank you for your invaluable insights into the writing process, especially around idea selection. Your excellence in the craft is an inspiration.

Zibby Owens, thank you for building such vibrant reading and writing communities and for including me in them. The vitalizing energy and soulful personal touches that you bring to every project are truly special.

Thank you to the other authors and friends who were particularly supportive of my last book, including Lynne and Valerie Constantine, Rea Frey, Tracey Garvis Graves, Emily Giffin, Caroline Kepnes, Liz Moore, Sarah Pekkanen, Carl Radke, and Wendy Walker. Wendy, you were the first to read it, and I will always cherish your reaction. Your warmheartedness is a superpower, and your ability to champion so many is an uplifting force.

In addition, thank you to the authors and friends who continue to support my work, showing great generosity of spirit and inexhaustible kindness, including Jennifer Bardsley, Lisa Barr, Jesse Bartel, Fiona Davis, Kristy Woodson Harvey, and Jill Santopolo.

Finally, thank you to none other than my in-laws! Jim and Julie, Francie and Will, Stephen and Mary Kate, and Betsy, thank you for loving me since the moment we met. I am lucky to call you family. Thank you to my mom ("Minkey") and dad, Parker and Michael, and Emil and Cara, who have always been my bedrock.

And most of all, thank you to my husband, David, who shared his passion for fine art with me when we started dating and has ever since filled my world with color.

ABOUT THE AUTHOR

Photo © 2021 Lea Cartier

Madeleine Henry is the author of four novels, including *My Favorite Terrible Thing*. Her work has been featured in the *New York Times*, the *Washington Post*, the *New York Post*, and *Entertainment Weekly*. Previously she worked at Goldman Sachs after graduating from Yale. She lives with her husband in New York, where she is at work on her next book. For more information, visit www.itsmadeleinehenry.com.